DOOM
IN THE
MIDNIGHT
SUN

DOOM
IN THE
MIDNIGHT SUN

AN ALASKA VINTAGE MYSTERY

EUNICE MAYS BOYD

LEVEL BEST BOOKS

Historia
ESTABLISHED 2019

To Ethel and Einar who introduced me to both Harding Lake and the Midnight Sun.

Praise for The Alaskan Vintage Mysteries

From 1944:

"As pretty, suspenseful and smoothly written a mystery as I've read in a long time."—Chicago *Sun*

"Grocer-sleuth F. Millard Smyth unriddles well-tangled murder plot with spy trimmings. Good entertainment."—New York *Herald Tribune*

"I frankly loathe stories laid in the Big Woods, or in the Great Frozen North. And I begin to get bored at the first hint of Enemy Agents. Therefore I picked up *Murder Breaks Trail* filled with misgivings. I put it down at 4 a.m. with a bad case of eyestrain...a *humdinger*!—Chicago *Daily News*

"An exceptional who-done-it, which won honorable mention in the third Mary Roberts Rinehart mystery novel contest, has been skillfully built into a book that is hard to put down until the last page."—Philadelphia *Evening Bulletin*

Chapter One

F. Millard Smyth snugged the magazines in the crook of his elbow, hitched the sack of jumbled clothes and groceries higher on his shoulder, and wondered how much farther he had to walk. A mile back, not traveled enough to make dust, the narrow road from the highway had rounded the hill and dipped toward the lake that gleamed like a green, watching eye in the distance. Now he was too far down to see it, and in spite of increasing pack-mule discomforts, he felt an unaccountable sense of relief.

"My gracious," he jeered aloud. "What are you scared of?"

Overhead, sly leafy whispers took up the sound of his voice, and he wished he'd kept still—that he hadn't come—that he wouldn't keep feeling, after what had happened last winter, that lakes and murders went together.[1]

The road curved sharply downward where it hit a blaze of sun, and F. Millard, stepping out of the dappled birch and spruce shade, twitched a whining platoon of mosquitoes off his head net and blinked behind spectacles at Harding Lake, now almost at his feet.

Through a cut in the bank a clearing led to the water. On either side the bank rose steeply seven or eight feet, and both right and left, as far as he could see through the trees, it was lined with cabins.

As the little man stood in the clearing, weighted down with magazines and lumpy sack, the thunder of planes brought his eyes from the lake. A deafening flight of bombers—almost too high for him to see the stars on their undersides—swept overhead and vanished against the sun—toward Fairbanks, F. Millard thought, trying to shake off his irrational mood of foreboding.

This close, the lake no longer looked like a sinister eye, but merely a body of green water shifting and glinting in the sun. In the center of the clearing, behind a huddle of boards on stilts that could only be a telephone booth, the road forked. To the left, it went up over the shoulder of a hill, with a studding of garages above the cabins on the lakeshore. The other fork ran along the level behind the buildings on the right.

Tom Blaine had said his cabin—F. Millard's for a week—was the last at the southern end of the road. It was hard to tell directions in Alaska with the June sun rising and setting so far to the north—what little setting it did in midsummer, but if the planes had been flying toward Fairbanks, northwest of Harding Lake, the road going over the hill would be north, and the level road south. He gave his bulging sack another hitch and trudged down the right-hand fork.

None of the houses he saw through the fringe of trees had a back door. Perhaps that made them all look deserted. A hodgepodge row—frame cottages and wallboard, tents and log cabins stuck side by side on the lake bank—and the farther he picked his way down the almost untracked road behind them, the more apprehensive he felt.

A sense of eyes dogging every step washed over him in prickles. Surely not all his prospective neighbors—reduced to eleven, according to Blaine, by the rubber and gasoline shortage—lived in the northern row of cabins.

Judging by the scarcity of tire tracks, most of them must have left Fairbanks the way F. Millard had, on the Valdez bus, and walked in from the highway. But it was funny he didn't even see a face at a window, while the feeling of being watched persisted.

In about half a mile, he came to the end of the road. So that last log cabin must be Blaine's. Awkward under his load, F. Millard fumbled for the overgrown path to the house and caught his toe on a rock. All the magazines spilled to the ground. Blaine had said to take only essentials, but F. Millard couldn't spend a week without detective stories. Guiltily he began to gather up a six months' accumulation of *Flatfoot*.

A group of round beach pebbles consorting with the flinty land rocks of the road caught his eye. Nature did funny things sometimes, he reflected; those beach pebbles almost made a pattern. They did make a pattern—some thing gnawingly familiar. Seven stones—the only thing he could think of was a giant meerschaum pipe—a flat-bottomed bowl outlined with four stones, and a jutting, slightly bent stem made of three.

Again, the sense of eyes watching prickled through him, and his feet scattered the pebbles as he groped for elusive magazines.

Crushing grass and low-bush cranberry plants, wading through blueberry bushes, he reached the front of the cabin. A trail ran along the lake bank close to the door in the screened porch, peering, to the other cabins whose backs he had skirted on the road. He saw no walls in the other direction, and the trail led into the woods.

With his foot, he smoothed a place in the path for his magazines, leaned the knuckly sack against the porch screen, and fished for Blaine's key. Not till his hand touched the padlock did he see it was hanging open. He blinked before he remembered that Blaine had said he couldn't recall whether he'd locked up or not the season before. To make sure he'd found the right cabin, F. Millard tried the key, and it fitted.

He crossed the screen porch and opened the door, also unlocked, of the cabin proper. Its one room was bright with afternoon sun just chair-seat high on the walls. A grocer by trade and instinct, the little man inventoried a dusty iron stove, a double-deck built-in bunk—complete with blankets, thank goodness—a dusty table, a dusty chair beside it, another a few feet away—a chair that wasn't dusty!

Behind his glasses, F. Millard blinked again. A chair that wasn't dusty in a cabin unused for a year! Involuntarily, he squinted *Flatfoot*-trained eyes on the floor. The dust was dotted with tracks. But no one as casual as Blaine would care if anyone entered his cabin. F. Millard had been reading too many detective stories.

To punish himself he decided to clean house instead of setting out to explore. But no hair shirt could keep him from looking around when he took a bucket down to the lake to dip water.

A panoramic glance still revealed no sign of life. Even his sense of following eyes was now gone. All those empty cabins along the bank made him feel uncomfortably alone. From Blaine's on the south, F. Millard's spectacles followed the curve of the hill to a rocky point jutting into the lake. At its end, crouching on the cliff top, a solitary cottage presented a two-windowed side of weathered gray-white boards to the little man dipping his bucket on the beach. No door was visible, but across several hundred yards of water, that house, too, looked empty.

His head swiveled back to the row of cabins. The three or four nearest stood out clearly. The others, at first only blurred by trees, were finally hidden in them. For perhaps a mile more along the bank, occasional landings and boat slips gave evidence of further habitation. Then even that evidence ceased, and the low green hills above the flat green water stretched into the wilderness.

By the time he'd had a sandwich and finished cleaning house, it was after ten o'clock. The flighty Alaskan sun, instead of setting in the west as F. Millard couldn't help feeling it should, had dropped out of his sight behind the highest northwest hill, but its light still yellowed the upper slopes across the lake. After ten p.m., even in broad daylight, was hardly the time to look up neighbors. Besides, years of long habit when his mother was alive had established ten o'clock as his bedtime.

Shaking out the blankets stacked on the lower bunk, he made up the cot on the porch and lay hearing the drone of mosquitoes outside the screen, staring into the trees, and feeling like a small boy put down for a nap. It was nearly eleven before the wash of gold on the southeastern hills disappeared and well after eleven before the daylight dimmed at all. Then the brightness was tinged with dusk, like a thin silk shade on a lamp, just too dark to read *Flatfoot* in comfort.

He made a face at the sky and turned over. Each night would be even lighter till after the 21st. Anyway, he hadn't come to Harding Lake to read, but to decide about buying Blaine's grocery. His own Nebraska grocery had been sold by correspondence three months ago, and he'd always wanted to live in Alaska. He thought of his early ambitions when the stampede had started for Nome. But his father was dead, and his mother had insisted he was too young to go at fifteen; when he overcame the age handicap, there had always been another excuse. After he'd saved enough money for a tourist trip to Alaska last fall before Pearl Harbor, the actuality, in spite of a couple of murders, had been better than the dream. Now, if he bought the Fairbanks grocery, he'd never have to leave.

He flopped on his back and reached for his glasses. This was the funniest midnight he'd ever seen—this eerie, dimmed-out brightness, with every color and leaf still distinct; he might as well have a good look. With an arm across his forehead, he shaded his eyes. Gradually, the hum of mosquitoes lowered his lids to half-mast. And it was while he lay like that—still, on his back, with glasses on and eyes nearly shut behind them—that he saw the red-headed girl.

She came stepping softly down the path from the cabins with no more noise than a squirrel or a bird. Something about her reminded him of a bird—her smallness beneath the trees, or her swift, quiet passage.

F. Millard didn't move. The girl's presence and silent progress down the path seemed part of all the strangeness, the way everything is plausible in dreams—the sight of her bright hair and yellow blouse in the middle of the night no odder than blue sky through green branches or the looming mass of green hillside reflected in the lake.

Just before reaching his cabin, she paused. Under lowered lashes, he watched her eyes search the porch. They stopped at his cot. But evidently, neither spectacles nor slit of eyeballs showed beneath his upraised arm, for after a minute, she darted on and knelt by the trail in front of his door, her face to the lake and back to the cabin. He could see her elbows move, and once she reached out an arm's length. Her hand and arm were bare. Didn't mosquitoes bite redheads?

Then she stood up in one quick, silent spring, and hurried noiselessly on along the trail to the woods. Her dark slacks, her shining hair, and finally the yellow blob of her blouse were hidden by trees.

Forgetting his glasses F. Millard firmly shut his eyes. Midnight might be the shank of the evening for a girl like that, but it was sleep-time for a middle-aged grocer.

He lay squeezing his eyes shut and hearing the buzz of mosquitoes. The buzz grew rapidly louder, from a hum to a pound to a roar. And three more planes zoomed over the lake, the fourth flight since F. Millard's arrival. He leaned close to the screen to see the Army stars on their undersides. The roar softened to a pound and then a hum. Finally, the only hum came from mosquitoes.

He lay back, very still. The lost thunder of the planes made the drone of mosquitoes seem hushed. The trees and lake were still. No wind rustled branches or made little waves lap at the beach. No boat rippled the water.

In the vibrant quiet he heard a scrape on the road behind the cabin. Another. Then only the buzz of mosquitoes.

Deliberately the man in bed relaxed tightened muscles. People had as much right to walk on the road as on the path before his door. Neither claws nor furry pads would scrape on rock. The sounds must have been made by shoes. But why had there been only two scrapes, and then silence, as if someone had muffled his steps?

All at once, his sense of being watched returned, disconcertingly stronger. Something seemed to have his head in a vise, holding it toward the spot where the girl had vanished and, at the same time, pulling it sideways, willing it to turn. Slowly, achingly, it turned.

At the screen door was a great furry head with pointed ears and gleaming eyes that watched, unblinking. Broad, shaggy, gray-tan breast; long shaggy legs, big paws—the creature stood motionless, staring, while the little grocer's stomach tangled with his windpipe.

The black nose wrinkled in a sniff. Then, with eyes still fixed on F. Millard, the brute's lips parted over long yellow fangs, a pink tongue lolled, and all but audibly, he laughed at the man in bed.

At last, the creature turned and trotted in a dignified way down the path the girl had taken.

"My gracious!" F. Millard said weakly. He'd forgotten about sled dogs, those malemutes and huskies that looked so much like wolves. But they were nearly always tied up or penned. Seeing that furry body with just a lake and trees as a backdrop, could anyone be blamed for jumping to the worst conclusion?

Right there at the door—F. Millard started. A wolf at the door! What if he bought the Fairbanks grocery, valued so much higher than his own—with a war on and danger of submarine sinkings—what if he couldn't meet the payments?

A flicker of movement caught his eyes near the trail past the cabins, down which the red-haired girl had come. The flicker stopped, then came again. Stopped. Came again.

Behind his spectacles, F. Millard blinked. Someone was gliding down the trail, slipping at intervals behind trees. This figure was no more silent than the first, but very much more furtive.

It was close enough now for him to see it wore a brimmed canvas hat with a dangling black head net, dark slacks, dark jacket, and gloves. This was someone who mosquitoes bit. Another girl, he decided; too slender for a man, too tall for a child. Her furtiveness made him wonder about the first girl. The redhead had been careful not to attract attention, but this one—was she stalking the first? It was none of his business. Anyway, what could he do—shout warning through the stillness of this eerily bright midnight? A fine way to get on with his neighbors! Besides, this girl, if she was up to no good (and it might be the redhead who was up to no good), was far slimmer than her quarry. For all the first girl's smallness, she'd looked strong, lithe, quick, and alert. This one was taller, so slim she seemed fragile, as if the small redhead could snap her in two.

She gave the cot and its motionless occupant only a glance; all her interest centered on the spot before the door where the first girl had knelt. F. Millard forgot to breathe as she bent nearer and nearer the ground just a few feet away. A fluff of something light under the net at the back of her hat might be very fair hair.

Then she was up and off, gliding, with that quick, recurring sidle behind trees, along the path the other girl had taken.

Apparently, both took his slumber for granted. Only the dog had given in to curiosity.

But by now, no dog could be more curious than the grocer. What was going on here? What had those two girls peered at so intently just outside his door? He swung his legs off the cot.

Though he closed the screen door softly, the waiting mosquitoes dive-bombed. But it was only a step, no need for a net. He slapped, took the step, slapped again—and his hand stopped in mid-air.

On the trail in front of his cabin, in the very spot he had smoothed a few hours before to retrieve his stack of *Flatfoots,* were seven stones in that same familiar shape he had seen on the road. The same flat bowl, the same out-jutting bent stem, only that stem had pointed toward the lake—this one pointed in the direction the girls and dog had taken.

Before he knew what he was doing he began to stumble through scrubby brush toward the road. He panted past his cabin and burst through the fringe of trees. There, where his spilled magazines had disarranged the beach pebbles, the pattern had been restored. Seven stones in that oddly familiar shape like a pipe. But the stem pointed a different way—now it, too, pointed the way the girls had gone.

[1] See MURDER BREAKS TRAIL

Chapter Two

In the morning, F. Millard surprised himself by waking. So he'd gone to sleep after all—in spite of the daylight and the traffic around his cabin. The turnip-type watch that had been his father's had ticked off half the morning. At least he wouldn't have to strain his patience waiting for his neighbors to get up.

He hurried down the bank for a fresh bucket of lake water and puffed back up, slopping it over the sides. At the door, he paused. Here, last night, both girls had bent over that strangely familiar arrangement of stones. F. Millard looked down, and water sloshed on the trail where the stones had been. There was no pattern now, just a water streak in the dust with a few scattered rocks beside it. He dropped the pail and hurried around the cabin to the road. The beach pebbles were scattered there, too, mixed with the sharp land rocks.

F. Millard only half chewed his breakfast before he reached for gloves and net-draped hat, crammed a rolled copy of *Flatfoot* into one hip pocket, and started down the trail past the cabins.

They looked even more deserted from the front than the back. Perhaps because now, he could see the closed doors: some padlocked, some boarded, some with locks that might be unlocked, like Tom Blaine's.

He had almost reached the clearing where the road came in from the highway before getting any indication that he wasn't alone among empty cabins beside a boatless lake. In the distance, he heard a shout. He quickened his step and heard more shouts, voices in noisy conversation, laughter, and, as he drew nearer, splashing.

At the second cabin, from the clearing, the trail spilled over on a wooden platform, apparently the sun deck of a boathouse, with a few canvas chairs and an orange umbrella. Over the railing, F. Millard saw three small boys and a man and woman diving from a float in the lake; on the beach below, a white-haired woman and two men, one in Army uniform, lay on a blanket over the pebbles, while two girls in bathing suits splashed in shallow water.

Gravel scraped under F. Millard's foot, and the three on the beach raised quick faces.

For a minute, they exchanged look for look, and then the woman said abruptly, "Come on down."

They watched each step as he clumped down the boat house stairs. When he reached the bottom, the woman stood up in a lithe, easy motion like a girl's, and the grocer tried not to goggle. Was this the second figure he had seen last night, the one who followed the redheaded girl? The light fluff beneath the net at the back of her hat that he had taken for very blond hair could have been white. This woman was tall, taller than he was, and very thin. She wore dark slacks and a man's blue shirt without a tie. In contrast to her hair, the eyes that examined F. Millard and the brows above them were dark; the lines in her face were deep but few, and her cheeks a weathered red-brown. "I'm Abby Thorne, mister," she said in a warm, strong voice. "Who the hell are you?"

F. Millard stammered his name.

"Smith don't mean a hell of a lot," she said frankly. "You a Fairbanks man?"

"I—I—" F. Millard stuttered. "It's spelled with a y."

The dark man in civilian clothes laughed. "That ought to make it all right then. Don't mind Abby. Just be glad she didn't greet you with a shotgun." His long, lazy length remained on the ground. He was one of the handsomest men F. Millard had ever seen, too masculine to be called pretty. "I'm Kingdom, from the University, and this is Ethan Frazee—Sergeant Ethan Frazee."

The man in uniform moved as if to rise, but merely sat up and held out his hand. F. Millard saw a deeply tanned face, darker than the blue eyes looking out of it or the light hair above it. This man wasn't handsome, and his grip made the grocer wince.

"Man of few words," remarked the civilian. "And here come the girls. The fat one's my wife—Mrs. Kingdom."

"Fat, indeed!" The two girls had come out of the water and stood just behind F. Millard. He didn't blame the dark one for being indignant. Mrs. Kingdom's every dimension was larger than any of his, but that didn't make her fat. The Juno-type, he catalogued: full busted, wide-hipped, rather beautiful in a large, quiet way.

Then she began to talk. "Oh, you're the F. Millard Smyth Tom Blaine's trying to sell his store to! You remember, Virgil, he was over the other day. He wants to go Outside on account of the war and arthritis—"

With animation and gestures, she reminded her husband of Blaine's conversation while F. Millard erased the word "quiet" from his mind.

Virgil Kingdom interrupted, rising on one elbow. "One side, Bella, Mr. Smyth wants to meet Jade."

The animation vanished from Bella Kingdom's face. Sharp discontent replaced it. She moved aside just as the other girl pulled off her bathing cap. Pale blond, almost platinum blond hair fell on slim shoulders. Wide, jewel-green eyes glanced obliquely at F. Millard from a delicately tinted oval face. The white-haired woman was no thinner than this girl, but Abby Thorne's thinness had the stringiness of age, and this blond fragility was all youth and curving charm. White hair, blond hair—stringiness, fragility—the second figure last night could have been either this girl or Abby Thorne.

F. Millard heard Virgil Kingdom's mocking voice. "They all want to meet Jade. Miss Lothrop, may I present Mr. Smyth, spelled with a y?"

The smile that sparkled in his direction was directed more at Kingdom than at himself. But before Jade could speak, Abby slapped madly at her forehead, yelling, "Damn it! Squirt me, King! Quick!"

The man on the blanket reached a lazy brown hand for a spray gun, and as the woman leaned forward with eyes squeezed shut, he sprayed her face, neck, hands, and the back of her shirt.

"Quick, Watson, the Flit," drawled Jade Lothrop. "When you finish Abby, start on me, King, before the mosquitoes do."

Both objected to mosquitoes, both these thin, light-haired women. In the woods without a spray gun, either would have worn a net, long sleeves, and gloves. F. Millard made sure his own net was in place.

Her face glistening with spray, Abby Thorne straightened. "All this fuss about mosquitoes—with men getting shot and bombed just a few hundred miles away! Bet Ethan's laughing his head off, unless it hurts his leg."

No wonder Sergeant Frazee hadn't stood up. Even more than the frequent plane flights or the bombing of Dutch Harbor, the cane F. Millard hadn't noticed before in the shadow of the soldier's long leg, brought the war close.

"That's why he can't go swimming," said Abby. "Though I tell the girls the lake's too cold for anyone with the sense God gave geese—ice hardly melted. Ethan was on a flight patrolling the Aleutians and got shot by some cruising Japs. He's out here resting up."

Ethan Frazee paid no attention to Abby and F. Millard. He made a more determined effort to get up, and this time succeeded, achieving an air of British nonchalance as he leaned on the cane. Virgil Kingdom, too, scrambled suddenly to his feet, and F. Millard felt smaller than ever. Unfolded, the soldier was tall, just under six feet, and Kingdom an inch or two over. Both pairs of eyes were fixed on the lake.

The five from the float were coming in, the little boys still swimming. The man was out of the water halfway down his ribs, and as F. Millard watched, the woman, too, touched bottom, revealing a straight pair of shoulders just taking on their summer tan, a mop of uncapped wet hair, and bright lips. She shook her wet hair, and F. Millard started. It was the redheaded girl, her burnished curls as sleek and dark as a seal's.

All five looked interestedly at F. Millard.

Surprisingly, it was Ethan who gave the girl's name. "Miss Christianna Thorne, Mr. Smyth." No nonsense about the spelling.

"Chris Thorne," she corrected gravely, offering her hand.

F. Millard glanced at the older woman.

"Abby's her mother," said Ethan.

The hand in F. Millard's was small and wet, with a grip almost like the sergeant's. The girl herself was as small as she'd looked last night walking, purposefully silent, under the trees, kneeling beside the trail. She and the three little boys in a standing row were the only ones on the beach shorter than the grocer.

The man with her was taller than Ethan, almost as tall as the lazy civilian. There was a faint similarity, like a family resemblance, between him and Virgil Kingdom, but no duplication of features: a good nose, not quite so straight; a good mouth and chin, not quite so clearly cut; brown hair receding slightly above the temples, instead of black; gray eyes instead of gold-flecked hazel. This man was as much like the handsome instructor as a dollar edition of a five-dollar book.

Virgil Kingdom confirmed F. Millard's guess. "Ethan only did half the job. This is my brother Benny."

The strength of Benny Kingdom's grip matched the redheaded girl's and Ethan's. "Scouts," he said to the boys, "shake hands with F. Millard Smyth. They're all named Bill, so we call them One, Two, Three, in order of size."

The grocer clutched successively three wet, limp hands.

Abruptly, the biggest and darkest boy demanded, "Say, are you the guy that was with that Senator's party, the one that—"

"The one where they had those murders?" shrilled the middle-sized Scout, who was also middle-colored.

The smallest and blondest gasped, "Why, you're the guy that figured it out!"

The adults were suddenly hushed. F. Millard heard himself swallow.

Abby Thorne's was the first voice out. "Why, damn it to hell, I'd no idea you were *that* Smyth!"

F. Millard felt a miserable flush sneak up under his collar. Then he realized, with relief, that head nets had other uses besides keeping off mosquitoes.

The others were still oddly silent. In the quiet, F. Millard heard a new sound, like snoring. Focusing his spectacles he saw, close under the bank in a dug-to-fit hollow, a mass of gray-tan fur.

"North! North! Wake up, old man," said Benny Kingdom. "Don't forget your manners."

The snoring stopped, and the fur unrolled. A shaggy head with pointed

13

ears raised itself from the hollow.

Bella Kingdom made his excuses. "He's so old, he's taken to snoring. He used to be leader of Virgil and Benny's best dog team. The last one they had, in their teens."

"He's not decrepit," her brother-in-law said quickly. "North's only twelve, and I've known dogs fourteen."

"They can't bear to give him up," Bella murmured to F. Millard. "And he really isn't decrepit. For a dog his age, North gets around—especially at night."

"I've met him," F. Millard smiled. "He called on me at midnight."

Another hush fell on the beach.

"You're supposed to sleep at midnight, mister," Abby said sharply.

"I can't get used to these daylight nights," F. Millard apologized.

"Thought you'd been in town all summer." Her tone was sharper.

"You can pull the shades down, there," the grocer pointed out. "There aren't any out here, and my cot's on the screen porch."

"You're staying in Tom Blaine's cabin?" Virgil Kingdom's voice was quiet but no longer lazy.

F. Millard nodded. "Mosquitoes are worse out here, too. Of course, I got to sleep in time, but not right away."

In time for what, the redheaded girl must be asking herself? To miss her noiseless passage by his cabin? Or to see it? In time to see her hover over those seven oddly spaced stones? Or see her destroy the pattern? And someone else must be asking similar questions. Either Abby Thorne, with her knotted white hair, or the glamorous blond, Jade Lothrop. And someone else besides, someone who had twice let his foot scrape on the rocky road. There might even be others. After all, F. Millard had finally gone to sleep. No telling who else among these intent listeners might have passed.

The silence lengthened.

"Did the old dog have far to go to get to my place last night?" the grocer asked at last. "Every cabin I passed this morning looked vacant till I came to the one with the sun deck over the boathouse."

"That's ours," said the redheaded girl in a firm little voice. "Abby and Jade

14

and I live there. North lives with the King—and Bella," she added quickly.

" 'The King?' " F. Millard repeated.

Chris laughed. Her red hair, drying at the edges, had begun to curl up and shine. "That's a hangover from childhood. We all used to call Virgil the King when we were little. Partly, I suppose, because his name was Kingdom, and partly—"

"He was the oldest and biggest," her mother broke in. "That made him leader. And of course with a name like Kingdom, what else would he be called? King to his face, and the King behind his back."

F. Millard's spectacles turned toward the younger brother. Naturally it would be the handsome, taller, older Kingdom who was called the King. Virgil, not Benny.

Bella Kingdom said suddenly in a low, tight voice, "That's not the only hangover from childhood."

Again, silence fell on the little group, heavy with unease.

"Did you three grow up together?" F. Millard asked.

Jade Lothrop shook back her long, near-platinum bob. "Not just those three, Mr. Smyth. We all grew up together, on the same tailing piles on the creeks."

"On Abby Creek," Chris Thorne enlarged. "The Abby Association."

"Association?" F. Millard repeated.

"Forgot you're not a mining man," Chris apologized. "An association's a bunch of claims joined to work together. Our families formed one on Abby Creek—the Thornes and Kingdoms and Frazees."

"And just Trigger Joe and me left," Abby murmured.

"Four claims," contributed Bella, "and only Trigger Joe's without children— Chris on the Thornes', and Virgil and Benny on the Kingdoms', and Ethan and Jade on the other Frazee claim. Jade's mother married Ethan's dad, so they're really stepbrother and sister. And my mother, who lived in Fairbanks, parked me with the Kingdoms every summer." She took off her bathing cap and smoothed the already smooth dark wings of hair from its center part. Her hands slid to the small of her back.

"Nothing tied there now, Bella," Jade said softly, her eyes glinting green in the sun.

"For the love of mud, Jade," the little redhead glowered, "lay off."

Her mother's voice rose strongly. "Those hoodlums on the tailing piles have turned out fine men and women. The King's a professor at the University—"

"Instructor," the handsome man amended.

"—and Benny sells insurance. Ethan's a gunner on a bomber, and my Chris a teacher. Bella makes a fine professor's wife."

F. Millard made a mental note that she hadn't mentioned Jade. The three boys had gone back to splashing in the water. They, and the six men and women who had grown up together, made nine; Mrs. Thorne ten. Tom Blaine had said there were eleven at the lake. One neighbor hadn't appeared.

"Guess I'll walk on," said F. Millard. "I haven't seen the rest of the cabins."

"North end of the trail's the Scout Camp," Abby told him, "and the south end's just past your cabin."

"Doesn't it go to that house on the point?"

"Have to go by boat." Did he imagine it, or did she snap that information?

"Or wiggle through the bushes," shrilled one of the Scouts, dodging a handful of wet gravel that hit Virgil Kingdom's broad shoulder.

"God help us," the instructor muttered. "Here's Trigger Joe."

A bent old man was stumping along the trail on the bank above them, coming from the direction of F. Millard's cabin. About a red face, sparse white hair stood out around his hatless head. Without slowing down, he began to complain in a high, irascible voice as thin as his body, "Now listen, you folks—I'm sick and tired of arguments. I'm not going to sell, and that's all there is to it. You might as well save your breath. Damn shame you look so much like your ma, Jade. Just so you don't get to be like her... "

His voice died in a mumble, but no one on the beach answered. All eyes, F. Millard's wide and astonished, followed the old man past the Thornes' cabin, almost past the next. Here, he paused. "One good thing this war did," he yelled down, "is make gas too scarce to bring all Fairbanks out here with outboard motors raising hell night and day."

Starting on, he flung back over his shoulder, "Now, remember, no use to argue," and stumped out of sight where the trail dipped into the clearing.

"For gracious sake," said F. Millard.

"Who's got cigarettes?" asked Jade.

Bella stood up. "It's nearly noon, Virgil." Her hands strayed toward her back, and she lowered them quickly, glancing at Jade.

"Time for lunch, Scouts," called Benny. "You can go by the beach if you want to. Come on, Mr. Smyth. I'll show you where we all live."

For all the comments anyone made, the old man might never have passed.

The boys splashed off in ankle-deep water. The three Kingdoms began to climb the boathouse steps. The dog got up with stiff dignity and followed. F. Millard hesitated. Then Bella, at the top of the stairs, turned the same way the old man had gone, and the grocer joined the procession.

They passed the Thornes' and the empty first cabin, dropped down the trail into the clearing, passed the telephone booth at the fork in the road, and climbed the path up the cut bank on the north—more closed doors and padlocked cabins, more beached rowboats, upside down and dry.

At last, Bella laid her hand on a doorknob. "Here's where we live, Mr. Smyth. Drop in sometime and tell us about your experience with the Senator's party last winter."

"You can tell me about the Senator's beautiful daughter," drawled her husband. "Here, North. Come here, boy."

F. Millard started on with Benny Kingdom behind him. "I'll find my way all right," he assured the younger man, "I'd hate to have you miss lunch."

Benny's laugh was unmirthful, "I'm not home yet. You didn't think I lived with the King?"

"Why, I—I didn't know. I didn't think. Your brother—"

The laugh came again, louder, no merrier. "An insurance agent quartered on the King? Besides, my brother's married now."

"Well, uh—"

" 'Well, uh' is right, mister. Any time you're hunting Benny Kingdom, don't go to the palace. I'm the Scoutmaster, even if only three mothers were willing to trust their offspring out of their sight in wartime. And I guess insurance agents are entitled to vacations just like University instructors.

17

So you followed me, old man."

At the change of tone, F. Millard looked curiously over his shoulder. Benny Kingdom had stopped to look back. Down the trail at an elderly trot came the old sled dog. He thrust his nose into Benny's hand, and the two walked on together.

"Didn't your brother's wife say the dog stayed with them? I thought I heard your brother call him."

Benny grinned. "It's a bitter pill for the King to swallow, but of course dogs are only dumb brutes—North prefers Benny Kingdom to Virgil. Can you imagine that? They fixed a down-cushioned bed, and cook him special gruel, and buy the best grade salmon strips from the natives—and still North prefers Benny."

The men and dog walked on in silence. They heard the three Scouts whoop on the beach. One of them yelled in a high boy's voice, "Benny! Hey, Ben, where are you?"

The man behind F. Millard gave an answering shout, and they passed two more empty cabins. Then Benny Kingdom's voice came again, half bitter and half amused.

"Epitaph for Benjamin Kingdom: Dogs and children loved him."

As F. Millard fumbled for a reply, the sound of motors drowned out the whine of mosquitoes frustrated by his net.

One, two, three bombers roared over the northwest hills. For a minute the stars on their silver wings were reflected in the lake. Then stars, planes, and motor-beats passed.

Ethan Frazee, reflected F. Millard, might have been flying over his former playmates if one flight hadn't brought him a cane.

Benny must have thought of it, too. He said, "Ethan's convalescing with his uncle. Old Trigger Joe Frazee's quite a lad. When he left the creeks, there were hardly any summer places out here, and he built himself a little cabin way off from the others to live in all year round. Then people began coming out and crowded right up to Trigger Joe and past him. The old man got so mad he built a high fence that goes out to deep water on both sides, so the trail can't pass his house the way it does everyone else's. Trigger Joe doesn't go for people."

F. Millard gripped the rolled copy of *Flatfoot* in one hip pocket. "Has he shot many men?"

"Sh-shot many men?"

"That name—Trigger Joe—"

Benny gave a whoop of laughter. "None that I know of. They call him that because of his hair-trigger temper. He gets so mad so often, it's a riot. There's the stockade."

Stockade, F. Millard thought stopping to stare while Benny and the dog went on was a good name for that enclosure—a double or treble row of birch poles with ends buried in the ground so close together no crack of daylight showed through. He pictured the old man behind it, shut off from noisy vacationers, alone with himself and his temper. Not alone now, for the weeks of his nephew's convalescence.

Quitting the shoreline he followed the trail along the fence almost to the road, in sight a few yards away through the trees, before it rounded the corner of the fence and passed a gate at the back.

Benny was waiting beyond the gate. "Here's the Scout Camp," he said, "the end of the trail."

The three boys came tearing up behind them and rushed Benny into the long, low-screened building in the center of the Scout Camp while F. Millard walked on, to the water's edge.

The camp lay in a curve of the lake shore, curved enough for the peering grocer to see, past Trigger Joe's fence, bits of the cottages and boathouses on the beach. He could see the float with its diving platform, the splash of orange on the bank that meant the Thornes' umbrella, and far away the house on the point. His spectacles followed on along the low, wooded hills and green water. Blaine said moose were shot over there, and bears got into meat at the cabins. The poor old misanthrope, Trigger Joe Frazee, had guessed wrong. If he'd built his cabin half a mile farther on, he'd have needed no stockade. Along the miles of untouched shoreline, there was only this short fringe of habitation—a raveling of civilization dropped on the wilderness carpet.

No trail led on from the Scout Camp, so F. Millard started home. As he reached the gate at the back of the stockade, it was flung violently open, and a figure sprang out to confront him—the bent old man who had passed on the bank, close enough now for F. Millard to see the wild gleam of his faded blue eyes and his almost toothless gums.

"So they've got someone else!" he snarled at the speechless grocer. "They knew they couldn't do it alone. Now I'll have you after me, too!"

The gate slammed in F. Millard's face.

Chapter Three

Because F. Millard couldn't sleep the second night, he smelled the smoke. It was midnight again and daylight. Two hours before, as he settled down on his cot, another flight of bombers had gone over. Watching the plane specks merge with the sky, he had first noticed the storm clouds. If it rained good and hard it might be dark enough to sleep, and the dry woods needed a wetting. When he came back this morning from exploring the lake, he had found Abby Thorne on her sun deck, staring at the sky. She had handed him the spray gun from the railing beside her, and absent-mindedly asked for a squirting.

"You'd think this long dry spell'd discourage mosquitoes, but they're thicker than ever. Suppose all we'll get out of it'll be a bunch of new forests fires."

And now F. Millard thought he smelled smoke. He admonished his too vivid imagination and turned over.

In the sky, the clouds were spreading, but it was still light enough to see, on the other side of the screen door, the spot where Chris had knelt last night, and Abby or Jade bent later. There was no pattern in rocks there tonight, and no one had come down the path. No more feet had scraped on the road that ended behind his cabin. The trail ended too, as Abby had said, not fifty yards farther on. He had followed it this afternoon till it disappeared in a clearing where someone had apparently prepared to build and then thought better of it. If Chris and the woman who had followed her, and whoever had walked on the road, went last night to the house on the point, they must, as the smallest Scout said, have wiggled through the bushes or gone over in a boat.

21

But the way the second figure had slipped from tree to tree made the thought of both women in one boat hard to credit, though the notion of two canoes, one following the other through the eerie daylit midnight, was even more fantastic, and a flotilla of three...

It would have to have been a canoe because F. Millard had heard no oars. But if a boat had been beached there last night, there would have been a mark on the pebbles, and this afternoon, when he'd been exploring, he'd hunted for an opening through the trees and slid down the bank in a cloud of mosquitoes—and had another surprise: a few yards farther on the beach ended too, as completely as the path. Water lapped right up to the bank, and tree roots dangled above it.

A boat could have waited beneath the bank for someone ashore to jump in. And perhaps his picture of three boats was only a little more farfetched than smelling smoke when he thought of fire.

The smell of smoke persisted, ridiculously real. He tried to turn his mind elsewhere to the picture of Ethan Frazee's wild-eyed uncle standing in the stockade gate raving at F. Millard. What on earth had he meant by, "They've got someone else?" How could F. Millard be "after him, too?" The poor old fellow must be completely off his rocker.

Anyway, it really was getting darker. If the storm clouds didn't blow over—

What made his throat sting? Something pungent and biting... He wrinkled his nose. Smoke! Not in his mind. It was in the air—in his nostrils!

F. Millard leaped out of bed. Jerking shoelaces into knots, without stopping to cover pajamas, he began to run. No time to get a head net either. Abby Thorne had been stewing over forest fires this afternoon. No rain since the snow left—fallen trees and dead brush like cured firewood—all these empty cabins—

Smoke swirled thickly around him. Then he saw flames. Midway between his place and the Thornes', a vacant cabin was burning—long spurts of flame that made the light night brighter. No time to wonder how it started—no use trying to stop it alone—he must run to the Thornes', send one of the women on for the Kingdoms and Ethan, and get back with the others to start a bucket brigade.

The air around the burning cabin scorched him. He crooked an arm over his face and tore by.

At last, the orange umbrella bloomed dizzily by the path. F. Millard pounded, wheezing, on the door. Chris Thorne opened it, rubbing her eyes.

The grocer gasped, "Fire—get boys—"

Chris, in her bathrobe, shot past him down the trail.

Abby, wearing lurid pajamas, collided with Jade as both dashed for buckets. In spite of his own excitement, F. Millard had time for surprise to see Jade Lothrop fully dressed. Then all three were over the bank, beach pebbles flying as they ran, filling buckets, panting up to fling their petty contributions on the blaze.

Time whirled by so readily that it seemed only a matter of minutes before the Kingdom brothers and Ethan Frazee, the three Boy Scouts, and Chris and Bella had joined the scramble; another minute before an orderly bucket brigade had been formed and helter-skelterness conquered.

F. Millard didn't know when they began shouting to let the blazing house go and save the others. Afterwards he tried to remember who had been most insistent. It was all a jumble of yelling and flames, sparks, smoke, and slopping water.

A sudden wind snatched in hot red gusts at the flames. The first fighters concentrated their buckets on the cabin to windward.

The wind increased. If it blew any stronger, in spite of the conveyor belt of buckets, the second cabin was doomed.

Then, another force took charge. The increased wind would have warned them if there'd been time to think of anything but the fire, though the ever-brightening flames kept back the growing dark. The storm F. Millard had seen approaching arrived. It broke above the lake with a violence even greater than the fire's. The bucket brigade became useless, each toss just a thimbleful in the sluicing rain. The next-door cabins were safe.

Reluctantly, angrily hissing, the spears of flame wavered, shortened, vanished.

With the brilliance gone from sky and cabin, night was suddenly there.

Not black night even yet—a gloomy gray, filled with the sound of whipping branches and the sputter and grumble of rain. The walls of the cabin that had blazed brighter than Abby's orange umbrella still stood, black and steaming in the downpour. The roof was gone, rain beating inside and out. The eaves of the other cabins bounced off cascades of water that the wind bent into silver bows. In the dim light, the bucket brigade was bedraggled and smudged. Abby looked exhausted and shaky. The others, except for Jade, in bathrobes, underwear, or pajamas, looked tired, dirty, wet, and exultant. Even the glamorous Jade had torn and smeared the smart green slack suit that matched her eyes; her cherished near-platinum bob was dripping and blown, sprinkled with black cinders.

No wonder Abby was shaking, F. Millard thought; he and she were years older than the others, except for the crazy old man. Where was Ethan's wild-eyed uncle? Wouldn't a fire, with Chris shouting for help at the gate, make even that old hermit come out of his cave?

He peered farther back in the shadows. Perhaps the old fellow had passed buckets with the rest, and then, when the storm took the job off their hands, had withdrawn. He could easily be watching now from the trees. He could even be on his way home, since the fire was out. He could—

There was no good reason for the apprehension that pushed against F. Millard's already pounding heart. An old man wanting solitude—

The grocer's eyes met Abby's, and he knew his apprehension was shared.

She spoke first. "Where's Trigger Joe?"

The others glanced carelessly around.

"He didn't come to the fire," piped the smallest Boy Scout.

"I haven't seen him all evening," said Ethan. The soldier's face was drawn. He had no cane, and his leg dragged when he moved it.

"He shouldn't go wandering around alone!" said Abby sharply.

Ethan looked surprised. "He's always been alone. Old fella'd be fit to be tied if I tried to take care of him."

"But now—" Abby stopped.

"It's since you folks have been here that he started going out." The soldier caught F. Millard's glance and pressed his lips together.

"I saw him headed this direction on my way home to bed," volunteered the middle-sized Scout, breathing faster. "He looked plenty mad."

"Now, kids," Benny cautioned. "You know Trigger Joe. There's nothing to get excited over."

F. Millard drew a deep breath. "How'd that fire start—in an *empty* cabin?" Someone gasped.

Ethan straightened. "I don't believe it. But I'm going in."

"You kids stay out," Benny warned the boys. The Kingdom brothers followed Ethan into the charred, still-steaming cabin.

The others waited, suddenly breathless, in the rain.

F. Millard heard a muffled exclamation and the scrape of iron.

Benny came to the door. The smudges on his face stood out blacker against new pallor. "You Scouts go on back to camp," he directed, blocking the lopsided hole that had been a doorway till the three pairs of curious young feet dragged reluctantly down the trail. "The old man's here, all right," he told the others tightly, "protected by the high-backed stove falling against the iron bed."

"You don't mean—?" It was Abby who spoke on an indrawn breath.

"Oh, no. He's not alive, but it kept the roof from falling on him, and he's not too badly burned."

"Lend a hand, Benny," called Virgil Kingdom from the cabin. "We'll bring him out."

Shaken, the others stepped back. The three men came out of the cabin, carrying another.

It was light enough when they laid him in the trail to see that most of the old man's clothes, and all his sparse wild hair and brows, had been burned away; light enough to recognize him in spite of the sickening changes; light enough to see on his left side—

F. Millard bent suddenly nearer. "What's that dark patch? Might be part of his shirt—but why, when the rest is all burned off—?" He put out an exploring finger, jerked it back. The patch, whatever it was, had a queer stiffness and stuck to the scorched flesh like part of it. Once more, he stooped, peering, then straightened. His eyes went from one to another of the silent group.

"Folks," he said slowly, "this man wasn't burned to death. He was shot."

Chapter Four

Nothing showed in the dismal light that fell on the dirty, wet faces but stunned horror.

"S-shot?" Bella quavered.

The grocer pointed. "You can see the hole. That one patch of cloth didn't burn because it was soaked with blood." Gently, he turned the body over. "Must have got him in the heart, and the bullet's still inside."

Suddenly, above the drumming rain and swishing branches, above the sound of labored breathing, Abby Thorne's voice rang out. "This isn't the first death, and it won't be the last. Trigger Joe and I were the only ones left. My husband killed! Ethan's father and Jade's mother! Both Kingdoms! Now Trigger Joe! Abby Association? It's the Death Association! I'm next!"

"Abby! Abby! Mom!" choked Chris. She gripped her mother's thin arm. "Get hold of yourself! Nothing's going to happen to you. All those deaths were accidents—except—" her eyes turned toward the pitiful thing on the trail. F. Millard saw her fight the shuddering that shook even her smudged bathrobe. "Nothing's going to happen to you, Abby. Poor old Trigger Joe must have done it himself."

Ethan Frazee raised a set, white face. "He's no suicide! Someone shot him!" His blue eyes blazed at Jade Lothrop.

The girl's green ones spat back. "Just because—" she started hotly.

"Forget it," Virgil Kingdom interrupted. "This is no time for a personal row."

F. Millard's voice held unexpected authority. "We'll look in the cabin. If he killed himself the gun wouldn't burn."

"D-don't you want to wait till morning?" Bella quavered.

"It's light enough," F. Millard said, still with that unfamiliar firmness. "We'd better look now."

Poking through the charred wreckage didn't take long. No gun had gone through the fire.

Abby's voice rose again. "I told you Trigger Joe was killed! Just like all the others. Just like I'm going to be. I'm next!"

Chris put her arm across her mother's shoulders. "I'm going to take her home, Ethan," she said. "The other girls'll help you—with him."

"I don't need—" began the soldier.

"You girls all go home with Chris," broke in Benny Kingdom. "We'll help Ethan take Trigger Joe to his cabin."

The women started down the path.

"I don't suppose it matters," said F. Millard thoughtfully, "as long as he's already been moved."

"Think I'm going to let him lie here in the rain?" demanded Ethan.

"I was thinking—about murder," said F. Millard. "You're not supposed to move the body."

The soldier snorted. He stooped over the old man's body. The Kingdom brothers and F. Millard bent for their share of the weight.

No sound came from the Thornes' cabin as the four men, leaning into the wind and rain, tramped by with their grim burden. Chris must have quieted her mother. The Kingdom house was as hushed as any vacant cabin they passed. The stockade gate banged hollowly behind them, and F. Millard thought of the other time he had heard it bang when the owner of the lifeless leg dragging at his hand had slammed the door in his face—the man who had thought F. Millard was after him too. For the last time, the old miner who hated neighbors was shut inside his stockade.

The enclosure they crossed was large enough to hold a wide-eaved log cabin and a high cache like a doghouse on tall stilts.

Inside the cabin, Ethan indicated one of the two corner bunks, and they laid their burden down. The grocer glanced curiously about the single room with everything as neat as a notable housewife would have kept it. Was the soldier nephew responsible for the squarely placed chairs, the cleared tabletop, and orderly shelves—or the old recluse miner? No dust kittens under the bunks, no powdering of flour between the cupboard and kerosene stove, and all litter had been swept off the hearth. Within the blackened rock fireplace, on the ashes of the last fire, was a little heap of torn paper.

F. Millard made an involuntary gesture toward the hip pocket his pajamas didn't have. He thought of the rolled copy of *Flatfoot* in the trousers waiting by his cot, and his fingers itched to take those scraps of paper out of the ashes and piece them together.

But even if murder had been done, it hadn't been done here. Though the murdered man had lived here, another man lived here too. The fragments of typing he could see by bending closer might be a letter from a girlfriend of Ethan's. Anyway, this was the marshal's job—not like the other murders F. Millard had been involved in, where there had been no marshal and no way to get one, where it had all been up to him.

If these torn scraps had any significance, he'd better not call attention to them until the marshal arrived. But what if Ethan lit a fire? It was chilly now, with the wind and rain; he shivered in his wet pajamas. Was it best to keep still—or not?

He burst out in the death hush of the cabin, "Who put those scraps in the fire?"

The Kingdoms and Ethan goggled. Then the grocer realized that tonight, the word "fire" meant only one thing to them.

"I mean in here," he pointed to the cold fireplace. "Who threw away those scraps of paper?"

"I did," said Ethan briefly.

F. Millard sighed. Lucky, he hadn't tried to piece them together. Flatfoot Flannagan—he blinked. The question Flatfoot Flannagan would have asked wasn't who threw them away.

The grocer straightened damp shoulders. "Did you tear it up?" he asked Ethan.

The blue eyes that were lighter than the soldier's tanned face measured the smaller man. "I don't see that it's any of your business, but if it worries

29

you—I found it torn up and threw it away."

"Your uncle did it?"

"I suppose so. He wasn't around to tell me. The pieces were scattered all over the floor."

"How long ago was that?" F. Millard asked.

"Fairly early in the evening, before the last bombers flew over."

That flight had been about ten. How long before the fire had Trigger Joe been shot? How long had the fire been burning before F. Millard smelled it?

"I believe," said the grocer slowly, "we'd better save those scraps of paper for the marshal."

"What the hell for?" scowled Ethan.

"It might have some bearing on your uncle's death. If he tore it up, it must have been one of the last things he did. It might give some clue to his murder."

"You must read detective stories, Mr. Smyth." Virgil Kingdom's tone was mocking.

F. Millard flushed.

But Ethan Frazee nodded slowly. "You may be right, at that. I don't know what the paper was, but if I built a fire—"

F. Millard filled in the soldier's pause: "If you built a fire, we'd never find out; the clue would be gone forever."

Ethan took an envelope from the table drawer and began to rake the torn scraps out of the ashes.

"Hadn't someone better call the marshal?" asked Benny Kingdom.

"You fellows go ahead," returned Ethan. "You'll want dry clothes and something to eat. One of you can phone him."

"You don't want to—stay here, do you?" asked Benny awkwardly.

Ethan stood up, laid the envelope of ashy scraps on the table, and dipped water into a hand basin. "Guess so," he said gruffly.

F. Millard cleared his throat. "Shall I take care of that envelope?"

"I'll keep it," said Ethan shortly.

The grocer blinked, then shrugged. At least there were plenty of witnesses.

Uncomfortably, the three filed out and left uncle and nephew alone. As the stockade gate banged, a tousled head ducked back to the Scout side of the fence.

"You kids get to bed!" The Scoutmaster followed his voice into the long, screened camp building. While his brother and F. Millard waited just inside the door, he shed wet pajamas for daytime clothes, and the humps in the three small sleeping bags lay still.

"And stay there till breakfast," added Benny.

"Aw," said one of the sleeping bags.

"I mean it," the man said quietly as the three adults stepped out in the rain.

F. Millard heard the patter of feet inside the screen. "Say," came a treble croak, "what happened to Trigger Joe?"

"He's dead," Benny said simply. "Now go to sleep."

A shadow rose to greet him from the shelter of the eaves—shaggy, gray-tan, and dignified. Benny's hand covered the wet black nose. "You ought to be warm and dry, old boy," he said gently. "Can I leave him in your house, King?"

"That's where he lives," said Virgil Kingdom shortly.

The men, with the dog close to Benny, slogged back down the muddy trail.

At the Kingdom cabin, F. Millard watched the Scoutmaster coax old North up on his down-cushioned bed while his brother changed well-cut, bedraggled pajamas for dry shirt, slacks, and a slicker. He shook back wet black hair and reached for the brown jacket he had worn the day before. F. Millard saw his body stiffen. His eyes met the little grocer's, and his hand dropped. Then he raised it again—to the overcoat on the next nail. "A long coat'll be more to the point, with you in those soaking pajamas. Better put this on till you get home."

F. Millard's quivering goose flesh was grateful for the warmth of wool, but his nose for detective stories, quivering too, demanded to know the reason for Virgil Kingdom's shift. Even a drink from the makeshift bar that tied F. Millard's unaccustomed stomach in a knot failed to distract him.

Then, the three men left the dog and continued up the trail.

Where the telephone booth stood small and dripping at the fork in the road, they stopped. Virgil Kingdom stepped in and reached for the old-fashioned crank, as if even as small a thing as phoning the marshal was his right. While wind swooped over the clearing unobstructed to the lake, and rain beat on his borrowed coat and Benny Kingdom's slicker, F. Millard listened to the lonely tinkle of the bell.

He thought of the clearing as it must have been in the summers before the war: cars parked to the edge of the trees, lodge picnics by the lake shore in the hundred yards free of cabins. Now, there were only eleven people—there had been twelve—and wind, and rain, and death.

A bell rang again. Funny, central didn't answer.

Benny said uneasily, "Line must be down."

His brother's only comment was another and harder ring.

Above the storm, F. Millard heard a door bang. The Thornes' was the nearest occupied cabin, second in the row where his was the last. Midway between, an untenanted cabin that hadn't been empty last night stood blackened and roofless in the storm—midway between the only two inhabited cabins. If it hadn't been for the rising wind that blew the smoke his way, no one would have known about the fire till the marks of killing had been burned from the old man's bones. No one but the person who set it.

Chris Thorne came around the first cabin, her hair covered with a bandanna, her small, raincoated body bent into the wind and rain. "Don't tell me the line's down!" she gasped.

The three men nodded gloomily.

"I'll walk out to the road," Benny volunteered, "and stop a car."

"I'll go," offered his brother.

"Doesn't anyone have an automobile?" F. Millard asked.

"King does," Benny told him. "But the engine's all apart. The rest of us came on the bus."

Of course, F. Millard caught himself thinking, the King wouldn't use the common bus, the King would have his own car—while he heard Chris say, "We made coffee. You must all come in and have some first."

"But I'm going to walk out to the road," Virgil Kingdom insisted.

"Oh, yeah?" his brother retorted.

Why were they making such an issue of who went for help, the grocer wondered? Was it just the old urge to play hero before the girls? Or something else?

Inside the Thorne cabin, the women were all washed and dressed and combed. The fire in the kitchen stove and the welcome smell of coffee should have made F. Millard forget for a while the flaming cabin and the pitiful body stretched out on the path, so pathetically like a singed chicken's, the near certainty that one of his neighbors was a killer.

But as he sniffed fragrant steam from the cup that Jade held out, he wondered if the slim hand offering it had raised the gun that sent the bullet into the old man's side. He took canned milk from Chris's hand and wondered if it had been hers.

Across the room, Bella Kingdom's voice rose, surprisingly high for a contralto. "Are you going outside again, Jade, now that you're rich?"

"Now we're all ri—" Jade began and broke off. Her green eyes slanted toward the grocer.

Benny Kingdom set down his cup. "Thanks, Abby. I'd better be going."

"Don't bother, Benny. I'll go." His brother shrugged into his slicker.

For gracious sake, if they weren't still arguing about that walk in the rain! Chris reached for the broom. "Why don't you boys settle it the way we used to?" She broke off two straws and held both hands behind her. "The long one goes. Which hand do you want, King?"

They weren't much more than kids yet, F. Millard reflected, in spite of the height of the men and the adult curves of the girls. He wished he might have seen them playing on the tailing piles when they were little, following their handsome young leader. All six were still in their twenties, and they still called the tallest the King.

Benny drew the long straw, and F. Millard felt a secret satisfaction that, for once, his younger brother had beaten the King. *King*, not *the King*, the little man corrected himself. He mustn't get into the habit of the others.

The Scoutmaster paused by his brother's wife. "If I'm late getting back, Bella, will you see the kids have breakfast?" Then, the storm swirled through the door, and Benny's slicker swung off toward the road.

They watched him go, Virgil Kingdom's brow dark.

Jade Lothrop's voice wove a sly thread through the eddying cigarette smoke. "Feeling for those strings again, Bella?"

"Oh, shut up, Jade," began Chris, but as Bella's hands jerked away from her back, her voice lashed at the blond girl:

"Well, at least I don't have to hold my hands up in the air to make them white!"

"King," said Chris gently, "remember that time on Abby Creek—?" They moved off to a farther window.

"Have another cup of coffee, Mr. Smyth," urged Abby Thorne. Was it possible that two hours ago this woman with smooth white hair and capable hands had given way to hysterics? That terror had leaped from her tortured eyes? Above the coffeepot her eyes again met F. Millard's, and he saw that the fear had not gone.

He had hardly begun his second cup when Virgil Kingdom put on his slicker. "I'll try phoning again. Central might have been out, or maybe they've fixed the line."

Kingdom left, and Chris joined her mother by the stove. The hands she held out to the warmth were shaking.

The grocer gulped the rest of his coffee. "Time I got my clothes changed, Mrs. Thorne. Mr.—uh—Professor— uh—the King loaned me a coat, but I've still got on wet pajamas."

They hustled him out with feminine clucks, and he stood for a minute in the rain. Off toward the fork in the road and the telephone booth, he heard the bell again, spooky and faint in the downpour. Heard it once, and no more.

He turned up the collar of his borrowed coat and started for home. The storm had lessened, and full daylight hovered back of the clouds. The unmistakable sharpness of wet, charred wood reached him before he saw the burned cabin. He stopped in the lopsided doorway. Nature had put a bad crimp in the murderer's plans. If it hadn't been for the storm, even though logs take longer to burn than boards, this doorway wouldn't be here, neither would the charred walls, nor the still recognizable, pitiful object that now lay on Trigger Joe's bunk. The bucket brigade could never have put out the fire alone.

It seemed as if the murderer had chosen a poor time for a fire. Something must have happened last night to make the killing advisable in spite of storm clouds, or it might have been a spur-of-the-moment affair when nothing but the urge to kill had counted.

Light gleamed in from the broken rectangle of the window above the high-backed kitchen range tilted against the iron bedstead where the body had been found. The old man must have been by that window. If he'd been shot somewhere else and carried in—but anyone with a body on his shoulder would attract a lot more attention than someone with a gun.

The bullet hole had angled forward. F. Millard stepped out and walked around the cabin. The ground rose slightly at the rear. It would be easy for someone standing behind one of those trees between the cabin and road to shoot through the back window.

He plowed through blueberry bushes. The soil near the lake was too sandy to retain clear footprints in spite of the rain. And of course the shot had been fired before the storm. But when he reached the road his eyes searched the ground just the same.

He almost jumped out of his borrowed overcoat— there, on the road, its stem pointing directly at the burned cabin, was that same design in rocks. Seven stones like a meerschaum pipe—no, this one had eight. The two stones defining the outer edge of the bowl had another stone above them.

Chapter Five

Gradually, while F. Millard bathed with water dipped from the lake and heated on the stove, breakfasted, and had time for a maddening amount of thinking that ran in circles; the rain slackened and stopped. Without its patter on the roof, the cabin was oppressively still, so that when a knock came on his door the grocer's pulse thumped too.

On the porch, the three Scouts were huddled in a bursting knot.

"Can we come in?" the largest asked. "We got something private to say."

F. Millard stepped back, and the boys filed in. The smallest, last through the door, made certain it was closed. The other two peered solemnly out of each window. Then, all three crowded close to the grocer.

"Look," said the first Scout firmly. "We know Trigger Joe was murdered."

F. Millard blinked. "Well, uh—guess he was."

"Soon as you guys left this morning after Benny changed clothes we went over and asked Ethan what happened."

"He didn't—you didn't see the body?"

"Naw. He wouldn't let us, but—"

"We got some clues!" piped the smallest Scout.

"We're going to keep watch on Ethan!" burst out the middle-sized one. "We haven't got anything on him yet."

"But—but," F. Millard gasped, "why should you?"

"He's going to get old Trigger Joe's money, ain't he?" the middle-sized Scout demanded. "Well, then!"

"Look here, kids," F. Millard said. "You mustn't get mixed up in this."

36

"We won't let no murderer get us," the biggest boy reassured him. "No one even seen us get the clues."

Number Two took up the tale. "When you guys left and we saw Ethan, we waited till Benny's brother got his clothes changed and you'd all gone. There was no one there when we went in, but the dog."

"You three went into the Kingdoms' cabin?" F. Millard wondered how the King—*No*, he corrected himself firmly, *King*—would like to be called Benny's brother.

"Sure," said Number One airily. "This is what we found."

He reached in his pocket while the smallest Scout gave an uncontrollable hop. In the first boy's grimy hand lay a shell from a twenty-two rifle.

F. Millard shivered. That small, blood-marked hole in the old man's side…

"We found it in Benny's brother's pocket—in the brown jacket he left on the nail."

The jacket King's hand had shied away from, that had turned his whole body rigid. The jacket he wore yesterday—when Trigger Joe had been shot.

"And we got another clue." This time it was the middle- sized Scout fishing in his pocket. "Off the floor by Benny's cot."

No one was sacred from their sleuthing, F. Millard reflected as Number Two wrestled with the contents of his pocket, not even the Scoutmaster.

Triumphant at last, the boy brought out a scrap of paper.

F. Millard's breath broke off in the middle. All those scraps of torn paper in Trigger Joe's fireplace—could this be related to them? He rushed to a window and held the scrap up to the light—heavy white paper, and on it two typed capital letters: E-M, and part of another letter before the E.

He turned back to the boys. "Where's Benny now?"

"Not back yet," said the largest. "Guess the storm washed out the road. They still kept trying to phone, but the line must be down."

"Now look here." F. Millard hoped he sounded stern. "You mustn't get mixed up in this. Murder isn't something to get a kick out of. It's bad business—dangerous, understand? Suppose whoever did it caught you snooping—"

The middle-sized Scout leaned forward dramatically, eyes lighted like

100-watt bulbs. "Our lives wouldn't be worth a plugged nickel!"

F. Millard choked back a laugh though his feeling coincided with the boy's. He tried to make his voice hearty. "Guess no one'd shoot a kid. But you might get a crack on the head to keep you from finding out something. And you mustn't take any chances before you're sent home." He looked at three pairs of bright eyes. "Maybe you better promise."

No answer. The three pairs of eyes were unchanged.

"Besides," the grocer added, "the marshal's office'll have charge of the case. If we try to muscle in, we might just ball things up."

"Are *you* going to keep out of it?" demanded the biggest boy.

"Why—yes, Bill." The grocer hesitated. "Didn't Benny say your name was Bill?"

"Yeah, and so's his, and so's his." The dark boy pointed at each of the others. "Just call me One, it's easier."

"I'm Two," said the middle-sized Scout.

"I'm Three," shrilled the smallest.

"Well then, One, it's like this." F. Millard turned to the largest Scout, man to man. "I had to be a sort of detective when I was out with the Senator's party because there wasn't any marshal, but when there's a marshal on the job, he's boss. If we know anything, we'll tell him, but we've got to keep hands off. You see the sense of that, don't you, One?"

The biggest boy nodded regretfully. "There ain't no reason why we can't keep our eyes open and notice things, is there? Just so we don't *do* nothing?"

Notice things…. "Might be a valuable help," F. Millard absently agreed. Murder—and the oddly familiar rock pattern that kept appearing and disappearing; murder— and the redheaded girl's silent walk and the slim girl or woman who had followed. Somewhere in the region of his stomach, he winced away from his thoughts.

"Whatever we see," the second boy declared, "we'll report to you."

This time, the man's voice was regretful. "Guess you better tell the marshal."

Three's chubby face twisted into a scowl. "Okay, if he comes himself, but if he sends one of those smart-aleck deputies, we'll report to you."

"Let's see if Benny's back yet," F. Millard suggested. "By the way, fellas, don't say anything about those things you found. I'll give them to the marshal when he comes."

They single-filed down the trail in front of the cabins. Just as well, thought F. Millard, to keep those kids off the road till the marshal saw that pattern in stones behind the burned cabin. The Scouts swarmed again through the ruins, but F. Millard kept his face averted. He didn't like those charred walls, or anything they stood for.

In the Thornes' three-room cabin, they found all the women and Virgil Kingdom—like a sultan surrounded by his harem. Neither Ethan nor Benny was in sight.

Now that the rain was over, slickers had been discarded. The handsome instructor wore the brown jacket he'd had on the day before. Involuntarily F. Millard's hand went to his own jacket pocket. That cartridge shell—as a married man, King wouldn't have the same ambition as Benny to play hero before the girls. But if he had gone alone to the road, he could have circled back to his cabin and picked up the shell.

Across the room, Bella Kingdom was holding forth. "Ethan won't let Jade in the cabin. She went down there and—"

"He just took one look," broke in Jade, her long, fair bob quivering, her eyes bright emerald fire, "and slammed the door in my face, and then yelled through it, 'I'll hand you that damn will!'—but he didn't. He was gone a long time while I stood out on the wet ground with the trees all dripping on me, and after a while, he came to the door and said he couldn't find it. All he could find was the old will, the one in his favor!"

So Trigger Joe had his will with him! "My gracious," the grocer began—but he'd think about that later.

"I tell you, it stinks!" ranted Jade.

Unconsciously, F. Millard sniffed.

"Not that kind," Virgil Kingdom said softly. The hazel eyes that met F. Millard's sparkled with dancing gold. There was something about what was going on that Virgil Kingdom enjoyed.

While F. Millard wondered what it was, Chris sprang to the soldier's defense. "Jade Mary Augusta Lothrop, you know Ethan wouldn't do that! If he says he can't find the will, he can't—and that's all there is to it! You know Ethan'd never gyp you out of anything—no matter how he hates you!"

Abby Thorne's dark eyes, without the copper-red tints of her daughter's, met the little grocer's. "Now, girls, you know Ethan doesn't hate Jade. It's natural for stepbrothers and sisters not to get along. What's Mr. Smyth going to think of us all?"

An abrupt silence fell in the cabin. F. Millard felt the converging gaze of all eyes.

Then Chris Thorne said grudgingly, "Well, it isn't fair of Jade to give the wrong impression of Ethan, or anybody. She's good at that."

"Now, girls," her mother said again.

Bella, beside the back window, cried suddenly, "Here's Benny."

The door opened, and the Scoutmaster plodded into the room and slumped down on a chair. He pushed his hat, with the black mosquito net rolled on the brim, back on his head. The two v's above his temples, where the fine brown hair had begun to recede, were damp with sweat.

"Whew!" he exhaled loudly. "These storms sure are spotty. It rained so much harder over the hill, the road's washed out and a lot of small bridges. I had to walk almost to Salcha before I could yell across a gully at the road crew to send word for the marshal. They said the telephone wire's down and the road's in such bad shape he'll have to come by plane. I began to think he'd beat me back."

"No plane yet," said his brother.

For a moment, the group in the cabin separated into its component parts, each walled away with his thoughts. Then Benny raised his head and looked across the room at the slender blond by the window where the light made an unhallowed halo of her hair.

"Well, Jade," he said quietly, "how does it feel to be rich?"

Almost the question, F. Millard reflected, that Bella had asked her this morning.

Before Jade could more than part her exquisite lips and raise the shallow curve of her breast with the breath of an answer, Bella laughed. "Now, won't your husband be sorry he was a brute?"

"Ex-husband," Jade said softly.

"I don't understand," burst out F. Millard. "Why is Miss—Mrs. Lothrop going to be rich? Did Trigger Joe leave her money?"

"Miss Lothrop," corrected Jade. "I took back my own name."

"He made her an heiress," mocked King.

"Was the old man rich?" the grocer asked.

"My God, no!" snorted Abby. "He was just as rich as I am—and that means he had nothing but his interest in the Abby Association. Your ex-'ll never hear about it, Jade," she said tartly, "way off in California. Unless you write him."

"Jade'll want him to know what he's missed." Bella's eyes held a brightening gleam.

The little redhead spoke up crisply. "Then the marshal may be along any minute, Benny?"

He nodded. "You girls got something to eat?"

Chris jumped up contritely. Bella hurried to help her. In the bustle, F. Millard heard the door close. Who, he asked himself quickly, had left the cabin? *Flatfoot* had taught him to keep his eyes open after a murder. They made a rapid circuit of the room. Chris and Bella were fussing over the stove, Benny still waiting in his chair. He heard the boys' voices in the north bedroom and saw that Jade still leaned on the window sill and King's long legs still extended from the couch. Abby Thorne was the one who had closed the door.

She was still gone when Benny started to sip his steaming coffee, still gone when he put down the empty cup. F. Millard stepped outside, closing the door behind him. He looked up and down the trail. No one was in sight. The door to the back yard substitute for plumbing swung back and forth in the breeze.

The road was wider and straighter than the trail. He'd be able to see for hundreds of yards. For some indefinable reason, he suddenly began to hurry through the wet, low brush. On the road, he shook both legs like a cat with wet feet and looked north up the track going over the hill behind the

Kingdoms' cabin. No one was on the hill or the level stretch below it with the telephone booth at the fork of the incoming road, no human legs beside the stilt-like legs of the booth. He turned his head south.

Abby Thorne emerged from the woods behind the burned cabin. Her thin body was bent forward, her eyes intent on the ground. Suddenly, she stooped. Both hands darted down, and she began to pick up something. Then she straightened, her arms drew back, and F. Millard saw a shower of something that looked like rocks fly through the air.

She followed them into the woods. Forcing himself to seem casual, F. Millard began to walk down the road. At the place behind the burned cabin where the design like a pipe had been laid, he looked down. All seven stones and the extra eighth were gone.

Chapter Six

F. Millard had hardly reached his cabin before he heard a plane. Not thunderous enough for a flight of bombers, it might be a single pursuit ship, or it might be the plane with the marshal.

He raised his head net for an unobstructed sight of the sky. A high speck appeared in the northwest—toward Fairbanks—and began to circle the lake. Not an Army ship, and it was landing. Eyes fixed on the sky, he began to stumble back toward the Thornes' on the path along the lake bank.

By the time he reached the sun deck, he saw all the others gathered on the beach. Pontoons hit the water as he clattered down the boathouse stairs, and the plane taxied toward the clearing where the road came in from the highway. Crunching through pebbles, the small boys, the Thornes and Kingdoms, Jade, Ethan, and F. Millard met the three men who clambered from the plane, all unknown to the grocer.

Everyone else seemed to know them. The tall man in the leather jacket was the pilot, who called the dapper man with the black mustache and silver fox hair "Doc." Was the big young man with his hat on the back of his head and black hair tumbled on his forehead a deputy marshal?

"Hello, Art," drawled Virgil Kingdom. "Marshal out of town?"

The mussy-haired man boomed, "Took out a party of insane last week."

F. Millard's eyes met the largest Scout's. If the marshal sent a deputy, the boys would report to F. Millard. Scout Number One winked.

"What's going on here?" demanded Art. "The message I got said a man had been murdered."

"Trigger Joe," said Ethan.

"Trigger Joe!" shouted Art. He looked slowly around the circle of faces, paused at F. Millard's, and then turned to the doctor and pilot. "So Trigger Joe Frazee's been killed. Now, there's nothing in the way of selling the Abby Association."

"Damn it, Art—" began Abby.

The big young man whirled on F. Millard. "Who's this little half-pint?" he demanded.

Chris Thorne performed the introduction. "F. Millard Smyth, Art Heggarty. Art's one of the deputy marshals."

"F. Millard Smyth," repeated Art. "You the guy that was with the Senator's party?"

The grocer nodded.

"Know Trigger Joe Frazee?"

F. Millard shook his head. "I just saw him twice—alive."

The deputy grunted. He turned back to the others, and again, his eyes swept their faces.

"Who killed him?"

For a moment, they looked at each other. Then Virgil Kingdom, spokesman, as usual, broke the silence. "We don't know, Art. Guess it's up to you to find out."

"Let's have a look at the body," broke in the doctor. "Down at his cabin, Ethan?"

The soldier nodded. He led the way up the bank to the trail, and the others fell in behind. Single file, those without head nets slapping mosquitoes, they wound their way through the trees along the lake to the old miner's stockade, tramped around it to the gate at the back.

The doctor, the deputy, and Ethan went in. The others waited outside.

F. Millard still resented being called a little half-pint. He stood between Chris and the Scouts to make himself feel taller. "What did that Heggarty fellow mean when he said that now there was nothing to prevent selling the Abby Association?" he asked.

Chris's brown eyes, repeating the burnished glints of her hair, sought Virgil Kingdom's, then rested on her mother.

"Go ahead, damn it," Abby directed. "You might as well tell him. Or Art will and make it sound worse."

"Abby and the Kingdom boys and Trigger Joe owned the Abby Association after Mr. Kingdom died. Arctic Dredging's been trying to buy it for two years, but Trigger Joe wouldn't sell."

"The others wanted to sell?"

"Hell, yes," said Abby.

"Were you offered a pretty good price?" F. Millard asked.

Abby's eyes turned wary. The grocer looked at the others. Each pair of eyes avoided his.

It was the stranger pilot who answered, leaning loose-jointedly against the fence. "Story around town was sixty thousand dollars[1]."

So that was the reason for those pointed remarks about wealth that they'd all been making to Jade. Each partner would get twenty thousand dollars. How much of Trigger Joe's would go to Ethan, and how much to Jade? The Kingdom brothers would divide their father's share. Abby would get a full share. Twenty thousand dollars, ten thousand dollars—and one old man holding out. Now, the old man was dead—murdered. With new interest, F. Millard examined the faces of his neighbors.

"Hey, Jim!" bawled a voice from within the stockade. "Lend a hand."

The pilot slouched inside the gate. In a little while, it opened again, and the big deputy, the pilot, the doctor, and Ethan carried out a blanket-wrapped burden.

Once more, the procession started, this time along the road. Up over the hill and down past the telephone booth in the clearing. Awkwardly, the blanketed figure was hoisted into the plane. The pilot climbed in, and the doctor, one foot on the nearest pontoon, looked inquiringly at Art.

Benny Kingdom spoke first. "Why not send the kids back in your place, Art?"

The deputy smashed a mosquito, drilling through the black hairs near his cuff. "I'd sure like to, Benny. The lake's no place for kids now. But there's no room in the plane. This small cabin job was the only thing on the river when your message came in. There's only a little bitty baggage compartment and barely room for two passengers. Doc and Trigger Joe'll take up all the space."

The boys began to grin.

Benny eyed them sternly. "Then you've got to keep clear of this mess. No playing detective yourselves. You've got to promise never to leave the cabin at night and to stick together in the daytime. Well, do I hear you promise?"

Grins more subdued, the Scouts promised.

The pilot leaned out of the plane. "Climb in, Doc. Okay to shove off, Art?"

Art Heggarty nodded. The propeller whirled, and the plane taxied down the lake. It gathered speed, rose above the water, above the trees, and darted off toward Fairbanks.

For a moment, F. Millard recaptured the pang of desolation he had known last winter when another plane rose from another lake and left him on the ground. He tried to laugh at himself. This was only for a day or two, four or five at most until the road was fixed. On the shore of that other lake had stalked murder and mystery and fear. He remembered the crackle of last night's flames, the patch of blood-soaked shirt on the old man's side, the pattern in stones that appeared and disappeared. He saw the set white faces around him—and knew that by this lake, too, stalked murder and mystery and fear.

Bella Kingdom drew an audible breath. Her words fell into the silence left by the plane. "Maybe you can track the man who shot Trigger Joe, Art. Do you suppose he's still hiding in the woods?"

Art Heggarty gave a short laugh like a fox's bark. "Don't kid yourself, Bella, or try to kid me. The old man wasn't in anyone's way except the other owners of the Abby Association—and they're all here. I don't guess whoever shot him's in the woods."

A sigh rippled over the beach.

Art took a stiff-backed tablet from his pocket. "Guess I'll start collecting alibis."

Abby roused herself. "Come up to the house."

Except for the grate of pebbles and leather-against- wood clump of shoes on the boathouse stairs, they walked in silence.

Inside the Thornes' cabin, Art drew a chair up to the table in the combined living room and kitchen. He laid his tablet on the table and licked his pencil point as the others gathered chairs and crowded in.

F. Millard blinked. Was he going to interview them all together? Flatfoot Flannagan examined suspects separately unless, of course, he had reason to think that the presence of others was an advantage.

"Okay, Abby," said Art, "this is your house. I'll begin on you. Doc couldn't tell without a post-mortem when Trigger Joe was shot. But it was sometime after midnight when you got him out of the fire?"

Abby nodded.

"Okay," he said again. "Ethan told us one of the Scouts saw the old man about nine p.m. walking toward the cabin that was burned. Where were you between nine and midnight?"

The white-haired woman drew a deep breath. The red had gone out of her weathered cheeks and left them a splotchy tan. "I went to bed early last night. Just before nine, I think."

"And you didn't go out again?" The deputy's Irish eyes were narrowed to blue smudges.

It seemed to F. Millard that Abby went a shade paler. "Once," she admitted, "right after some planes flew over. All that racket made me jumpy."

"Where'd you go?"

"Just up and down in front of the cabin and out to the clearing once or twice as far as the phone booth, and then came back to bed."

"Go anywhere near the cabin where Trigger Joe was found?"

"Damn it, no!" snapped Abby.

"See anyone?"

"No," she said defiantly, as if she'd been braced for that question.

Art tapped his pencil on the oilcloth. "Which room do you sleep in, Abby?"

"North bedroom."

"Anyone sleep in this room?"

"Chris. She gave up her room to Jade."

"You come through here to go out?"

"Sure I did. There's only one door. Think I climbed out a window?"

Art grinned. "I wouldn't put it past you, if you didn't want to be seen. Both those bedrooms have low windows. Chris here when you came through?"

As Abby hesitated, her daughter said quietly, "It must have been while I was out, Abby. I didn't see you."

F. Millard heard the woman's half-strangled inhalation. Then she threw up her white head with a mixture of pride and terror. "Yes, Chris," she said softly. "It was while you were out."

The deputy made painstaking notes in his tablet. He turned a page and faced Chris. "So you were out, too, last night, between nine and twelve?"

A little smile pulled at the corners of the red-haired girl's bright mouth. "Nine's a bit early for sleeping."

"Where'd you go?" Art demanded.

"Just for a walk. Out to the highway and back."

"Alone?"

"Yes." Chris Thorne spoke as defiantly as her mother.

Art asked, as he'd asked Abby, "See anyone?"

Chris moistened her lips with her tongue. "I saw the King—at a distance."

"Sure you didn't go out to meet him?"

Her copper-brown eyes blazed. "Art Heggarty, you must have forgotten he's married now!"

In the quiet room, F. Millard heard Bella's sigh.

The deputy marshal flushed. "Sorry, Chris. I was thinking about old times."

"It's different now," she said shortly.

"After you came back, what did you do?" Art asked.

"Went to bed. Mr. Smyth woke me shouting about the fire."

Art licked the pencil and did some more writing. He turned the page and looked at Virgil Kingdom. "Where were you headed, King, when Chris saw you?"

The University instructor opened his chiseled lips, but no words came. He tried again.

Jade Lothrop laughed. "He was coming to see me."

Bella Kingdom's gasp made even the chubby Scout start.

"How long'd it take him?" Art asked gruffly.

"To see me? About half an hour. We met at nine-thirty in that clearing beyond the Blaines' cabin where Mr. Smyth's staying. I came away just before those bombers flew over, if anyone knows when that was."

"Ten-twelve," supplied F. Millard. "I was winding my watch to go to bed."

Art turned back to Jade. "You and King left together?"

Jade's green eyes sparkled. "I'm afraid he didn't want to be seen with me. I left first."

"How'd you go? By the trail?"

"The road," she answered. "Going and coming."

"By the way, Jade," said the deputy suddenly, "didn't I hear that Trigger Joe put you down in his will?"

Her delicate color was unchanged, but her eyes gleamed with triumph. "Half and half with Ethan."

Art turned to the black-haired instructor. "How long'd you stay in the clearing, King, after Jade left?"

"Five or ten minutes, to give her time to get out of the way."

"What was so hush-hush about meeting Jade?" Art's eyes were narrowed again.

Red darkened Virgil Kingdom's handsome face. He shot a lid-lowered glance at his wife. "We had some business to discuss that was private."

"Business?" Art echoed incredulously. "With Jade?"

Jade laughed, and Virgil's flush deepened. "Business," he repeated sharply.

"See anyone else except Chris and Jade?"

"No," returned King shortly.

"What'd you do then?"

"Went home."

"What time?"

"Don't know."

"Know when your husband got home, Bella?" Art looked at the dark, tense girl who sat two chairs away from F. Millard.

She, like Chris, had to moisten her lips before she could speak even a monosyllable. "No."

"You—er—" Art looked embarrassed "—you sleep in separate beds?"

F. Millard saw her hands clench as she drew a deep breath. He wondered if she counted ten, because her voice, when it came, was steady. "In separate rooms," she said coldly.

Art still sounded embarrassed. "Were you out last night, too?"

Bella shook her head and said clearly, "I was home all evening. I sewed for a while, and read, and went to bed at ten."

"I don't—er—suppose you've any way to prove it?"

Her eyes scorched the deputy briefly before she lowered them. "I have no way to prove it. But that's what I did."

Art wrote heavily on several pages while the others sat looking at their hands or stealing surreptitious glances at each other.

At last, he turned a fresh page. "While we're on the Kingdom family, Benny, how about you? Where were you between nine and twelve?"

"I got the Scouts to bed at nine, then I read a while, and went to bed early myself."

Art turned to the boys. "Can any of you kids prove it?"

All three Scouts blinked. Two, the middle-sized one, swallowed. "I didn't go to sleep right away. I saw Benny reading, and then he blew out the lamp, but of course, it was still light. Then I began to get sleepy, and the last thing I remember was Benny sitting on his cot rubbing tonic on his scalp like he does every night before he goes to bed."

Once more, Jade's laughter rang out, and Benny's face flushed scarlet. F. Millard tried not to look at the receding v's above his temples.

"Guess that puts you to bed, all right, Benny," said Art after his own guffaw subsided. "Any of you boys wake up before midnight?"

Three's chubby pink face grew pinker. "Those bombers woke me up when they went over."

Art turned to F. Millard. "That was at ten-twelve, you said, Smyth?"

The grocer nodded.

"Benny in bed then, was he, kid?" Art asked the smallest Scout.

Three nodded. "I sat up to see the planes, and all the sleeping bags were full—One's, and Two's, and the biggest bump was Benny."

Art grinned, and the chubby Scout leaned back, still pink.

"What about you, Ethan?" asked the deputy marshal. "What did you do last night?"

A muscle in the soldier's tanned cheek twitched. "I was out the early part of the evening, paddled across the lake to see if I could get some ducks, but I got back at nine."

"Duck season's not open yet," said Art sharply.

The soldier grinned.

"Anyone see Ethan's canoe? Asked the deputy marshal.

All but Abby shook their heads. Abby said she saw a canoe about half-past seven, too far away to recognize the paddler.

Art turned back to Ethan. "Were you out between nine and twelve?"

"I walked for about half an hour right after the bombers went over."

"Where'd you go?"

"Out to the highway and back."

"Isn't that quite a walk for a man with a leg wound?"

The muscle twitched again as Ethan's jaw hardened. "Got to toughen up."

"See Chris on the road?"

Ethan's blue gaze rested gently on the redheaded girl. "Wasn't that after you came back?"

F. Millard thought Chris's answering smile held gratitude. "Oh, yes. I'd been home quite a while."

"You didn't see anyone else?" Art persisted.

"The soldier hesitated. "Well—I don't know who it was. I just caught a glimpse of an arm and leg disappearing around the first righthand cabin, the one next to the Thornes.'"

"Man or woman?"

"The leg wore pants and the arm a sleeve."

"But with all the girls in slacks," demurred F. Millard, "and they all wear sleeves, except Miss Thorne, on account of mosquitoes..."

Art nodded. "Could be anyone but Chris—and she could of put on a jacket. Didn't see the guy again, did you Ethan?"

"I went right home and didn't see anyone else till Chris called me for the fire."

Art made some more notes, then turned, with a clean sheet, to F. Millard. "And what did you do last night, Smyth, besides winding your watch at ten-twelve?"

"I read *Flatfoot* all evening till ten and then got ready for bed." Behind his spectacles, F. Millard's lashes batted as he tried to remember details. Lucky the marshal was asking him about last night instead of the night before. Goodness knew what sort of hornet's nest he'd stir up if he had to tell about the two women's silent passing and their strange behavior in front of his door where he found the stones—

His breath caught. Chris—her dainty, sturdy figure kneeling beside the trail—the movement of her elbows, the way one arm had reached out... That very minute, right under his eyes, she might have made that rock pattern— placed the seven stones herself, while he was watching.

"Well," said Art impatiently, "did you spend the rest of the night getting ready for bed?"

The grocer blinked. But he was telling about last night, not the night before. "I just lay there trying to go to sleep till I smelled smoke and ran out to see why."

Art looked around the room now blue with cigarette smoke. "Guess that covers everyone."

F. Millard guessed so, too—covered everyone with a blanket of suspicion. If he could only get out of his own head the picture of those rocks on the road behind the burned cabin—and Chris's elbows moving.

Funny he hadn't heard Jade and King pass his cabin on their way to the clearing, even though they went on the road. But, of course, when they met at nine-thirty, he'd been deep in a story in *Flatfoot*, and when they came back separately during the time he was getting ready for bed, he'd been moving around himself.

His memory of Chris kept nagging. Even if she hadn't made the rock patterns the first night, she wouldn't have spent all that time hovering over the one before his cabin without some special knowledge of that peculiar arrangement of stones. Chris, and the woman who had followed. The reaching tentacles of F. Millard's mind recoiled.

"Let's get back to the shot," Art was saying, and F. Millard tightened his grip on the chair-arms. "The hole between Trigger Joe's ribs was made by a small caliber gun. We won't know till Doc gets the bullet, but my guess is a twenty-two."

The grocer sat very still. He mustn't let his hand seek the pocket that held the twenty-two shell, not with Virgil Kingdom in the room.

"The lake's so still, now that most of the cabins are empty," the deputy went on, "and you folks wandered around so much last night, didn't any of you hear a shot?"

Slowly, each head shook.

"A twenty-two wouldn't make much noise," began Ethan.

"But think how God-awful quiet it is out here," repeated Art.

Still, each denial was firm.

F. Millard jumped to his feet. "Those b-b-bombers! He could have been shot with an elephant gun when those six planes went over, and no one would have heard."

"God damn it, of course!" cried Abby. "You've got your head screwed on right."

Art grudgingly nodded. "Guess so. Someone would've heard it any other time. Anyway, we'll know for sure after Doc's report. He ought to be able to set the time from the food in the old man's stomach. Trigger Joe still eat on the stroke of six, Ethan?"

But F. Millard's mind was deep in calculations of its own. If the marshal's office fixed the killing at the time the bombers went over, that left only one of the group in this room with an alibi. The smallest Scout had seen Benny Kingdom in bed—but wait—he hadn't seen Benny's face, only a hump in his sleeping bag. The schoolboy trick of stuffing a bed was long ago hoary with age. Benny had no alibi either.

"What about those scraps of paper?" began Virgil Kingdom, and F. Millard blinked—how could King know F. Millard had been thinking of that scrap by the Scoutmaster's cot? "The stuff Ethan raked out of the ashes," the instructor went on. "He was going to give it to Art."

All eyes turned to Ethan, who slowly reached into his pocket. He brought out an envelope, and—reluctantly, the grocer thought—handed it to Art.

The deputy dumped the smudgy scraps on the table while everyone crowded around him.

He waved an authoritative hand. "Look out! I'm doing this. No one else is going to touch it."

Beneath his big fingers, the jigsaw puzzle grew. Where several typed words came together, Bella read over Art's shoulder, " '—appoint my said nephew exec—' Why, it must be a will!"

Jade's sharply drawn-in breath reached every corner of the room.

" In the name of God, a—,' " read Chris.

"'I, Joseph McCorkle Fraz—' It *is* a will!" cried Benny.

"It isn't—oh, God, don't let it be the one—" Jade babbled frantically.

"Where's the rest of it?" demanded Art. "Where's the other pieces?"

"All there is; there ain't no more," shrugged Ethan.

F. Millard looked up sharply. This was the first time he'd heard Ethan be flippant.

Sergeant Frazee leaned forward and pointed with steady hands. "You can make out the date—May 14th, 1942. This is it, Jade. Here's your name, and 'share and share alike.' "

"You don't—you don't mean—" her hands caught at her slim white throat, and her voice was strangled. Suddenly, she leaped to her feet. "I don't believe it!" she screamed.

"What's become of the other pieces?" bellowed Art, pounding on the table till the scraps of paper jumped.

"It's the will in your favor, all right, Jade." Bella Kingdom's voice was full of venom. "And it's been destroyed."

[1] One dollar in 1943 is worth about twenty dollars in 2024. The $60,000 would be worth approximately $1,200,000.

Chapter Seven

Jade screamed, "You did it, Ethan Frazee! You couldn't bear for me to get half your uncle's money. You destroyed that will yourself!"

"Don't be ridiculous, Jade!" said Chris sharply. "You know Ethan wouldn't do that."

"Ethan wouldn't destroy a will that keeps him from getting ten thousand dollars?" Jade cried hysterically, her long fair bob shaking. "To keep *me* from getting ten thousand dollars? Ethan wouldn't—My God, my God, Art, I'll bet he killed Trigger Joe! Destroyed the will, and killed him, so he couldn't make another!"

The whole roomful sat rigid, staring at Jade, whose eyes were like green-hot dollars spitting sparks.

"That's a pretty serious accusation, Jade," said Art slowly, forgetting to bellow.

"I make it just the same!" the blond girl shrilled. "Who else would kill old Trigger Joe, but the man who gets his money—all of it under the will that's good now! Not a cent for a penniless girl—left all alone in the world."

"Shut up, you little hell-cat," said Ethan tightly.

"'Hell-cat!' " she shrieked. "He calls the girl he defrauded a hell-cat! A man who killed his own uncle, so he—"

Chris jumped up, her bright curls no higher than Jade's eyes. One small brown hand clamped down on the taller girl's arm. "You come in here, Jade Lothrop," she ordered fiercely, tugging her toward the south bedroom, "and stay there till you get control of yourself!"

The door shut behind the two girls.

The others exchanged glances that seemed to F. Millard long and knowing.

Virgil Kingdom stood up with a stretch as full of grace and power as a panther's. "Now that's over, what do you say to a swim? You through sleuthing for a while, Art?"

"Guess I'll have plenty of time. The stage won't get through for days. Go ahead and swim. I'll have a look at the burned cabin."

"I'll show you," F. Millard offered. "It's on my way home." He fingered the cartridge shell and scrap of paper in his pocket.

Art replaced his hat on the back of his head, and the grocer put on his, pulling the net down over his face. Sunshine was cracking the clouds as the two men stepped outside. The trees no longer dripped, and the sandy trail along the lake bank, which had been running almost like a creek when they carried Trigger Joe to his cabin, was now only damp. A storm's life and death, F. Millard reflected, treading on the deputy's heels, was like a man's. All bluster and hullabaloo, then nothing but mute reminders— washed-out roads and bridges, torn scraps of paper in a fireplace.

Funny, this storm that had saved perhaps a whole row of empty cabins might cause the death of a man. If the fire hadn't been put out in time to preserve the marks of Trigger Joe's wound, no deputy marshal would be here now to hunt a murderer.

Art Heggarty stopped at the blackened cabin, and the grocer stopped, too. The deputy stepped through the gaping doorway, and F. Millard followed.

"How the old boy ever got out of this in as good shape as he did—" mused Art.

"Rain," said F. Millard simply. "The iron helped too, of course." He led the other man to the window above the stove and bed. "He must have been here—"

Art grunted.

"You saw where the wound was," the grocer hurried on. "If someone had been outside that window—"

"Don't let me keep you from your swim," the deputy muttered, "or whatever you want to do."

"Oh, I'll be glad to help," F. Millard said happily. One hand sought his bulging hip pocket to flick the pages of *Flatfoot*. "I've got a couple of things that might be clues."

Art turned around. He reached up and tipped his hat forward, far over the tousled black hair. His eyes, like blue slits below it, cut into the little man. F. Millard's hand fell away from the highly colored, rolled face of Flatfoot Flannagan.

"You may have stumbled onto a murderer once, my little banty, but that doesn't make you a detective. All that rigamarole I heard about what went on with the Senator's party sounded like the goings-on of a nuthouse to me. I'm not going to have you or anyone else messing up my work —see?"

F. Millard blinked. Involuntarily his hand moved once more toward *Flatfoot,* and fell away. "You don't think I could help?"

"No, I don't," Art said brutally. "You stick to your detective stories and leave real murders to me. Now I don't mean you're not to tell me anything you know. If you got any facts tucked under that head net, I want them, but leave the deducting to me. Now what was that you said about clues?"

Sighing, F. Millard drew out the shell and scrap of paper.

Art pounced. "Where'd you get this twenty-two shell? You know it might've been a twenty-two—"

The grocer explained. And this time, the deputy listened.

He held up the scrap of paper. "This looks like part of that torn-up will."

"Does to me, too," F. Millard agreed and told the rest of the Boy Scouts' story.

Art pocketed the treasures, still warm from the grocer's keeping. His eyes narrowed again. "I'll have a little talk with the Kingdom brothers... Got anything more like this?"

"No, but there was something queer—" If he told about the rock design that kept appearing and disappearing—

"Just facts, remember," cautioned Art. "I'll make the deductions."

Behind his spectacles, F. Millard's eager eyes hardened. He'd tell about the design on the road behind the burned cabin; it might have some connection with the murder, and he wouldn't be withholding evidence. But Abby's destruction of it, Art might consider deduction. After all, F. Millard hadn't been able to see from such a distance whether she actually picked up those special rocks.

And as for the other rock patterns—the ones he'd seen the first night—Chris and the woman who stalked her— there hadn't been any murder that night. Art didn't want deductions.

Stiffly, he told about the design on the road behind the burned cabin. The deputy pushed his hat once more to the back of his head, and his heavy brows slowly approached his tumbled hair as the grocer talked. Slowly a grin spread over Art's face.

F. Millard flushed.

The deputy gave a roar of laughter. "That's just why I told you to leave detecting to me. I'll bet you haven't once thought of the kids at the Scout camp. They're always tying knots and watching birds and playing games of one sort or another. But if one of their rock signals points toward the burned cabin, you get all hot and bothered to connect it with murder. Good God, man, if those kids ever find it out, you'll never hear the last of it!"

F. Millard's flush scorched him. Praying his head net hid it, he made his five-foot-six as tall as he could and withdrew. Art Heggarty could have those charred logs all to himself and soak his own trouser cuffs in the wet brush to find out where the murderer had stood.

Severely erect, he stalked toward his cabin. But his shoulders drooped as he neared it. Then, the stiffening sprang back when he saw someone move behind the porch screen. The smallest Boy Scout pushed open his door, and the other two rose from the cot and laid down copies of *Flatfoot*.

"What'd Art have to say?" asked Two. "You working with him?"

"The marshal's office," said F. Millard stiffly, "doesn't want any help."

"No amateurs, huh?" asked One. He exchanged sly glances with Two and Three.

"Now look here, kids," F. Millard reminded them. "You promised Benny to keep out of this mess."

"No sneaking out at night," recapitulated Two.

"And stick together in the daytime," Three finished.

"But we can use the old bean," cried One. "Especially if no help's wanted in the marshal's office. That just about leaves it up to you and us kids." He grinned at F. Millard.

"You promised—" the grocer began.

"Well, you didn't!" One's boy-voice was almost scornful. "You don't have to stay in nights. With what we can pick up days and you get nights, we ought to make out a case—with all the practice you've had."

All three pairs of young eyes shone. F. Millard caught himself giving the boys a conspiratorial nod. "Remember, it's not only big things that count. You can't hope to find a cartridge shell in every pocket. You know these folks better than I do. If anyone does something he wouldn't ordinarily do or says something odd, tell me about it, will you?"

Three winked at Two and One, his chubby face pink with delight.

"But remember," the grocer warned, "you mustn't get yourselves in trouble. You owe it to Benny, and your families, and all of us to keep out of danger. Besides—if anyone gets the notion you're watching, your usefulness would be over."

One's thin, dark face nodded solemnly, and Two bobbed his straight, mouse-colored hair.

"Let's get going, you guys," urged the chubby Scout. "No telling what we could pick up right now."

F. Millard watched the boys pile over each other down the trail. If they made that much noise when they stuck together, they ought to be safe in the daytime, and at night they were staying inside. But he'd feel a lot better when the road was open again.

He felt better now than he had when he left Art Heggarty. There was something about the admiration in those young faces that restored lost confidence. The marshal's office might not want help, but you couldn't expect a man to go around with his eyes shut where there'd been a murder. His thumb flicked *Flatfoot's* pages.

After lunch, he'd watch the swimming. Yesterday, he'd heard enough while his neighbors were gathered on the beach to start all sorts of speculation. But when he reached the Thornes' sun deck, he looked down at only one figure.

59

Three blankets had been spread on the pebbles, but of all the persons who had mussed them, only Bella remained. In a bathing suit, she sat with her knees drawn up, arms clasped around them, and head bowed on their hump.

What if Bella had searched her husband's brown jacket before the Scouts took the cartridge shell? Then F. Millard remembered this morning's revelations: the separate rooms in the Kingdom household, the meeting last night between Jade and Bella's husband.

On tiptoe, he headed back for the trail, but loose gravel rolled under his feet. Bella's head swung up.

"Oh, I—I'm sorry," he stammered. "I thought you were asleep."

As if she had taken both hands and pulled her mouth into a smile, her teeth flashed in the sunshine. She stretched out her legs, straightened her back, and raised one arm in a comradely gesture.

"I don't usually sleep sitting up." Her voice was gay, and he wondered how much the effort to make it gay cost her. "I was just thinking—about a sunbath."

Sunbaths weren't usually taken all folded up, either, F. Millard thought, but he said, "I was only looking for company."

"Come on down," she smiled. "We can pretend we're at the ocean, watching the wild waves—hundreds of miles—thousands—from Harding Lake."

The only part of that little speech that rang true, F. Millard reflected, clumping down the boathouse stairs, was the mileage, her wish to be far away.

"We must be making a terrible impression on you, Mr. Smyth." She patted the blanket beside her, and F. Millard sat down. "You mustn't judge us by the way we behaved this morning. After all, when someone you know has been—let's face it—murdered, you don't—well, you don't act quite the way you would if it was some other summer, just an ordinary summer at the lake."

"Murder," F. Millard said dryly, "does have peculiar effects."

Both sat quietly, watching the quiet water.

Another pseudo-smile began to contort Bella's face. She opened her mouth, but F. Millard beat her to speech. "What was Mrs. Thorne talking about last night when she—"

"Abby's a darling," Bella broke in. "You know, she's been a widow for years, ever since Chris was little, and she'd be so much happier married to someone who's not too domineering and has had some other experience besides mining—a businessman, someone who owned a dress shop perhaps, or—or a grocery store."

F. Millard's jaw sagged, his eyes wide behind their glasses.

"You know, when we sell the Abby Association, she'll have money, too," added Bella.

What was this buxom brunette up to? Did she think that recruiting F. Millard into their ranks would make him think twice before investigating this murder? Bella and Abby weren't related, or the Kingdoms and Abby. But they all seemed bound up together.

With determined obtuseness, he pursued his own course. "What did Mrs. Thorne mean about all the other partners in the Abby Association being killed?"

Bella dropped her artificial air. "I hadn't thought about it till Abby got to raving, but you know, it *was* odd. The Association started with Abby and her husband, Virgil's parents, and Trigger Joe and his brother. Right after they went in together, Abby's husband was killed in a rockslide. Then Ethan's father and his wife—Jade's mother—sold to the other partners and went Outside. They were in one of those terrible nightclub fires and didn't get out. That was the year we were married. If it hadn't been for his wife, Mr. Frazee would still be alive; she was just like Jade."

Bella's face darkened. "The Frazees just came back to Alaska once, the summer Jade was seventeen." Her voice died away while her fingers squeezed the robe she sat on into folds.

"What about the Kingdoms?" F. Millard prodded. "What happened to them?"

She sighed and relaxed. "Mrs. Kingdom was killed in an automobile accident on the Circle road. And Mr. Kingdom was just killed last yea—" She broke off, and F. Millard saw her body stiffen in its revealing bathing suit. She drew a long breath, and finished abruptly, "—last year. And now,

61

Trigger Joe. I don't blame Abby for being upse—"

"You didn't say how Mr. Kingdom was killed."

"Oh, didn't I? Well, as a matter of fact, he was shot, too."

"Shot?" F. Millard sat up straighter. A year ago! For two years, Chris said, Arctic Dredging had been trying to buy the Abby Association.

"Oh, it wasn't murder. Just a hunting accident. But the coincidence suddenly struck me. You can see why Abby—"

The grocer interrupted again. "Did he fall on his gun?"

"N-no." Bella reached for the package of cigarettes beside the spray gun. F. Millard hadn't seen a knot of hair like hers for years. It suited her classic beauty. But her next words, as she found the package empty and threw it down, knocked all thoughts of beauty from his mind. "He—I guess someone mistook him for a sheep. They were hunting mountain sheep, and he wore a white shirt —and in the distance—you know how it is."

"Don't they use binoculars?"

"Yes. But whoever did it might have forgotten his or seen the flash of white and not waited to look."

Or had a good look, ticked something in F. Millard's mind, and then shot. "Who did it?"

"They didn't know; they all said they'd shot on that hill, but either missed their sheep or carried them to camp." Bella's fingers were tight on her knees. She shot a quick glance at F. Millard and handed him the spray gun. "Will you spray my back, Mr. Smyth? Bathing suits weren't made for this time of year in Alaska."

F. Millard accepted the spray gun, but he lowered the nozzle instead of starting to pump. "Who was on that hunting trip, Mrs. Kingdom? Any of the folks that are here?"

He saw the smooth back tighten. Once more, her fingers dug into the rug. Her voice, when it came, was faint. "Why, yes. Ethan was there—and Abby—and—and Virgil."

"Hmmm," said F. Millard Smyth.

Bella turned back to the grocer. Synthetic gaiety again curved her lips but failed to hide the apprehension in her eyes. "You were smart to leave with Art this morning, Mr. Smyth. Jade blew a gasket. She went on swearing Ethan tore up the will and killed his uncle so the old fellow couldn't make another. She and Ethan always fought like cats and dogs, but I never thought—"

Suddenly, she stopped. Forced gaiety and apprehension vanished as her eyes went round and bright with speculation. "Why, Jade might have done it herself. *She* might have killed Trigger Joe to make the will effective! I wouldn't put it past that green-eyed vixen! And then when she found the will was destroyed—whether Ethan did it, or Trigger Joe—no wonder she was seething!"

Her eyes shone with vindictive mirth. F. Millard discovered with surprise that they weren't brown at all, but deep smoke-blue. Did that mean fire behind them?

He sat looking at her. "You dislike Miss Lothrop a lot, don't you, Mrs. Kingdom?"

The girl beside him started. The hard brilliance in her eyes blazed into fury. "I hate Jade Lothrop more than anyone in the world! She's a tramp. She's a no-good, tow-headed devil!"

F. Millard blinked.

"She had no business at the lake. She only came because of Trigger Joe and—and—"

Was the name Bella couldn't speak her husband's?

"There wasn't even room for her at Trigger Joe's; Abby had to put her up. But she *would* come. And I thought—I kept telling myself she'd come because of the money. And then—"

F. Millard sat as intent as a biting mosquito, equally unfeeling too, he thought, waiting for a girl to tear out her heart.

"This morning—" her voice was husky "—when Art asked—I found out she and Virgil had been meeting. That clearing—how many other times—in houses—Oh, my God, I thought it was Chris I had to fear! At least Chris would fight fair."

All at once, Bella slumped sideways on the robe. Her cream-smooth back quivered, and sobs like a child's shook her dark knot of hair.

Brushing off mosquitoes and letting her sob, F. Millard waited. When the worst violence subsided, he laid a gentle hand on her shoulder. "Don't take it so hard, Mrs. Kingdom. The deputy marshal's questions just showed they met once. Perhaps that was the only time. Give your husband the benefit of the doubt."

"You—you don't know Jade." Her voice was smothered in the blanket. "Or—"

Or Virgil Kingdom, thought F. Millard.

"She'd never let me keep the thing I want most in the world—if she wanted it too." She sat up as abruptly as she'd fallen over, her face splotchy with tears, but the sobbing had stopped. "I grew up with her. I know. I knew them all. Jade and Chris were the ones who got all the attention, even then. I was fat—a fat little girl! They— they called me Belly-flop and Belly-ache! Even if I've taken off the fat and learned to do my hair and dress right, how can I keep a man like the King—if Jade wants him or Chris?"

"But, my dear," F. Millard said timidly, "you're lovely. You—"

She reached for a handful of pebbles. The tear splotches were almost gone, and no more drops spilled from eyes that were now only pools of misery. She began to breathe faster as the pebbles ran through her fingers. "He—he chose me when he could have had either of them. That was before Jade's marriage and divorce, and Chris was just waiting for him to ask her. She's always waited for Virgil—never looked at anyone else. But he married me! It was me he wanted—then. Why can't they leave him alone?"

Her voice broke, and F. Millard, in terror of more tears, searched wildly for words. None came, but they came to Bella in place of the weeping he feared.

She dumped all the pebbles on the blanket and, with each gasp, picked one up and plunked it down beside her. "Chris didn't need a vacation after teaching. She has a defense job waiting in town. But, no, she has to join her mother at the lake for a rest—a *rest*, with all that swimming and hiking! But if one of them has to be after my husband, I'd rather it was Chris than Jade. That Jade—"

At each gasp she plumped down a pebble with the full force of one muscular arm, till F. Millard looked to see if she'd pushed them through the blanket.

He looked—then stared.

On the robe beside Bella Kingdom lay the seven stones of that strangely familiar design that had been haunting him. Seven stones so precisely placed, and in the girl's hand an eighth.

As he watched, she plunked it down… The design behind the burned cabin.

Chapter Eight

Perhaps F. Millard made some sound as he goggled at the rocks on the blanket, or his frozen stillness penetrated Bella's abstraction. She looked up, and at the sight of his face her eyes flew wide open. Then they dropped to the blanket. He heard her gasp, and her creamy-tan cheeks went white.

"What—what's that?" the grocer pointed.

"Why it—it—it—" she stuttered. "It's the Alaska flag."

Of course! The seven stones were the seven stars of the Big Dipper, in that rough outline like a pipe. The eighth stone, above what he'd called the outside edge of the pipe bowl, was the North Star.

The eighth stone—the Dippers he'd found near his cabin hadn't had the eighth stone. But the one with the stem of the pipe, the handle of the Dipper, pointing to the spot where Trigger Joe had been murdered, had had the North Star. Once more he looked down at the blanket. The Dipper beside Bella Kingdom was complete with North Star.

"Mrs. Kingdom—" his voice was hoarse "—why did you do that?"

"Why, I—I—" hers trembled, and she ran her tongue over her lips "—I wasn't thinking of what I was doing. That must be what they call doodling—with—with rocks instead of a pencil."

He leaned forward, intent on her face. "If doodling is something involuntary, habitual—why did you make the Dipper?"

She drew a long breath—counting ten again, he supposed. "I've been making the Alaska flag." Her voice, that came in a little rush, was steadier, but her face was still without color. "The University put on a pageant just before we left—Virgil and I've only been out here a week—and the Professor's wives had to make goodness knows how many flags—the Alaska flag with the Dipper and North Star. And I got so in the habit of it that I just did it without thinking."

For a moment their eyes met. Through his spectacles and head net the little man looked deep into those smoke blue eyes of Bella's that might have fire behind them. That almost certainly had.

"That—that's why I made it," stammered Bella. "Don't you see? Just because I'd been making so many—at the college."

F. Millard said, "Oh."

Bella's smooth arm swept away the pebbles. Her color was coming back, and she forced her lips once more into that pseudo-smile. "Isn't it funny what people will do unconsciously? It makes one think more than ever about behaviorism and psychiatry and things."

She waited, watching F. Millard.

"Yeah," he said absently. His mind was already occupied with behavior—Bella's, Virgil's, Benny's, Abby's, Chris's, Ethan's, and Jade's.

Bella picked up the spray gun and rose.

"Wait a minute." He held out his hand before he realized she had no skirt for him to catch at. Warmth crept up under his collar at the thought of grasping her snug bathing suit. "Do you know Art Heggarty pretty well?"

"He was one of the big boys when I started school."

"Who do you think he suspects?" F. Millard watched her closely. "Surely not one of you women?"

Anger flooded red in her face. "He certainly has no right to suspect me! I told him just what I did last night."

"If he believes you," the grocer murmured.

"If I was going to kill anyone," she burst out, "it'd be Jade or Virgil, wouldn't it—after what came out this morning? Why would I kill Trigger Joe?"

Why indeed? Except that he was keeping her husband from getting ten thousand dollars. She might have other reasons for wanting money, but ten thousand dollars would take the Virgil Kingdoms a good many miles and oceans away from Harding Lake—and Jade Lothrop and Chris Thorne.

F. Millard hesitated. "You don't think the deputy marshal suspects me, do you?" Maybe that would bind them together.

But Bella Kingdom stood tall and scornful above the little man who sat clasping his knees on the blanket. "I think you're perfectly safe, Mr. Smyth. You didn't even know Trigger Joe. … I can't stay another minute among all these mosquitoes."

Watching her run up the stairs, F. Millard was glad she hadn't turned the spray gun on him.

He got up and sauntered down the beach with a jingle of pebbles. Once more, he had that prickling sense of being watched. But not even the Kingdoms' dog showed his nose.

At Trigger Joe's fence, F. Millard climbed the bank and followed the trail. Even in the Scout Camp beyond the stockade, everything was quiet. Were they all trying to avoid him? Had Art turned them against him? Or had they seen him with Bella and been afraid she'd talked too much?

He started back by the road. The trail along the lake bank was as level as the beach, but the hill that the road climbed behind the Kingdom cabin was steep. Since King was the only one who had brought a car, the garage halfway up with tire tracks going under the door must be his, as hushed now as any empty cabin on the lake shore.

At the top of the hill, a rapidly loudening throb announced the approach of planes, and F. Millard stopped to see three pursuit ships dart birdlike over the hill and vanish southward.

Mosquitoes whined around his head net as he looked down at the lake. In the crowding green of birch and spruce, only roof corners showed of the fringe of cabins on the shore, parts of walls, or the gleam of windows. Last night, in one of those cabins, a man had met death. Last night six roaring bombers had covered the sound of a shot. Who could tell what other shots another flight might cover? Perhaps these very pursuit ships racing south.

He shivered. The hill he stood on hid the high white range of mountains he had watched coming out on the stage, spread in fantastic glitter beyond the Tanana. The press of green around him—the low green hills, the lake like a green Cyclops eye—was suddenly suffocating.

He shivered again and began to walk—fast, and then faster. At the foot of the hill, he hurried by the telephone booth at the fork in the road from the highway, down the level stretch toward his cabin, by the Thornes'—its doorless back wall making it look as untenanted as any in the long row of empty cabins he was passing. And he wondered anew if one of them was not empty—today.

Unconsciously, his nose crinkled to sniff for smoke. But no second house had yet been set on fire.

By the time he reached his own cabin, he was running. As the screen door banged behind him, he sank down, panting on the cot, pushed his head net over the brim of his hat, and tossed the hat on a chair. His arm remained extended, body bent, as he peered at the stack of magazines on the next chair. The top cover showed Flatfoot Flannagan overpowering a masked figure. But the last magazine F. Millard had read was the one with the picture of Flannagan shooting a Tommy gun. He remembered laying it on top of the pile—and by gracious, the stack itself had been on the other chair, the one where he'd just tossed his hat!

Someone had been in his cabin.

For gracious sake, he told his quickening pulse, what if someone *had* been looking over his copies of *Flatfoot?* The Scouts had read them this morning. But his pulse didn't slow, and almost without volition, he found himself warily approaching the wooden door leading into the one enclosed room.

The door was shut, and he'd left it open.

He stopped for a minute, holding his breath, then pounced on the knob and flung the door wide. No one was in the room now, but someone had certainly been there. The straight chair F. Millard sat on for meals had been moved away from the table, in the cupboard the plates were on the wrong side of the cups, the iron lifter that he hung on a nail had been left in one of the stove lids, and the blankets on the bunk were no longer tucked under the mattress but hanging over the side. Nothing was topsy-turvy or badly disarranged, but to the neat storekeeper who kept his house like his grocery, too many changes were apparent.

Had it been one of his neighbors, he asked himself, or the deputy marshal?

Flatfoot Flannagan would have left everything as he'd found it, and surely Art would too.

Outside the screen porch, a twig snapped.

F. Millard whirled in the doorway.

Art Heggarty was striding down the trail from the cabins with a purposeful, heavy tread.

"I saw you come back," he flung out.

F. Millard didn't contradict. Was it Art's gaze he had felt? But a man who has just had his dwelling searched has use for a deputy marshal. That dusted chair the first afternoon—the Dippers around his cabin—he had nothing to do with the murder, but what about his cabin? He held the door open.

Art tossed the other man's hat to the cot and sat down on the chair it left clear. He got his question in first. "What you been up to now?"

"Why, I—I've just been sitting on the beach talking to Bella Kingdom, and afterwards took a little walk. I haven't been up to anything."

Then he squared his shoulders. What right did Art Heggarty have to demand an accounting from him? F. Millard wasn't a suspect. And after the way he'd talked this morning, Art had the nerve to expect from the grocer even decent cooperation!

"What have you been up to, yourself?" he countered. Whatever the deputy had been doing, he hadn't been able to keep someone out of F. Millard's cabin. "Have you found out about that shell in Virgil Kingdom's pocket? Or the scrap of paper by Benny's cot?" Good gracious, why had he spoken like that?

But Art's scowl only deepened. "Benny explained that piece of paper all right, but King's story was pretty thin. Said he saw that shell on his way back from the clearing, shining in the bushes along the road—says he can't remember just where—and picked it up for defense metal."

The little grocer made a sound just too faint for a snort. "Can you see Professor Kingdom doing salvage work?"

A grin lightened the deputy's face, then the scowl settled down again. "Benny says that scrap of paper must've fallen out of his clothes. Says he dropped in to see Trigger Joe somewhere between eight and nine last night, and the old man was in a rage. He was raving about no-good, worthless folks and so generally foaming at the mouth that Benny couldn't make out what it was all about. The old man had so many of those spells, Benny said he didn't think anything about it, and when he saw he couldn't get him calmed down he started to scram, but the old fellow grabbed something off the table and let fly. Benny said he thought he was going to get hit with the coffeepot or a plate of beans, but it turned out to be something, like a snowstorm. He beat it out of there as quick as he could, but one of those flying scraps of paper must have dropped in his pants cuff."

F. Millard stared. "You think it was the torn-up will?"

"I know it," said Art. "It's the E-N and half the M in AMEN. Benny's story corroborates Ethan's about coming in at nine and finding scraps of paper all over the floor."

"Of course, Ethan might have burned up the scraps he found on the floor," the grocer said thoughtfully, leaning against the door jamb, "and torn up the will in Jade's favor himself and thrown it in the fireplace. But that's kind of farfetched."

"I'll say it's farfetched," Art scoffed. "Sounds like an amateur's logic. Trigger Joe was mad at someone. Why not at Jade? He could of just had a fight with her and torn up the will to get even."

F. Millard nodded slowly, overlooking the remarks about amateur's logic. "Funny, Benny didn't mention it before. He was there when I pointed out those scraps, and Ethan raked them out of the ashes."

"Nothing funny about it," retorted the deputy. "If you'd stop to think about life for a while instead of Flatfoot Flannagan, you'd know anyone'd keep still before he got mixed up in murder. Benny says he would've spoken if it could've done any good, but he didn't know what the torn-up paper was, or even what the old man was talking about. When you found those scraps, don't forget Trigger Joe had been killed, and Benny knew if he admitted he'd been talking to a man just before he was shot, he'd be involved, too. Benny's lived in a small town too long not to know that wouldn't look so hot for a Scoutmaster."

"What about the gun?" cried F. Millard. "Did you find the gun that shot

71

him?"

Art Heggarty tipped back smugly in the chair that had held the grocer's hat. "Sure, I found it. We can't tell if that's the gun till they dig out the bullet, but there's a twenty-two, with one cartridge out of the magazine, in Trigger Joe's cabin."

"Trigger Joe's cabin? His own gun?"

Art nodded. "But that don't necessarily mean Ethan. He was out from right after supper till nine o'clock; anyone could've dropped in and swiped it."

Anyone could have dropped in at Trigger Joe's cabin—someone had certainly dropped in at his own. "I've got some news for you, Mr. Heggarty." F. Millard tried to sound casual, but his tone put each word in italics. "Someone went through my cabin while I was out."

Art didn't move, except for his eyelids, which narrowed again till his eyes were blue splinters. "What makes you think so? Anything missing?"

"I—I don't know."

"Then what makes you think it's been entered?"

"Too many things out of place," F. Millard said promptly. "The dishes, and blankets, and stove lifter, and a chair—"

A different sort of gleam crowded out the first in the deputy's eyes. "Your cabin's neat as a pin," he growled.

In the doorway, F. Millard started. "How do you know? You're only on the porch. You haven't been inside… Or have you?"

Art's chair clattered against the screen as he rose. "Sure I have, you little runt. I searched your cabin."

Flatfoot Flannagan would have fired such a careless operative, F. Millard told himself in the second's pause before Art went on, "And I found what I was after. I told you to keep out of this. So what were you doing with these in your cabin?"

He pulled an envelope out of his pocket. Leaning over F. Millard's cot, he dumped out a handful of torn scraps of paper.

"Here's the rest of that will."

Chapter Nine

F. Millard stared at the scraps of paper on the cot. "For gracious sake," he cried, "they're all over ashes! Someone took them out of the fireplace after Ethan threw them in. But who—why—?"

"Okay, Smyth, why did you do it?"

"Why did I do it?" he gasped. "I didn't!"

"Then what were they doing in your teapot?"

"Teapot! I d-don't drink tea," F. Millard stuttered.

"You'd hardly hide anything in the pot if you did."

"But who—? I don't know any of these folks. How would they know I don't drink tea?"

"I'd like to know what you're up to," said Art. "Tampering with evidence is a pretty serious offense."

"I didn't do it," F. Millard yelped. "I'll admit I wanted to work with you, but certainly not against you. You must think I'm crazy if I don't want to get this murderer in handcuffs. Here I am—all by myself, clear down at the end of half a mile of empty cabins, and I can't leave till the road's fixed. Do you think I want a murderer to shoot through one of *my* windows? Or burn *my* house down some night?"

Art's stubborn, blue-black jaw was a little less out-thrust. "Well, then, suppose you didn't hide the stuff— though it looks mighty queer to me— who did? And why in hell put it in your teapot?"

"He must have deliberately wanted to turn suspicion toward me. Unless he knew I didn't drink tea and thought my place would be the only one, you wouldn't search."

73

"Then that'd mean he wanted to be able to lay his hand on it later; just get it out of the way for now."

"Then why didn't he hide it somewhere else? Out in the woods where he wouldn't run so much risk of being seen? No, sir, the funniest thing to me is why he put it in my teapot. I've never said anything to anybody here about not drinking tea."

Art, his jaw hardening again, watched the little grocer.

Suddenly, F. Millard straightened. "Suppose he didn't know I didn't drink tea! Suppose he thought if he put the scraps in my teapot, I'd be sure to find them. Suppose he wanted them found!"

"Then why didn't he just leave them in the fireplace," returned Art practically, "and let Ethan save them with the rest?"

"But that's why!" F. Millard rushed on. "He wouldn't know they were going to be saved. These scraps must have already been taken when we carried the body to Trigger Joe's cabin. Someone was afraid Ethan would build a fire and grabbed a handful out of the fireplace first to make sure we'd be able to identify that torn paper."

"Hogwash," said Art. "There goes that farfetched amateur logic again. Someone who *didn't* know you *didn't* drink tea—someone who hid a handful of papers to make sure they'd be found, instead of leaving them in the fire place and seeing to it they were found—someone— Baloney, *you* knew you didn't drink tea, and *you* thought your cabin wouldn't be searched. You're still the logical suspect."

But the big deputy's conviction had begun to waver by the time he finally slammed the screen door and flung off down the trail with his hat on the back of his head.

F. Millard watched him go. Above the lake, he saw more storm clouds gathering, but his mind didn't stay long on the weather. Why on earth would anyone hide those scraps of paper in his teapot? Someone who knew he didn't drink tea and put them there so they shouldn't be found, or someone who thought he drank tea and put them there so they should be found?

He paced the floor, thinking and blinking and getting nowhere. When he finally gave up and reached for a copy of *Flatfoot*, the afternoon was nearly gone. By the time he stopped reading and shoved the magazine into his pocket, the clouds were thicker and blacker and higher in the sky.

His stomach and watch said it was long past dinner time. He lit a fire in the old range so like the one that had shielded Trigger Joe's body, heated a can of beans, and carried his plate to the porch. Munching, he sat on the edge of the cot while his eyes traveled over the storm clouds, down the green hill to the house on the point.

Something about its weathered loneliness teased his imagination. Before he left, he had to fix up Blaine's boat and row over it. From here, he could see no space between the front of the house and the cliff. At the back, a stretch of boulder-dotted, untimbered ground led to the woods.

The black clouds laid a shadow-like dusk on the landscape. Through the deepening twilight, F. Millard's eyes, on the space between the cabin and trees, caught a flicker of motion. A forkful of beans dropped back on his plate. Over there, dodging among the boulders toward the cabin—was it Benny's dog—or a bear—or—?

Not upright like a person, bent over like a creature on all fours or a crouching man, it slipped from rock to rock. No color showed. The figure blended with the rocks, motion all that made it visible as it approached the cabin and disappeared.

Would the Kingdoms' dog approach the house so furtively, or a wild creature go there at all? Fingering *Flatfoot,* F. Millard knew instinctively, as he'd known all along, that the figure he'd seen was human.

He laid down his plate and stood up. Why couldn't Art Heggarty have made his visit now instead of this afternoon? By the time F. Millard could get hold of him, that furtive shape might be gone. But if he went himself, right now—

With his hand on the door, he paused. This might be the perfect opportunity to find out who was up to what among the empty cabins—but last night, a man had been murdered. If, in the lonely woods, he came face to face with a murderer—F. Millard Smyth, alone, unarmed, fifty-six years old, and five feet six inches tall...

But someone on foot—along a narrow tongue of land, with no boat to cross the lake, there was only one way to return. If F. Millard hid in the bushes, he could see who came out.

He crammed *Flatfoot* deeper in his pocket, reached for his hat and head net, and didn't let the screen door bang as he hurried through.

He zipped off a hundred yards till light from the empty clearing washed in on the end of the trail. Just a few more steps of smoothed pathway—

F. Millard stumbled to a stop. There, at the end of the trail, was another Dipper. Seven stones—no, this had eight; this Dipper had the North Star.

The Dipper again! Now he *had* to go on. Its handle pointed forward.

He raced across the clearing and dived into an opening in the brush. Bending under leaning trees, climbing over the fallen ones, working his way around brushy patches, or thrusting through them, he went on. Every few yards, he crouched behind cover and listened. Since plunging into the woods, he'd had no clear view of the house on the point. Whoever had approached it so stealthily might even now be on his way back.

Halfway there, he squatted behind a thick clump of young alders, bent forward with fingertips on the ground like a racer about to run. He stilled his own panting breath. For a minute that held no sound he was smothered in wilderness quiet. In the distance, a bird gave a raucous squawk, and a squirrel chattered angrily back. Like Bella and Jade, thought F. Millard. Then he heard another sound.

A humming throb, too pulsating for the mosquitoes that hovered hopefully outside his net. More planes. Through the tangle of spruce and alder branches, he caught the flash of two army bombers flying into the storm clouds. This was a funny country—dark for so long in winter and so bewilderingly light in summer that the only stars to be seen were on government planes, the only constellation picked out in rocks on the ground.

The throbbing died away. F. Millard gathered his muscles to start for a blueberry clump farther on.

Still crouching, his muscles froze.

Another sound came through the woods' quiet. Rustling, crackling, the loud pop of a stepped-on twig. F. Millard thought of that sneaking approach to the house on the point and the wound in Trigger Joe's side. He held his breath and bent lower.

The rustling and crackling drew nearer. Something moved beyond the alders. In front of a white-barked cluster of birch trees, a shadow appeared. Then the crouching grocer saw it wasn't shadow, but substance—a person in dark clothes. It glided nearer, and he caught back a gasp.

This was the same slender figure in dark slacks and jacket, black head net, and gloves, that had followed Chris the night she passed his cabin. At least it looked the same; it was hard to tell with clothes like that, but such slim height must belong to either Abby or Jade. Both were women—but a woman's finger could pull a trigger as well as a man's.

Even then, the first night, he had sensed the need to shout a warning. Now, he felt the presence of evil so strongly that he tried to shrink smaller behind the screen of branches.

For an instant, the dark figure paused. F. Millard's breath stopped too. Utterly immobile, head on one side, she listened.

What if he'd been stumbling over logs and crashing through bushes, F. Millard thought weakly, as the woman stood intent? What if they'd met face to face? He reminded himself that Art Heggarty had the gun that had killed Trigger Joe, and no second gun was in the hand of that tense figure. But an automatic could be carried in a pocket.

The face behind the head net turned his way.

Then he drew a long breath as her head turned back and she started on, filling the hush once more with rustles and crackles. Like a lurching reveler a spindling spruce, half uprooted, caught her head net as she passed. She gave an impatient jerk, but the spiny, dead branches held fast. She jerked again, and hat and net came off.

In spite of the clouds and the leafy tangle through which he peered, F. Millard knew that head. No one else had that delicate jawline or that long, curled-under blond bob. The stealthy figure stretching up in a slender arc to detach her net from the tree was Jade Lothrop.

The net came loose. She shook it out, settled the hat once more on her telltale hair, and glided on.

The last rustle had died away, and the woods had been still for long minutes before F. Millard straightened cramped muscles and stood up. He began to run toward the house on the point. No need for caution now. That furtive presence on the point had gone.

He ran till he had to stop for breath. Everything was still, the woods beneath the storm clouds darkly hushed. Silence pressed on his eardrums. Then he let out his breath in a whistling snort. Jade and her aura of evil—the fire last night and the dead man—what if the house on the point—?

He began to run again. At the edge of the woods where the promontory thrust, treeless and rocky, out into the water, he leaned, gasping, against a tree and felt smooth birch bark under his fingers. But no smoke feathers, no spears of flame rose from the lonely cottage. He tried to scoff at himself. It was just the return combination of storm clouds and bombers and his urgent feeling of danger that had made him fear a repetition of last night's horror. Anyway, now that he was here, he wasn't going to turn right around and go home. He'd have a look at the place and have it, if possible, unobserved by his neighbors.

He drew a step farther back in the woods, feet sinking in the deep pile of moss and leaf carpet. The light was dimming by the second. In the birch he had just left a bird twittered drowsily, and with no rush of wings for warning, another bird shot past him like a baseball.

He jumped and strained his eyes through the thickening dusk to examine the twenty yards or so of open ground between the trees and house. Some of the rocks were shoulder-high. Hunched over, like the figure he had watched from his porch, with the light so dim and his clothing dark, it was unlikely that anyone in the row of cabins across the water would see him.

As he chose the first boulder to make for, rain began to fall. Big drops at first, that streaked the white birch bark near him and splashed on the unsheltered rocks. He broke into a crouching run, and the few drops changed to a torrent. Thank goodness, this cabin had a back door, so he wouldn't have to take a shower bath all the way round to the front. Zigzagging from rock to rock, he reached the house, and the wet china knob slipped in his hand as he pushed the door squawkingly open.

He blinked his eyes to get used to the denser interior dusk. This was the first separate kitchen he'd seen at the lake. A range, a cupboard and table, a few straight chairs, and a makeshift sink peered back at him in the murk. Two doors led into other rooms. The one on the north opened into the front of the house. The one to the left, on the western wall, was closed.

F. Millard still clung to the back doorknob. He felt a peculiar reluctance to step farther into the room, to go through either of those two waiting doors. The rain drummed, loud, on the roof.

He shook himself impatiently. It was people yielding to such fancies that gave old houses bad names. If Jade had left behind her any of that sense of menace he had felt when she passed him in the woods, the girl herself was gone.

He released the knob and took a tentative step toward the closed door on the left. His eyes darted to the one that was open. The gloom ahead looked bad enough, but there was something about opening a door that had been shut...

Nonsense, he told himself, marching firmly across the kitchen; he was going to look over the house, and the closed door came first. So he'd open it first. He laid his hand on the metal knob and paused again. A little shiver ran down his spine. Then he made himself turn the knob.

A sigh of relief escaped him. A bare iron bed, with bare wire springs, and the bare floor showing through, a straight chair by the window, a flimsy table—no bodies, no crouching evil. A curtained stack of boxes substituting for a bureau stood by the door. Hardly knowing what he expected to find, he raised the dusty-smelling cloth. The boxes, too, were empty.

With another sigh, he backed into the kitchen. That door was going to stay open, he promised himself, while he was in this house. He looked with satisfaction at the oblong of lighter dusk and made for the door on the north, remembering, as his head net brushed his chin, to push it up on his hat brim. Now everything was brighter.

The next room was as small as the others. He saw another door on the left—open, thank goodness. The square house, bisected twice, must have been built by an amateur because, in this room, the door to the west opened outward, flat on the wall beside him. This must have been the living room, with a dilapidated couch and Morris chair and a table with a kerosene lamp. On the north wall near the east corner was a closed door with glass in the upper half.

He crossed to peer through the glass and drew back almost dizzily from the proximity of the cliff. Through the slanting gray rain, the lake seemed just outside the door—and alarmingly far down. The grocer blinked and backed off.

There was still the other west room to examine. He stepped across the threshold: another bedroom, with another unblanketed bed and stack of boxes for a bureau, another chair, and a table. He hurried to the west window. The cliff was near here, too, but not so dizzily near as in front. Across the roughened, dark water the other cabins showed through steel-tape bands of rain: his own the nearest, then a row of empty cabins, the burned one, more empties, the Thornes', with the orange umbrella glowing bravely through the rain; the clearing where the road came in; another row of untenanted cabins, the Kingdoms', more empties, Trigger Joe's stockade, and last the Scout Camp. His eyes ran back along that fringe of habitation and stopped with a jerk midway between the Thornes' cabin and his own.

From across the lake came a flash of light. But in a storm like this, lightning shouldn't surprise him. Funny, he hadn't heard thunder, though the rain on the roof made a lot of noise.

But the drum of rain was softer now, and the storm perceptibly slackened. The flash came again, and still, he heard no thunder. Then his fingers clamped on the gritty windowsill. That wasn't lightning across the lake! A flashlight or a lantern suddenly covered—

Someone was signaling from one of those empty cabins near the one where they'd found Trigger Joe.

It might be Morse code, but the grocer knew no code. There were several quick flashes, and a few times the light was held steady and clear. Then it disappeared, and the dusk seemed almost like darkness.

Now, the rain fell more and more lightly, like the claw feet of walking blackbirds. Over the patter came a groaning squeal that brought F. Millard's head around so fast the net fell off his hat brim. *Squa-awk!* In the lonely house on the edge of the bluff, the little man felt his scalp prickle.

He knew that sound—though he'd heard it only once. The back door had opened and closed!

Nailed to the floor, he waited. Then he remembered the window behind him, outlining his whole upper body. With an effort as hard as lifting a sack of potatoes, he heaved himself to one side. Tight to the wall, he waited.

The rain had turned to a drizzle now that made no sound on the roof. The house was as still as the woods had been when Jade passed. No footfall came from the kitchen.

In the smothering hush F. Millard could faintly hear the watch that had been his father's ticking in his pocket.

There was still no sound from the other rooms. The little man drew a shaking breath and, with the palms of his hands, pushed himself away from the wall. He couldn't stay there forever, waiting to be found.

He tiptoed a few steps out in the room, and stopped again. Still no sound but his own labored breath. Under his weight a board creaked.

By gracious, this couldn't go on! He'd spring out there and face the intruder!

He dashed across the bedroom and out into the living room before he stopped again. The open door into the kitchen revealed no other presence. But the open door didn't show all the room. Someone might be lurking by the wall or in the other bedroom, the one that had been so hard for him to enter. Clamping his jaws together, he made himself take the remaining steps to the kitchen.

No one there. Then he saw the door to the bedroom he'd entered first. He'd left it pushed almost wide open. Now, it stood at right angles to the wall. Every nerve pulling in the other direction, he drew a step nearer. Just one peek—and he'd bolt through the woods for home. But if someone was hiding in that bedroom, why hadn't he shut the door?

No one showed through the open door. He crept forward another step, and more of the room was revealed. Still no one. Through the wide crack between hinges, he saw no one by the south and east walls. That left only one corner unobserved. Keeping as near the back door as he could, F. Millard stepped nearer and craned his neck. The room had no one in it.

"For gracious sake," he muttered. His voice started sly echoes in the empty house—inhuman and ghostly.

Trying not to shiver, he surveyed the bedroom that twice had made him so obscurely uneasy: curtained boxes, flimsy table, bare bed, straight chair—

F. Millard gulped. A few minutes ago, that chair had been by the window. Now, it stood by the bed.

But no one would sneak in, silently move a chair, and sneak out again. Besides, the back door had creaked only once—one opening and closing. Whoever had been in this house had been here all the time! He had just gone out, not come in.

Something shuddery and crawling crept up F. Millard's spine. While he'd stood in this very doorway, someone had been in this room. He stared around him once more, and his hand went out to the door. Back there—he gave it a push—was the way he'd left it, not quite against the wall. Not quite—

His gasp quivered through the still house. He hadn't been able to push the door against the wall because someone had been behind it!

He turned and dashed across the kitchen, dragged open the groaning back door and shot through it. Heedless of possible watching eyes on the strip between house and trees, he leap-frogged the smaller rocks he had tried to hide behind earlier.

Wet branches slapped at his face as he tore through brush and slithered down slopes of moss and leaves. He stumbled and fell, slipped, slid, got up, and ran on.

Once, to catch his breath, he lay where he'd dropped beside a fallen birch. Its white bark gleamed ghostlike in the twilight. He shuddered and turned his head. The soft drip of rain-washed leaves was the only sound in the woods. He lay on his back in a cleared spot with sky instead of trees overhead. No rain fell on his upturned face, so he knew that the storm was over. But the trees dripped on—*plunk, plunk, plunk...*

That was how steps sounded on bare floors in empty houses—*plunk, plunk, plunk.* He sprang to his feet and tore on through dripping trees.

When he finally burst into the clearing near his cabin, the wheezes and gasps that served him for breath were almost sobs. He stumbled across it and paused where the trail began to take one last look at the Dipper... It was gone. Instead of rocks, only scratches showed on the trail.

F. Millard wavered over the place where the Dipper had been. A small pool of water in the path reflected pale sky—a clear pool, with one beyond it muddy. Behind spattered spectacles, his *Flatfoot-trained* eyes narrowed. The trail's damp sand resisted footprints, but someone had just passed by.

As he stared at the puddles, he heard the dry, grinding rattle of pebbles. Someone was on the beach.

F. Millard hesitated. Only Benny's dog, he told himself, while his mind raced back along the sliding, stumbling way he had come to the house on the point—the moved chair and the groaning back door. Whoever—whatever had muddied the pool in the trail—perhaps the person who had been on the point—would still be in sight on the beach.

The thought of his cabin, snug and safe after the last tingling hour, pulled at F. Millard like a magnet. But if he let this opportunity slip—

He tore down the trail toward his cabin, but instead of lunging for the door, he sprang down the path over the bank.

Someone was crunching through the pebbles—not on four legs, but on two. Close under the bank, crouched out of sight of the row of cabins, a man in swimming trunks hurried along the beach. He walked fast and carried no cane, but he walked with a definite limp.

F. Millard's eyes narrowed again. It would be easy to imitate a limp. Could a man with a leg wound walk so fast in loose gravel without a cane? But only one man at the lake had blond hair like that—and that man was Ethan Frazee.

Chapter Ten

That night F. Millard slept in the cabin instead of on the porch, with the door locked and the bureau shoved against it. When he took off his clothes his father's old watch read midnight—the third midnight he'd met with wide open eyes. But he'd no sooner tucked the blankets over his outside ear than his eyes began to close.

When he woke the sun was warm, raying in his north east windows, toe-dancing on the lake—just as if there hadn't been another storm, or evil loose in the woods—just as if there hadn't been a murder. If last night's rain had washed out more road and kept the stage away longer...

He shivered and jumped out of bed.

A morning like this ought to bring everyone to the beach—all that queer little interlocked group tied together so firmly by blood or marriage, shared childhood and economic necessity, by love, and equally closely by hate.

In the midst of a stove-heated bath dipped out of the lake, the soap slid from the grocer's hand and splashed in the galvanized washtub. Last night, with someone behind the back bedroom door of the house on the point—when F. Millard looked into that room, had he stood right in the doorway? Could anyone flattened against the wall, with even his breath sucked in to stand flatter, have seen F. Millard through the crack? He'd dived in once to raise the curtain on the boxes. His spectacles were the only pair at the lake. But he hadn't raised his head net till he went to the front of the house. In dark clothes and net-draped hat, would he be any more recognizable than the figure he had watched zigzagging among the rocks or Jade when she slipped through the woods till the tree raked off her hat? The rooms had been heavy with dusk, but he might have been recognized.

Goose flesh rose, and he bent for the soap. He'd just have to watch and test reactions—watch very, very closely.

But when he reached the Thornes' boathouse and looked down on the beach, only Ethan lay on the blankets, fully dressed in Army suntans with one arm over his eyes and the cane beside his game leg.

F. Millard clumped down the boathouse stairs and crunched across the pebbles. "Hello," he said tentatively.

"Hello, Smyth."

Had Sergeant Frazee been watching under that arm?

The little man sat down on the edge of the blanket and looked at the strained mouth below the defensive arm a few inches from his own knee. The tanned skin of cheek and jaw had a yellow look, though the gunner's outdoor convalescence should have kept his tan from fading. F. Millard's eyes traveled on to the cane. "How—" he cleared his throat "—how's your leg?"

But Ethan only grunted without rising to the bait. A man of few words, Virgil Kingdom had called him. He was a man of no words this morning.

F. Millard changed the worm on his hook for a grasshopper. On the sunny, still beach by the sunny, still lake, he quoted abruptly, " 'The King can do no wrong.' "

Ethan's arm flopped away from his face. The thick lashes, only a shade darker than his hair and far lighter than his brown skin, batted rapidly while his bright blue eyes held the grocer's. Then his arm flopped back. "The hell he can't," he growled.

"You don't share the general admiration for the King?"

"I know him too well."

"The girls seem to think he's pretty grand," F. Millard murmured, "Bella and Jade and Chris."

A spasm rippled the taut, straight mouth.

"Even Abby," said the grocer. "Aren't you and Benny lodge members too?"

"What do *you* think?"

"His wife strikes me as ambitious," F. Millard remarked. "I wonder if she's satisfied with his present job?"

The tight mouth almost relaxed. "You can't get Ph.D.'s without money. Kingdom got his M.A. last year while he was teaching, and put most of this year's salary in a car. Bella must have been fit to be tied. She helped him graduate, gave up her college education to sling hash."

"Is that what Miss Lothrop means—no waitress apron anymore when Mrs. Kingdom's hands go to her back?"

Ethan nodded. "Bella developed social yearnings after the King got his university job, and reminding her she was ever on the receiving end of tips burns her up. My God, if I could do for anyone, I loved what Bella's done for Kingdom—" Ethan's mouth lost its tautness and looked gentle and oddly sweet "—well, I wouldn't be embarrassed about my social standing."

"Do you think Mrs. Kingdom really is? Maybe it's her husband who's embarrassed—and she knows it. I wonder —if they had money—" F. Millard paused.

"They'd go Outside like a shot. Bella'd see he got his Ph.D. at the ritziest place, and they'd never come back where folks knew she once waited tables to help her husband through college."

Then Bella did want money for more reasons than removing King from Chris and Jade. But the cartridge shell had been in her husband's pocket. How much did he want a Ph.D.?

"If I had a lot of money," F. Millard mused, "I'd buy Tom Blaine's grocery. What would you do, Sergeant, if you had?" And that, he congratulated himself, was smooth—Flatfoot Flannagan couldn't do better.

Again, Ethan's arm came away from his face, and his bright eyes stared up at the grocer. Suddenly, he grinned. "Trying to establish a motive for the heir? Well, I'll just fool you and tell. I'm going to buy a dairy ranch. I was stymied before, because they wanted twelve thousand, cash, but now… There's a going concern in the Matanuska Valley that one of the colonists wants to sell. I've tried mining and fishing and trapping, and I want something permanent—something definite to fight for, not just Alaska, or America, or democracy—something of my own. It's not like I had a wife."

"I'm surprised you don't have a wife, an upstanding young fellow like you," said the grocer. "You and Benny'd both make better husbands than the professor, if I'm any judge."

The look of peace that had gradually come to the gunner's face turned bitter. "Anyone who marries the King is out of luck. Anyone in love with the King—"

Steps grated pebbles, and both men turned. Bella and Virgil Kingdom were walking up the beach.

"Here comes the ball of fire." Ethan felt for a cigarette.

Behind King, a gray-tan furry head nosed forward. The dog's preference for Benny didn't mean he never followed the older brother.

A step on the sun deck brought F. Millard's head around. The three women from the Thornes' cabin were coming down the boathouse stairs. The Abby Association was gathering.

More blankets were spread on the pebbles. Jade dropped her Hollywoodish beach robe, the same shade of green as her eyes, and joined the other girls at the edge of the water, and Benny and the Scouts dashed, whooping down the bank.

Someone picked up a flat stone and skipped it over the water. In a minute they were all skipping rocks, all except F. Millard and Ethan, who lay with his arm still over his face. Even Abby ran down to the water's edge and sent rocks as far as King's.

The little grocer watched the yelling, posturing line-up. It didn't seem possible that one of them was a killer.

Slowly, his eyes turned south, over Chris's burnished curls, hardly higher than the scrambled black thatch of the tallest Scout, to the house on the point. Paintless, square, and solitary, it stared unwinkingly back. Something about its defiant isolation seemed sinister even in sunlight. He shivered, recalling how it had felt last night in the dusk and rain, and his eyes dropped to the silent figure sprawled beside him. Last night Sergeant Ethan Frazee had been coming from that direction, walking fast, without a cane. Today, he looked drawn and tired. Was it Ethan who had been in the house on the point? A wounded man could be easily overtaken. His leg must be nearly well for him to swing along with the unaided stride F. Millard had watched last night. And those bathing trunks—when everyone said Ethan's wound wouldn't let him swim.

The night of the fire—F. Millard, remembering, started—Ethan had fought all through the blaze without a cane. At the time, F. Millard thought the excitement lent him strength, but maybe the excitement made him forget to hide his strength. Not till the fire was out and they all stood hearing rain sizzle on still hot logs did the gunner's leg begin to drag—not till he must have remembered he was under observation.

And the hunting accident when Mr. Kingdom had been shot—Ethan had been on that hunting trip. F. Millard's eyes picked out the two fully dressed figures among the bathing-suited line-up on the beach. Abby and King had been on that hunting trip, too.

His eyes slid to Jade. Those flashes last night from an empty cabin—was she friendly enough with anyone here to signal to him? Not Bella, certainly, or Chris, who had bawled Jade out too often to suggest collusion. And Abby patently doted on Chris. That left the men. Jade and Ethan were all but at each other's throats, and the morning Art's questions brought their meeting into the open, King had looked at the long, near-platinum bob as if he hated its owner. Benny seemed to avoid her. He swam with Chris, and yet—blinking, F. Millard realized that if he had to single out the girl Benny seemed most interested in, he'd have chosen Bella Kingdom, the girl his brother had married.

But who could Jade—? Suddenly, he swallowed so loudly that Ethan must have heard him. What if it wasn't one of the line-up on the beach or the man beside him? Jade had expected to come into money. If she'd arranged matters with some boyfriend, maybe even her ex-husband, then the signals and her aura of menace both would be accounted for. He thought of the blade-slim dark presence that had passed him last night, with just a few bushes between them, and shivered in the sunshine.

The rock-skipping contest had ended. Chris, Benny, and the Scouts were swimming toward the float, Jade and Bella splashing each other in the shallows. The two in dry-land clothes were coming up the beach.

Abby made for the blanket on which F. Millard sat. He felt his facial muscles go rigid. Abby Thorne might be an accessory to murder or a murderer herself, but Bella's hint about marriage had unnerved him.

He shrank closer to Ethan, but Abby sat down, tucking the spray gun companionably between them. "God damn it," she said cheerfully, "if the stage don't get through pretty soon, we'll be out of meat, even last winter's caribou."

"Last winter's?" F. Millard marveled.

"Lake ice," she said briefly. "Trigger Joe rigged up an icehouse with a bear-alarm of tin cans that sounds like an accident to a garbage truck. The Scouts got mixed up in it once. I'll bet you could've heard it clear over on the point."

F. Millard gave inaudible thanks that no one had tangled with it last night.

In the shallow water, Bella turned her back on Jade and dripped up the beach toward the blankets. Her crunch, crunch in the pebbles, seemed strangely loud, almost doubled.

"Art didn't take *my* twenty-two," said Abby calmly. "Think I'll see if I can get some birds this afternoon." She turned to F. Millard. "Want to come along?"

"I—I—" he stuttered. Catching Bella's smoke-blue gaze, his collar felt too small. "No thanks. I've got some things to do this afternoon."

"What things?" said a heavy voice behind him.

"Hell's fire, Art," scolded Abby, "you oughtn't to sneak up on a fellow like that. Look how you made Mr. Smyth jump."

So it had been Art's feet in the pebbles that had seemed like an echo of Bella's.

"Go ahead, Mr. Smyth," urged Bella, sitting down.

"Abby's a wonderful shot. She can take the head off a ptarmigan with a twenty-two."

Could she hit a man's heart through a cabin window while she stood so near the road that the shell had fallen where Virgil Kingdom said he found it? The others were waiting for his answer. "Is it ptarmigan season?" F. Millard wondered audibly and feebly.

"Art's not a game warden," said Ethan.

"What were those things you had to do this afternoon, Smyth?" Art

Heggarty persisted.

F. Millard sighed unhappily. Jade had followed Bella out of the water and now sat dripping a yard away. Her green eyes were added to the concentrated gaze that ringed the little grocer.

"I—I was only going to read a serial in *Flatfoot*," he said miserably, "I guess I could do it some other time."

"Okay," said Abby, unoffended. "Drop by the house about four."

Bella Kingdom must have put Abby up to this hunting trip, F. Millard fumed.

"Watch us race!" came a boy's thin yell from the lake, and five figures dived off the float.

Out of the confusion of splashes, bobbing heads, and plunging arms, Benny Kingdom emerged yards ahead and flung himself down beside Bella.

Chris, with her hair seal-wet the way it had been the first day, dashed up the beach, and the boys, like dripping puppies, stopped to water-fight in the shallows.

But something—was it the presence of the deputy?—had cast a shadow over the beach. Half an hour ago when the Abby Association gathered, F. Millard had been struck with how carefree all but Ethan seemed—carefree, two days after a murder. Now, the only heedless chatter came from the Scouts at the edge of the water.

F. Millard glanced around the silent circle of adults—some faces pale, some darkly flushed, all gloomy. With their animation discarded, he could see that these people weren't sleeping well nights, that they all showed watchful tension.

Jade shattered the brooding quiet. "Why can't we get this murder settled and get away—clear out of Alaska? You people wouldn't care if you never went Outside. But think of me! Without my money—mine by rights—" she stopped to glare at Ethan "—I'm stuck here too! Wasting my time in the sticks!"

"Willful, wicked, wanton waste of Hollywood talent," drawled Virgil Kingdom. "But you won't be stuck long, Jade. Not with all the officers and Big Business Boys commuting from the States."

"You can pan Alaska now, Jade," said Ethan shortly. "It's too late to make yourself solid with Trigger Joe."

"And anyway," added Bella, "you're not the only one who's been Outside. We all have, except Chris."

Jade gave a jeering laugh. "Pardon me, Bella, I forgot the trip you made to Seattle when you were twelve."

The dark girl flushed. "Well, Virgil's gone twice. For first year high school, and again last summer, before we got into the war. And Benny went out after Virgil and I were married and stayed all winter. You should talk about all the time you lived Outside when Mr. Frazee took Ethan out the same year your mother took you!"

"And he ran away and came back to Alaska in six months," hooted Jade.

"He went out again for your—for his father's funeral the year I was married," Bella reminded her.

"Okay, okay," said Jade impatiently, "so you've all been Outside, except Chris. But none of you've lived there year in and year out like me. As long as you've got a gun, or a fishing rod, or a pair of skis, you don't care about the theater or restaurants or good clothes. You don't—"

"Did someone say you were a model, Miss Lothrop?" broke in F. Millard mildly.

"For one of the very best shops." Jade tossed back her fair hair. "And I might have been in the movies now, if I hadn't gone and got married!"

"Did marriage spoil your chances?"

"That guy'd ruin any girl's chances," Jade answered viciously.

Then she'd hardly collaborate with her former husband, F. Millard told himself, to make Trigger Joe's will effective. Seeing her last night didn't prove Jade had made the signals, anyway.

"Jade's Hollywood phase," remarked Chris, "reads just like the movie magazines. She was a model in Seattle till she tried to crack Hollywood, and got married in Las Vegas just like the stars."

"And came crawling back the next year to Seattle," added Bella cruelly, "when she found she couldn't twinkle like the stars."

"Well, at least I got nearer than you ever would," flared Jade. "If I hadn't been so broke I had to get married—"

"So it was economic pressure, not romance," sneered King.

"Because I had to eat!" Her blond bob quivered with emotion. "The poor sap thought he was going to get the hand that rocks the cradle and darns socks. But I showed him."

"Perhaps," put in Benny Kingdom, "the poor sap thought he was going to get a wife." There was a white line around his mouth as his eyes left Jade and sought Bella.

"How did your husband spoil your career, Miss Lothrop?" F. Millard asked.

"He beat up on a Joe that took me out to dinner, fellow that knew all the right producers."

"Where was the dinner, Jade?" asked Virgil Kingdom dryly.

"What if it *was* in his apartment?" she flung back. "A girl has to get her start some way."

King grinned. "That's the wrong way if she's got a loving husband. Was that when Goo-Goo became the Big Ape?"

For an instant, the girl's green eyes blazed into his. Then she laughed and turned away. "You wouldn't know about Goo-Goo, Mr. Smyth. Maybe Art doesn't either." Her green eyes slanted up at the deputy. "My ex was so mushy at first, I called him Goo-Goo. Honestly, you'd have died—the things he said and the way he pawed me—"

"I don't believe Mr. Smyth and Art are interested in your love-life, Jade," broke in the little redhead crisply. "And the rest of us have heard about it—several times." She jumped up. "Who'll race me to the float?"

No one moved.

Bella said softly, "You were married about the same time I was, weren't you, Jade? It's sad to think how some marriages turn out."

But Bella couldn't take the others' attention away from the slender blond. Only Benny continued to look at his brother's wife, with gray eyes that were dark and unhappy.

Virgil Kingdom laughed. "Bella's sorry for you because you didn't have the good luck she did."

92

"Phooey!" Jade blew out geranium petal lips. She was enjoying herself, F. Millard decided. "I wouldn't have stayed married to you as long as I did to Goo-Goo."

Bella broke in hastily, "You must tell us about California some other time, Jade. The rest of us only went to Seattle."

"Seattle means Outside to most Alaskans," Abby explained to F. Millard.

He turned suddenly to Art. "By the way, Heggarty, where are you staying? I didn't know where to find you." Then he could have punched himself.

"You didn't know—were you looking for him?" Abby's voice, almost in his ear, sounded hoarse.

Chris sat down abruptly.

"That red wallboard cabin between Thornes' and Kingdoms'," Art's heavy voice returned. "Did you want to see me?"

"Why, I—I—" Why hadn't he kept still? Now every one was waiting, thinking he'd found out something, wanting to know what it was. Someone, maybe more than one in this intent group, had a reason to listen intently.

His mind flew back to the night before. If he hadn't been recognized there was still a chance.

"Been trying to find me?" repeated Art.

Still a chance that whoever had been in that house last night didn't know F. Millard had been there too. His voice, thank goodness, came firmly. "Oh, no indeed, I haven't been trying to find you. I only wanted to know where you were, if I—After all, when there's been a murder..."

His words trailed off. When he started out last night, he'd had a rolled copy of *Flatfoot* in his pocket; he remembered shoving it farther down after he put on his hat. He didn't remember seeing it when he undressed last night and hung his trousers over a chair.

He'd done no reading this morning. After his bath and breakfast, he'd hurried to the Thornes' beach. He hadn't crammed any magazine in his pocket this morning. If the one he'd put there the evening before wasn't in his pocket now—

His mouth felt suddenly dry, and the hand he forced toward his hip was as stiff as a doll's, as heavy as a shovel. If that magazine wasn't in his pocket now, he'd dropped it last night in the house on the point or between there and his cabin. Even if he hadn't been recognized, *Flatfoot* would give him away.

At last, his hand reached his hip pocket. No magazine was there.

Chapter Eleven

Thank goodness, F. Millard thought weakly; his firm answer had made the others lose interest in him. Bella resumed her bickering with Jade, who sat church-steepling her hands with green eyes glinting through them—hands up, F. Millard remembered Bella's accusation to keep them from getting red; Benny took up Chris's challenge to race; King stretched his lazy length on the blanket; Abby, Ethan, and Art began some sort of hunting discussion right across F. Millard's legs; and the boys—

Tangled in a snarl of arms and legs, the Scouts were making violent faces. Not at each other, F. Millard saw—but at him.

They must have something to report. He'd better stop that grimacing now before anybody noticed. He pried himself upright. "Hey, kids, how about showing me that bear-pit Trigger Joe rigged up?"

The arms and legs unwound, and the boys trod on his heels as he started for the boathouse stairs.

"It's not a bear pit," explained One, his thin, dark face earnest. "There's a bunch of wires strung around the tunnel where the meat is, with cans tied every few inches, and when a bear goes after it, he runs into the cans, and the noise scares him away."

"The moose and caribou's got to stay froze," Two enlarged, "so after the weather gets too warm to use the high cache, Trigger Joe cuts ice from the lake for the tunnel—I mean he used to."

They had passed the central clearing and were walking by the north row of cabins. "They can't hear us now," said F. Millard. "You can spill what you have to tell me."

DOOM IN THE MIDNIGHT SUN

"Gosh, you *are* a good detective!" Three's face was pink with admiration.

"I thought you really wanted to know how Trigger Joe kept his meat," cried One.

"Sure I do. But we couldn't let anyone think we came for anything else. Okay, shoot."

"I had the first shift," Two began, "because I stay awake easier than the others."

"Shift?"

"Sure," broke in One. "When Benny wouldn't let us go out nights, we decided to keep watch on him and Ethan right in camp. Ethan gets all Trigger Joe's money, don't forget."

"So I had the first watch," Two hurried on. "I kept my eyes almost shut till Benny went to bed, but as soon as I heard him snore a few times—"

"Don't tell me Benny snores," F. Millard murmured. He'd be willing to bet King never did.

"Hardly ever," Three said loyally.

"He did last night," Two returned, "for a little while. So when I knew he was asleep, I put on my sheepskin and sat up."

"But what about Ethan?" F. Millard asked. "How could you watch Ethan if you didn't get out of bed?"

"The gate! That fence goes clear out to deep water, and there's only one gate—but you can see it from the Scout Camp; and, mister—" Two paused dramatically "—it didn't open last night."

F. Millard stumbled, and his teeth came down on his tongue.

"Here's the tunnel," said one of the boys. "You see how the wires and cans—"

Vaguely conscious that they'd passed Trigger Joe's fence, crossed the road, and climbed part of the hill, all the grocer could think of was Ethan's untanned body gleaming in the clouded night-daylight above his swimming trunks.

"Doesn't Sergeant Frazee have a boat?" F. Millard asked.

"Just a canoe," said the middle-sized Scout, "and Art's had it since yesterday noon."

Then Ethan had swum around the fence. A wound no one knew was healed would make a perfect front—for someone who needed a front.

But some detective stories said the most unlikely person. The boys had kept watch on the Scoutmaster, too, and Benny's sleeping bag could have been stuffed the night of the murder. Why had he suppressed the story of the torn paper? F. Millard turned back to the boys. "Did you see Benny's face last night when you thought he was sleeping? Do you *know* he was there all the time?"

"My gosh," cried Two, "I saw him undress and go to bed! And he didn't get up during my watch. I had my eyes wide open all the time, and as soon as he went to sleep, I sat up."

"Who had the next watch?"

"Me," said One. "I sat up too, to keep awake. He sure didn't get up then! He always sleeps snuggled down in his bag like Three, but he turned over two or three times while I was watching, and I saw his face."

"Me too," shrilled Three, "I had the last watch and sat up like the other fellas. I saw his face several times. And he didn't get up till breakfast."

So that was that, F. Millard thought. Well, the most unlikely person had never been Flatfoot Flannagan's theory. But those kids taking turns watching…

"Look here, Scouts," he said firmly, "when Benny made you promise to keep out of this, he meant you to keep out of everything about it. What if one of you sitting up there watching had seen something incriminating? Suppose the murderer found out? Then where'd you be—with your families depending on Benny? What can he or any of us do, if you don't take care of yourselves?"

"Aw, you're not going to say—" begged the smallest Scout.

F. Millard's answer was sincerely regretful; he knew how much he was asking. "We can't let you take chances. You've got to carry out your promise in the spirit as well as the letter. I'm sorry, but I'm afraid you'll have to stop this watching business."

The boys kicked their toes against the ground. Number Three hit a can with a tinny pop. "Hell!" Number One said loudly.

F. Millard jumped.

Voices came through the silence. On the trail below, Ethan and Benny were returning from the beach. Old North had attached himself to the Scoutmaster again like a loving, gray-tan shadow. The soldier opened the stockade gate, and Benny called the boys.

F. Millard sighed and turned homeward. It was a dirty shame to take away the kids' fun, but murder wasn't a game. If they stumbled on something, and anything happened, he'd never be able to meet his own eyes in the mirror again. And just think of shaving every morning!

Not wanting to pass as close as the trail would take him to Art's cabin, he started up the road. Though with that magazine lost between his own place and the point he might have to turn to Art for protection. Climbing the hill in the sunshine, he shivered.

At the top, he stopped, as he'd stopped the day before, staring down at the lake—green water, green hills, green choking smother. Mosquitoes swore at his head net.

A patch of alien red marked the deputy marshal's cabin. If Art had only taken a different attitude, what fun it would have been to work with a real detective, to be in on all the fitting of pieces and laying of plans, to be on the side of the law. But he was on the side of the law. However, Art might react to his offer of help, F. Millard Smyth was still on the side of the law. He gave his head net a virtuous waggle.

If he kept Ethan's recovery secret, was he staying on the side of the law? And the Dipper that had appeared again last night—with the same number of stones as the Dipper behind the burned cabin?

Then what about Chris and the seven-stone Dippers? Little bright-haired, spunky Chris.

That theory of the most unlikely person—a few minutes ago he'd applied it to Benny. It would fit Chris equally well. On the side of the law...

Without stopping to look for a trail F. Millard leaped off the grade and went plunging down the hill toward the patch of red. To be on the side of the law he mustn't hold anything back. No telling what scrap of information might supply the missing answer. No matter if Art laughed.

He reached the red cabin, lathered and panting.

Art met him at the door. "You look like a feller just one jump ahead of a man with a gun. Met up with the murderer?"

F. Millard could only gasp and shake his head.

Art watched through narrow eyelids. "Kind of thought you had something to tell, and now I damn well know it. Come on in."

Still panting, the little man followed the big deputy, and this time, Art didn't laugh when he heard about the Dippers, but he still refused to be convinced. "If you could prove one of these folks was a murderer, Smyth, I'd believe you. Somebody killed Trigger Joe. But I swear they've outgrown kids' games. It's just too bad the Scouts are here. They make things more complicated—for an amateur."

F. Millard flushed. "What about Chris kneeling so long by that Dipper in the trail? Her arms moved. I saw them. What if she made it?"

"Hogwash," said Art. "The first time you saw it in the road, you were interested, yourself. If that was the first time Chris ever saw it, there's nothing funny about her getting right down close, maybe tracing it with her finger —that'd make her elbows move."

"But Jade or Abby, whoever followed Chris, bent down and examined it too," F. Millard objected.

"They'd be just as curious as Chris," returned Art. "That Jade—she was always a snooper."

"You actually think all those Dippers were just coincidence? Even the one behind the burned cabin? And Bella made one yesterday right in front of my eyes."

"And she told you why she did it. If you'd sewed dozens of Alaska flags, you'd be making Dippers too. Haven't you ever spent a day working with figures and gone home and dreamed about them? God, I have," Art finished with feeling.

"And then again last night—"

"What about last night?" demanded Art sharply.

So he heard the story of F. Millard's trip to the house on the point, from the sight of the furtive figure across the cove to the disappearance of *Flatfoot*.

Art's scowl got blacker and blacker. "So Ethan doesn't have to walk with a cane and stay out of water."

"B-b-but," stammered the grocer, "that doesn't necessarily mean he killed Trigger Joe."

"Look here, fella," said the deputy marshal. "If Ethan wasn't up to something, why didn't he go out his gate like a man? Why'd he swim around the fence and plow through all that loose gravel under the bank? No, sir; he didn't want to be seen."

"But—but, Art, we mustn't jump to conclusions. Maybe there was something else, nothing to do with the murder—"

"Maybe so fella. And maybe not. Ethan's the likeliest suspect. The old man's share from the sale of the claims'll go straight to him. With that will destroyed, he won't even have to divide with Jade."

My gracious, the little man worried, *what have I done?* Such actions as Ethan's didn't look innocent, but how could F. Millard know what lay behind them?

"He's always been a funny guy," Art went on. "Ran away when he was twelve and didn't like it Outside and got back to Alaska as a deckhand. He never cared what folks said. If he wanted to do a thing, he went ahead and did it."

And he wanted a ranch, thought F. Millard, and couldn't afford it unless the Abby Association was sold and he got his uncle's share.

"N-no one was killed last night," he faltered, "the night we know Ethan was out. How about what Bella said, that there might be someone hiding in the woods?"

Art snorted. "You know why Bella said that—either she's afraid King's involved, or she's involved herself. But it's shaping up like Ethan."

"Those signals," F. Millard ventured, "prove two people are working together."

"Not on murder. Everyone's present and accounted for today."

"But if two people killed Trigger Joe, they'd have plenty to talk over. Listen, Art—you know how Jade talks about her ex-husband. What if that's all front? What if she's still friendly with him—and he came to Alaska after she got

Trigger Joe to make a will in her favor—to get the old man out of the way?"

"Goo-Goo?" Art gave a hoot of laughter.

"Well, maybe some other boyfriend," the grocer persisted.

"I told you to leave the deducting to me. Now you listen for a while—" the deputy paused impressively "—Alaska may look like a big place, but think of how you get here— boats and planes, only boats and planes, till the International Highway's finished late this year or next, and then the same rules'll apply. It was hard enough to get in or out in the old days, but now, with a war on, and the Army helping the marshal's office, there's no boat or plane from Outside and no boat or plane or train or stage inside Alaska, that we don't know all about everyone on it. And if he somehow managed to cross the Alaska-Canada line on foot, where'd he be? Lost in the wilderness, that's where. No, sir, Jade's husband or any Outsider's all washed up."

Drooping, F. Millard rose. Art followed him to the door.

"No, sir," he said again. "It looks more like Ethan every minute. And listen, Smyth, don't go snooping around anymore by yourself. Forget about those Dippers, and try to keep from getting killed."

Keep from getting killed, echoed in F. Millard's brain as he stumbled down the path, walking sideways like a skittish horse as he passed each empty cabin—one of them might not be empty, like the night Trigger Joe was killed, like last night when he had heard, himself, that squealing door.

Keep from getting killed, he thought, pulling open his own screen door. Involuntarily he paused to listen before he stepped inside and took a quick look in the cabin before he sat down on the porch.

Today his canned beans might have been warm sawdust for all the flavor they had. He hated to give up his theory about Jade's husband. Trigger Joe's will in her favor had been dated May 14, 1942, a month and a day before he was killed. There would have been time for an accomplice to come from California, but only by plane or boat, and both were too closely watched. F. Millard sighed, shook his head, and began to wash dishes—the murderer was here at the lake, living in one of the cabins, swimming and eating with his friends, laughing, talking—signaling to one, murdering another.

Ethan might be the most logical suspect, but the grocer didn't like the way

Art's mind had fastened on him. *My gracious,* the little man stewed, *should I have told Art, or kept still?* He might smugly feel that now he was on the side of the law, but if easing his own conscience got an innocent man in a jam… F. Millard straightened his shoulders. Now he had to find out the truth.

As the afternoon ticked on, he turned to a more personal problem—his hunting trip with Abby Thorne. Why hadn't Bella minded her own business? Though perhaps she felt that getting him attached to the Abby Association was her business. Mrs. Thorne's profanity paled his own "my gracious" into pernicious anemia, but he might have become conditioned to her "damn's" and "hell's fire's", he might have been able to enjoy some aspects of that hunt this afternoon, if it hadn't been for Bella. Drat the girl, and the woman, both. Besides, if Ethan was innocent, the murderer might be Abby herself. What a fine situation F. Millard would be in if he went shooting with a murderer!

Abby had been involved in one hunting accident. Mentally he put the words, *hunting accident,* in quotes. Abby, or Ethan, or Virgil Kingdom had shot King's father for a mountain sheep.

But F. Millard knew he couldn't get out of going hunting. He'd tried hard enough this morning, and not only were Bella and Art determined that he should go, but Abby herself seemed determined. When four o'clock came he started reluctantly down the trail.

Abby was closing the door of her cabin when he arrived. "Just going after you," she said in the warm, hearty voice she swore with. "Time to get started if we want to bring back any birds for supper."

In her hand was a twenty-two. He thought of the hole between Trigger Joe's ribs and followed her with a pounding pulse to the center clearing and up the north fork of the road, discovering, to his secret embarrassment, as he fell into step beside her, that he had to lengthen his stride.

"Chris'll have everything ready by the time we get back," said Abby, "and clean and skin the birds. It's mighty nice when you get to be our age, mister, to have a daughter like that."

She swung up the hill half a stride ahead of F. Millard. "I—uh—wouldn't think you'd take kindly to coddling," he panted.

"Chris is too damn smart to coddle me." She shot him a quick glance. "Bet you're only jealous because you haven't got a daughter."

"My—my gracious no," the little man said swiftly. "I wouldn't know what to do with a daughter." Or a stepdaughter, he added firmly in his mind.

"No joking, mister," the woman insisted, "Chris is a wonderful girl as well as a wonderful daughter. She worked her way through college—the University out here— and got a job in the Fairbanks school plenty of Outside girls wanted. She gets a fine salary without being beholden to any man."

"How—uh—how nice."

"Damn right, it's nice. And hasn't hurt her either. She's still the same honest, unaffected, good little sport she always was. Why, by God, mister, that girl's a downright gentleman... Here's where we take to the woods."

They had reached the summit of the road. Abby made a running leap up the bank and watched F. Millard climb it. They set off uphill through the trees.

The woman had plenty of spare breath for talking. "Chris'd never do an underhand thing or take advantage of anyone."

Had Abby brought him out here just to brag about her daughter? She was working harder to sell him, Chris, than Bella had to sell him, Abby, herself.

The sight of a ptarmigan on a rock hushed the eulogy. The woman rolled up her head net, and while F. Millard's eyes were still on her knot of white hair. The gun cracked through the quiet, and he saw the bird on the ground.

She bent as if to pick up something, dropped her net, and strode forward. "Right through the head," she said proudly, stuffing the warm, feathered handful into the game pocket of her jacket.

F. Millard swallowed. Right through the head—a small head and a single, small bullet.

They climbed a few yards farther and saw another ptarmigan pecking on the ground. Once more, Abby raised her head net, and F. Millard saw the bird's head flop almost at the instant the twenty-two barked.

Once more, Abby stooped before starting for the bird. "What are you finding?" F. Millard asked curiously.

She opened her hand. In its calloused palm lay a twenty-two shell. "We been doing it ever since we got in the war. Can't afford to waste metal, you know. It gets to be automatic if you shoot much—fire, eject the shell, and pick it up before you get your game."

Fire, eject the shell, and pick it up…

"Does—does Virgil Kingdom do much hunting?" F. Millard sounded breathless.

"Why, yes—" She broke off, and looked at him sharply. "Damn it, why didn't you sing out? We been climbing too fast; you're all winded."

But F. Millard had his answer. Virgil Kingdom did a lot of hunting, and habits were motions you went through without thinking, even if the game you stalked was human.

But doodling was a habit. And when Bella Kingdom doodled, she made a Dipper.

"Anything the matter?"

F. Millard looked up to find Abby watching him closely. "You look all steamed up," she explained. "And I can't believe the hill did it. You may not be so big, but you don't look soft."

"I—I—no, it's not the hill," he stuttered. "I was thinking."

"Look here, mister," she said abruptly. "You may say it's none of my business, but it's certainly not yours. If you're stewing about murder, leave it to Art. That's what he's paid for."

"Why, I—I—"

"My advice is "Keep out!" Her tone was cold, all the warm heartiness gone. Gradually, before F. Millard's batting eyes, her body tautened, weathered cheeks paled, and the dark eyes staring out of her rigid face looked tormented.

"If anyone has a right to sweat about that murder, it's me!" Her voice went up the way it had the night they found Trigger Joe. "I tell you the Abby Association is doomed. They've all been killed—every one of the others! And I'm next!"

"Oh, no, no, no, Mrs. Thorne," said F. Millard helplessly, "You mustn't feel like that."

"Mustn't feel like that—when I'm next to go? When I know they'll get me, too? I'm next, I tell you! The next to die!"

The little man shivered. Trigger Joe, too, had said someone was after him, some mysterious "they." Then, as he tried not to look at the distraught woman, came another idea. Every time F. Millard had seen her, except today and the night of the murder, Abby Thorne had shown iron control. What if—the little man blinked— what if this hysteria was a mask to be put on or off at will?

Even as he turned the notion over in his mind, Abby regained her control. "Listen, Mr. Smyth," she said earnestly, all shrillness gone, "whatever's going on around here, Chris isn't in it. I can guarantee she has nothing to do with it. And I haven't, either." Abruptly she stooped for her second bird and began to climb the hill.

Before they reached the top, she shot another ptarmigan. In silence, F. Millard watched her pocket her third shell and pick up her third bird, again neatly drilled through the head.

When they reached the top of the hill, for the space of a gasp the little man forgot cartridges and wounds, forgot death and the dealers of death. Beyond stretched the mountains: past the near greenery, miles through blue distance, they scalloped the sky—all wind swept cleanness and peace.

"Not bad, are they?" Abby observed. "Like a shot in the arm." She drew a bead on her fourth bird.

As they went down the hill, with Abby's game pocket bulging, F. Millard said thoughtfully, "I'm surprised Virgil Kingdom isn't in an officers' training camp. Of course, I wouldn't expect him to be just a non-com like Ethan—"

"Think how handsome he'd look in uniform. But to do him justice," Abby admitted grudgingly, "he's no coward. Guess Bella's afraid to let him out of her clutches."

"Perhaps the draft'll get him," said F. Millard. "Married men without children'll go next. What keeps Benny out of the war?"

"Deferred. Flat feet or too much bridgework—one of those things you don't notice. He pretends not to care but he won't even talk about it. Nearly kills the poor boy not to be as perfect as the King. To my notion, he's got a damn sight more to recommend him."

"Oh, well," F. Millard consoled her, "they'll get over being so particular.

Maybe Benny'll get to be a hero before King."

Chris was waiting for them at the door of the Thornes' cabin. "I have a place set for you too, Mr. Smyth," she smiled, "and Jade's got on her best slacks."

"Of course, we're expecting you to supper," said Abby.

"Uh—" F. Millard cleared his throat "—I don't think—"

But Chris's determined little hand drew him inside. Her copper-bright eyes had an extra sparkle. Had she been talking with Bella? Or did she want to make sure of his presence here while something happened somewhere else?

No mouthful of the crisply browned bird laid on his plate tasted as good as it should have. Another flight of planes roared over the lake, and he didn't even look out the window. When Abby offered him tea, he absent-mindedly started to take it before he remembered he didn't like tea and thought of those scraps of paper in his teapot. Could this offer of tea be a test?

As soon as the meal was over and the dishes washed, Chris left the cabin. And a few minutes later, Jade followed.

A tete-a-tete with Abby inside four walls was too much to expect of F. Millard. A hillside in the sunshine with all outdoors to flee in had been bad enough. Bella Kingdom's devilish hint was almost as disconcerting as the thought that Abby might be the killer. Her gun was in the house now, leaning behind the door, with the two of them alone. And in an empty cabin two nights ago, Trigger Joe Frazee had been shot.

F. Millard's hand sought his hip pocket and the copy of *Flatfoot* that replaced the one he had lost. Abby said "they" would get her, and Trigger Joe had said "they" were after him—one of those vague "they's" meaning no one special, or "they" in the sense of two or more? It might refer to two Kingdoms, either man and wife or both brothers; it couldn't refer to the Thornes, since Abby had used the expression. Neither Ethan nor Jade was a part of any "they" group, unless—

F. Millard squeezed his magazine. Both Abby and Trigger Joe belonged to the first generation of the Abby Association. What if all the second had banded together to get control? Not, of course, to kill Chris's father when they were children, or Ethan's father and Jade's mother who died in a night club fire, and perhaps Mrs. Kingdom's death in an automobile accident had been really accidental. But after that? With only Mr. Kingdom, Trigger Joe, and Abby left, what if the second generation had taken a hand?

An irresistible longing caught F. Millard to see again those high, white mountains, to feel again their austere purity and peace.

He got to his feet. But this was no country to wander around in alone. Last night should have taught him, if Trigger Joe's murder hadn't. Well, he wouldn't have to go alone, he'd invite Art for an evening stroll.

He heard himself say something to Abby that he hoped was polite, then he was trying not to run down the trail, trying not to pound on the red door of Art's cabin.

But no one answered his knock. He tried the door and looked in. Art wasn't home.

The little man felt cheated. His heart had been set on the sight of those mountains, and he couldn't go alone. Neither could he go back and ask Abby; Chris and Jade had disappeared; he didn't want King or Bella; and Ethan—you couldn't ask a man with an injured leg to climb a half-mile hill without giving away too much knowledge about his wound. That left the Scouts and Benny.

Skirting the Frazee fence, he heard boys' shouts on the hill above Trigger Joe's icehouse. He must remember to give those tin cans a wide berth, F. Millard thought, crossing the road and starting to climb. Wasn't the tunnel toward the right? He turned half left and stopped short.

Beneath a cluster of birches stood a figure—motionless, dark, large. The figure swayed, and he saw it was two— a girl wrapped in a man's embrace. That dainty body, that flaming hair—Chris Thorne—and the man was King.

F. Millard stumbled blindly to the right, and a New Year's Eve clamor broke loose.

Chapter Twelve

"My God, you damn fool, what are you trying to do?"

F. Millard disentangled both feet from the mess of wires and tin cans that Trigger Joe had strung together to protect his meat from bears. Scarlet, he looked up into Virgil Kingdom's furious face, thrust down an inch from his own.

The shouts of the boys on the hill above, now risen to shrill yelps, were coming closer. A man's voice called from somewhere near, and down by the lake, a woman screamed.

"Too bad you don't have a siren!" snorted King. "God, Chris, I'll have to scram."

He was gone before the first Scout burst through the trees.

"Oh, I—I *am* sorry, Miss Thorne," F. Millard stammered, and then the Scouts surrounded them, Benny and Ethan hurried up—the soldier limping heavily on his cane—Jade slid noiselessly out of the woods, glistening green eyes avid, and Bella came panting up the hill.

As the little grocer tried to make himself heard above pelting questions, he saw Abby run across the road and Virgil Kingdom and Art striding down the wheel tracks.

"For gracious sake," F. Millard muttered, "there's nothing to get excited about. I just miscalculated the place where the icehouse was and caught my foot in the wire."

"I thought the kids showed it to you this morning." There was an odd note in Ethan's voice.

"They did," the grocer said quickly, "but only that once, and I—I was

108

thinking of something else and didn't notice."

"What were you doing up here, anyway?" The sergeant's tone was sharper.

"Nothing. I mean, I was looking for Benny and the boys to go for a walk."

"Then," gasped Abby, who had just come up, "there wasn't another murder?"

"My gracious, no," F. Millard twittered, "I was only—"

"Someone take a crack at you, Smyth?" demanded Art Heggarty, pounding up with King who was trying to look as curious as the others.

"No, no, no!" F. Millard cried. "There wasn't any murder. There wasn't any attempt. There wasn't anything, but me not paying attention and stumbling over this wire. No wonder the bears run away!"

In the close pressing circle about him, he heard at least one deep sigh.

"Well, for God's sake," said Art gustily, "watch where you're going after this. You scared the bejasus out of me."

"You'll give us all the screaming meemies, Mr. Smyth," Jade said slyly. "If we haven't got them already."

Even his head net, F. Millard thought wretchedly, couldn't hide a face as hot as his. Or maybe the net had burned off.

"You still want to go for a walk?" piped Scout Number Three.

F. Millard shook his head and started down the hill. At the moment he wanted nothing so much as to get home and shut the door.

The others followed, Virgil Kingdom, the grocer saw, walking with his wife. At the trail, the Scouts and Benny turned toward their camp and Ethan toward the stockade. At the Kingdom cabin, King and Bella left the procession, and Art left at his. Abby and Jade stopped at the Thornes'. But calling over her shoulder, "Be back in a minute," Chris kept on with the grocer.

They passed three empty cabins before she spoke again. "I'm sorry you—saw what you did, Mr. Smyth," she said slowly, "but I can't say I'm sorry it happened. It—it's the first time since they've been married. And it's been—so long."

F. Millard walked faster, but he heard the girl's steps behind him in the narrow path. Her mother had called her a gentleman. But did gentlemanly girls kiss other women's husbands?

"He—" Chris hesitated. "You see, it's always been the King and me till—till Benny discovered Bella."

F. Millard stopped so suddenly that Chris bumped into him. He turned around and stared. Her cheeks were pink, and her eyes as luminous as last night's clear pool of water beside the muddy one in the trail.

"Benny discovered Bella?" he repeated stupidly.

"The King never would have noticed her otherwise. She'd always been underfoot and kept trying to wear bouffant clothes and curl her hair."

F. Millard thought of Bella Kingdom's smooth, straight hair with its center parting and simple knot. All the girls wore slacks at the lake but hers were dark and plain and especially well cut.

"We were all in college a little older than average on account of spending so much time on the creeks," explained Chris, "but Benny only went a year and then started selling insurance in Fairbanks. Ethan, Bella, and I had been at the University of Alaska for two years and the King three the summer he and Benny fell for Bella. The King was so broke, he thought he'd have to put off graduating, but—well, he got married anyway." She paused, then hurried on. "Benny fell for her first, and you never saw such a change in anyone in your life. Bella blossomed out in everything right—the way she looks now—stopped trying to curl her hair and began to wear simple, severely-cut clothes. She was actually lovely."

F. Millard began to walk again toward his cabin, and Chris tagged along. Her voice came in jerks.

"I—I guess the King saw she was lovely too, or maybe he couldn't bear to have Benny beat his time. Anyway, before I'd even got used to his taking Bella out instead of me, they were married."

The little grocer heard her catch her breath, but she kept on coming. They reached his cabin, and he turned around again. "So Bella and King were married, and she quit college to work so he could graduate." He spoke accusingly, and a bright flush rushed up in her face till it almost hid the child's handful of freckle dust over her nose.

"I—I told you it was the first time he'd kissed me since they've been married, and—and I'll see it won't happen again while—if they stay married. Oh, damn, damn, damn!" she burst out suddenly. "Why didn't she stick to Benny? They would have made such a good combination! She ought to've known better than take on the King."

F. Millard blinked. According to Art, Benny hadn't told about the scrap of paper in his slacks and his visit to Trigger Joe because he knew nothing that would help solve the murder. But if he did know something—knew it involved Bella, he'd keep still.

The flush had faded from Chris's face, leaving it wistful. It was a shame, F. Millard silently agreed, that Bella hadn't married Benny and let Chris have King; then there might have been two happy couples instead of one unhappy couple and two unhappy singles.

"Couldn't—couldn't you and Benny have made it up to each other?" he suggested timidly. "Or you might have married Ethan. They both seem like nice young fellows."

"They're grand," Chris answered warmly, "for some other girl. I'm sorry, Mr. Smyth, but I'm afraid it's the King or no one for me. It always has been."

"I noticed you stuck up for Ethan when Jade was raving about the will. What's Sergeant Frazee like, behind that poker face?"

Chris hesitated. "In a way, he's like his uncle, old Trigger Joe—completely self-sufficient, and he doesn't give a whoop for convention. Only Ethan's more practical. Even when we were children he admitted the right of the one who could lick the others to be leader, but he said no one had to belong to the gang. He was one of the King's gang when he played with us, but mostly Ethan went off by himself. He was a realist even then, but not all realist."

She paused, and F. Millard saw her eyes soften. "He used to say—I can remember him now perched on the very top of a tailing pile with his skinny brown arms around his knees—he said there were other kingdoms besides the King's, and if I wanted him to, he'd let me in his."

"And you didn't want him to?" the grocer asked quietly.

Chris sighed and shook her head. "It was always the King or no one for me."

"I suppose he's a good gunner? Usually gets his enemy, and that sort of thing?" F. Millard held his breath.

"I don't think Ethan could miss. He's a wonderful shot—" She broke off and raised eyes black with fright. "Oh, I didn't mean anything by that! He never would have shot Trigger Joe; Ethan loved him. Mr. Smyth, please forget what I said. I *know* he didn't do it!"

"He admitted being out the night the old man was killed."

"But he was back from duck hunting and in the house before those planes went over when you all figured Trigger Joe was shot. He didn't go out again till they'd gone!"

"So he says." The grocer paused. "He can't prove it."

"If he says so, it's true, Mr. Smyth! And when those planes went over, I know just how he felt—he had to get right back into the fight! He rushed out—just as he said—and took that walk to toughen his leg."

F. Millard studied the flushed face before him and the fiery, earnest brown eyes. Evidently Chris didn't know that Ethan's leg had already been toughened.

She caught the grocer's sleeve with a strong, brown little hand. "He didn't do it, Mr. Smyth. I know he didn't! And—and about the King—what you saw tonight—please forget it. At least it had nothing to do with the murder." She turned and ran toward home.

Long after the glow of her hair was gone F. Millard went on staring down the trail. There were dark forces working at the lake. How could Chris be sure King's kiss had no connection with them? And how could she know, as she insisted, that Ethan hadn't killed Trigger Joe? Could anyone be so positive—who wasn't on the inside himself?

The little man sighed and went into the cabin, pulling out his watch. Twelve after ten—two nights ago, at this very minute, the roaring flight of six bombers had covered the sound of a shot. Two nights ago, at this minute, a man had met death.

When the road was passable again, would Art let them all go back to town or keep them at the lake till he made an arrest? Would a resumption of normal living ease the wire-stretched tension that kept everyone here, including himself, strung so taut? Or would something in one of them, something that had driven him to kill, go on festering even in town and break out again in murder? Chris and Abby, Bella and Jade, King and his brother, Ethan—there was something against each one. But good gracious, if they were all in cahoots, he and Art Heggarty were alone in a den of rattlers!

Careful, F. Millard admonished himself; might as well be murdered as die of fright. Murdered—

That was the trouble. Murder was in the air, lurking in these empty cabins, breeding in tortuous mind-paths. Murder—

If someone found the magazine F. Millard had lost last night—someone who wouldn't want to be spied on at the point or anywhere else—someone who wouldn't dare to be spied on—someone who would kill to make sure...

A drink of cool lake water might take the dryness out of his mouth. He crossed the room and lowered the dipper into the water bucket on the table. With a splash and a clatter, it slipped through his fingers. A dipper—like the Dipper in the sky, like the Dipper on the Alaska flag, like the Dipper in stones on the ground—the Dipper that pointed to death.

Nonsense, he told himself sharply and gulped down a drink with his teeth clamped on the granite ladle. And that was that! That might be that, his treacherous thoughts retorted, but how long would it be before the missing copy of *Flatfoot* got into dangerous hands, how long before the road was passable, how long before another taut and still tightening nerve-wire snapped, and the killer struck again?

The thing to do, he told himself briskly, was to think of something normal, unconnected with death, or Dippers, or the green, watching the lake. Blaine's grocery, of course. He'd come to the lake to decide about buying and got mixed up in murder. The thing to do—

His glance fell to the table, and his whole body went rigid. There, spread face down, thickened and welted with rain, was the missing copy of *Flatfoot*.

Chapter Thirteen

F. Millard stretched out his hand. It hovered over the magazine and fell back, while everything inside him turned upside down and cold. Could it—his mind grasped frantically at straws—be some other issue of *Flatfoot?* But he remembered that cover—Flannagan shooting it out with a saboteur. That was the copy he'd been reading and crammed in his pocket before he warmed his dinner beans and saw that furtive figure sneaking toward the house on the point beneath the spreading storm clouds. And if he needed further proof, rain had swollen and blistered the pages.

No use trying to kid himself—this was the copy he'd lost.

With a shaking hand, he picked up the magazine and turned it over, and he saw what he was meant to see. Where it had been spread open, on a page that was partly blank at the end of a story, was a crude pencil drawing, like a child's. A square house with square windows on top of something that looked roughly like a skirt with wavy lines beneath it. Wavy lines meant water, the skirt was a cliff, and the house—was the house on the point.

Beside the picture a strip of Newspaper had been pasted across a heavy perpendicular line like a sign on a post, on the strip a printed warning: KEEP OFF THE GRASS.

No handwriting or characteristic wording to give away the sender. But he might find the paper it had come from in someone's cabin.

Then he recognized a KEEP OFF THE GRASS sign from a cartoon in the local paper that had come out before he left Fairbanks. The sheet from which it had been cut would be burned. Any of his neighbors—all local people—would have the local paper.

114

Would there even be fingerprints? Probably the maker of the drawing had worn gloves. Anyway, he would save it for Art.

He stepped to the door and looked through the porch screen, out past the trees and over the water to the square, weathered cottage on the bluff. The late sun had sunk low enough behind the hills to leave the bluff, the house, and the whole point of land in shadow. This morning, in bright sunshine, F. Millard had thought the place looked sinister; now, in the spreading shade, in the breathless lake-and-woods quiet, it looked like murder itself.

He stepped quickly back inside and shut the door. Who wanted to go over there anyway? He didn't need a warning to keep him away from a place like that.

His eyes dropped to the magazine in his hand. Tomorrow he'd take it to Art. Not tonight. Sunlight still lingered on the southeastern hills, but he'd had enough of wandering at night about these lonely woods and cabins.

Taking down an old newspaper from a yellowed stack on the shelf above the dishes, he wrapped it carefully around the blistered copy of *Flatfoot* and pushed the package under the stack. He told himself that he wouldn't let this warning scare him, wouldn't even let it interfere with his usual routine—that ought to show the fellow that sent the message, or if it didn't show the fellow, at least it ought to show F. Millard he wasn't scared. And to prove it, he'd undress right now and go to bed.

Perhaps he'd sleep in the cabin again instead of on the porch. But it would be silly not to lock the door. Trying to make the gesture seem casual and accustomed, he clicked the key. Funny how all the buttons on his clothes eluded him tonight, and his shoelaces, instead of pulling loose, jerked into tighter knots. After all, he didn't actually know that this warning had come from the murderer. Perhaps someone in all innocence had found the magazine and sent the message to tease him. But the stark finality of murder wasn't likely to give rise to practical jokes.

It might be someone's idea of humor—F. Millard gave the bureau a shove—but he couldn't make himself believe it. With a final push, he maneuvered the heavy piece in front of the door and determinedly climbed into bed.

But he didn't feel sleepy. Must be the daylight, he told himself. It was three days nearer the longest day than his first night at the lake, and there were no clouds in the sky. Everything in the cabin stood out almost as plainly as at noon.

If there were only shades at the windows! And it seemed so stuffy in here. He got up and put on his spectacles, padding to one of the windows. Out of doors, it was even brighter. Every birch and alder leaf, each needle of spruce, even the tiny low-bush cranberry leaves, stood out with daytime distinctness. At least it would be hard for a murderer—for anybody, F. Millard quickly amended, to go about unobserved.

The quiet was as hard to bear as the light. Nothing but the mosquitoes' tireless hum. No bird, or squirrel, or meat-scenting bear broke the stillness that roared in his straining ears. That, too, would make a murd—anyone's passage more easily marked.

F. Millard sighed. Well, maybe he could read himself to sleep by this light that kept him awake—it *was* the light, he told himself sternly. Picking up the last three issues of *Flatfoot,* he settled himself on the bunk.

He read half a page, and his head bent forward, tilted to one side. What on earth was he listening for, he asked himself sharply? He wasn't out in the woods tonight, knowing there was someone else there too whom he had to avoid. He was safe—well, anyway, snug—in his cabin, with the door locked and the bureau against it.

He raised the magazine again, and his eyes traveled down a dozen lines. Then what would ordinarily have been a normal sound on the roof—a soft thud and a scurrying patter—knocked *Flatfoot* from his hand and sent both feet to the floor.

"My gracious," he whispered. If a lighting bird or a squirrel's jumping from a tree could bring his heart up past his pajama neck like this…

He followed his feet out of bed. No use trying to read. Not even *Flatfoot* could hold his attention tonight. He walked to the north window. The empty trail came past the brown logs of the next cabin, empty as well, and the lake glimmered beyond.

What made him so restless? He stepped to the table where he'd left his watch. Twelve-thirty. Too late for so much light, but not, apparently, late enough for sleeping. At least this was one midnight that had managed to pass without a flock of planes pounding overhead, or anyone stealing past his cabin (at least in sight), without a fire or murder.

F. Millard moved to the south window. The trail led on, still empty, but on this side, no cabin interrupted the woods. He pictured it all as he'd seen it last night—the end of the trail, the rectangular clearing where no house had been built, the long stretch of untenanted woods, the point with its rock-strewn neck, and the four-room cottage on the bluff. He thought again of that groaning door, and, trying to erase the thought, rubbed his hand over his mouse-colored hair, slightly sprinkled with gray, and walked toward the west window.

The fringe of trees behind the cabins cut off most of his view of the road. Only a short stretch between two dark spruce trees was visible from the window. As his eyes rested on it, something as dark as the evergreens, coming from the direction of the cabins, walked across the space and vanished. But not too fast for F. Millard to see a dark jacket and slacks and a canvas hat with a net, or to see both hands go to the belt of the slacks in the back.

The grocer began to shiver. Only one figure, he reminded himself, to the rattle of chattering teeth, it had been but one figure that passed on the road. And it takes two to make a murder—two to make a murder—two to make a murder.

The words went on and on like a stuck phonograph record as he jerked on his clothes. He'd been at that window only a minute—how did he know a second figure hadn't passed, or might be coming now while he fumbled for the other trouser leg?

And why was he dressing, anyway, he asked himself furiously, reaching for his shirt? The figure had been walking toward the house on the point, and F. Millard certainly wasn't going there alone tonight, or even outside his cabin. Something about dying with his boots on flitted briefly across his mind, and he told himself even more furiously that he wasn't going to be the next victim; maybe he could be in at the death with his boots on—only he was going to stay in his cabin.

Then, he was pushing the bureau aside and turning the key in the lock.

With his hand on the doorknob, he paused. Maybe this was just what that moving figure had counted on—getting F. Millard outside. Maybe that was why he had walked in sight instead of skirting the cabins through the woods. Perhaps he'd been patrolling this stretch of road, sure that sometime the grocer would see him and leave his cabin to investigate—come out and be shot, like a sage rat from its hole. Two to make a murder—that figure, plus F. Millard, made two.

He went back to the table for his watch. Ten minutes of one. He waited by the inch-open door. No sound, but the whine of mosquitoes came in through the cautious crack.

Five minutes of one—one o'clock—still no sound but the insects' drone.

During the seconds of its passage between the trees, F. Millard hadn't been able to tell whether the figure was man or woman—fat or thin, tall or short. A canvas hat didn't indicate sex. The girls and men both wore them to keep the veiling away from their faces. And that gesture— those hands at the small of the back—had been like Bella's hard-to-break habit of straightening the bow of the apron she no longer wore.

Ten after one. If he could only get Art! If there were only some way to telephone! He couldn't dash out of his cabin—leave cover—to make himself a target on the trail!

Eighteen after one! What if his prudence was even now costing a life? What if the murderer wasn't after F. Millard, but after the figure that had passed? Or if that figure was the murderer, he could have found someone else, he could even now be lifting a gun...

Or was he waiting outside this cabin?

Half past. Twenty-five of two. Then it came—the sound that he must unconsciously have been waiting for—a thin, shrill, terrified scream— suddenly—chokingly cut off.

Chapter Fourteen

F. Millard snatched open the door and leaped through.

That terrible scream, so far away and thin, could only have come from the house on the point.

He tore down the trail past empty cabins, past the Thornes', equally silent, past the telephone booth—but not quite past. He whirled to a goggling stop.

The telephone was ringing. *Tingggg—tingggg— tingggg*—thin and far-sounding in the early morning silence, like that scream. The last time he had heard it ring had been in the wind and rain after Trigger Joe was murdered.

No one was in the booth now. That meant the line had been fixed. But the grocer couldn't stop. With that scream still ringing in his ears high over the tinkle of the bell, there was no time to answer the phone.

Then at last he was pounding on the door of the red wallboard cabin and Art's sleepy grunt was answering. As a key turned, F. Millard felt a twitch of something that hours later he had time to identify as satisfaction that the big deputy too, had locked himself in.

When he was able to make sense from the grocer's gasps, Art stopped only long enough to grab his shoulder holster, then dashed to the beach in his peppermint-striped pajamas, scraped a canoe down the shingle, and jumped in. F. Millard barely got one foot in the boat before water widened behind him.

Art pushed a paddle at him and dug deep into the lake with the other. The canoe shot forward in swooping glides.

"Hell, if we only had gas for an outboard!" the deputy mumbled. He spoke only once more on that frenzied crossing. "See anyone tonight, Smyth?

Anyone pass your cabin?"

F. Millard, fumbling wildly with each dip of his unfamiliar paddle, grunted out his story. Then, both drove their paddles deep, without words.

A wide band of sunlight trimmed the hill behind the point, and past his shoulder, F. Millard saw the sun itself craning over the northeastern horizon. He'd always thought of murder and violence with darkness, of evil abroad in the night. Here, night came without darkness, but evil and murder came with it.

As they approached, the cliff spread out and grew taller till, at last, it loomed above them, all but the roof of the house on top hidden by its bulk. Above them a line that must be a path angled along the north face. Art wagged his head to the right and bent farther over his paddle. On the west, the line was longer, and the deputy headed for the spot where it touched the water, leaped out, tied the canoe to a rock, and went lunging up the ledge-like trail.

F. Millard followed blindly, trying not to slip, trying not to look at the restless water gleaming farther and farther below. Iron posts cemented to the rock showed where rope had once been stretched, but the rope was no longer there. The path led dizzily toward the front of the bluff where he had first seen it from the boat, and he followed it around to the east face before a sharp switchback turn landed him at the front door near the east corner of the square, waiting house. No screaming came from it now, no sound of any kind.

Art flung himself against the door. With an affronted wail, it gave. For an instant F. Millard shut his eyes, then stumbled after the deputy marshal.

But the dingy living room told them nothing, neither did the bedroom from which last night F. Millard had watched the blinking lights. The kitchen, nothing. Art stepped to the other bedroom door and lurched to a stop. The little grocer peered under his arm.

The west window was open, a canvas hat flung down before it. The small table and the chair that had been moved last night were tipped over. The bed had been dragged from the corner. His eyes turned toward the box bureau, and F. Millard gave a noisy gulp.

A woman's hand and part of her arm protruded beyond the faded curtain half ripped off the tottering boxes.

A woman's hand—Abby had said they would get her. She knew she was going to be next.

Art drew an audible breath and walked toward the still hand. F. Millard, his own hands knotted into fists, slowly followed.

A slim arm flung out with the sleeve pushed up—then he saw the crumpled body, the purple, distorted face, the witch-wild hair—not Abby's. The next victim was a woman, but the body on the floor was Jade's.

Jade Lothrop—just a girl, and a beautiful girl. For a minute, while his head and stomach churned, F. Millard remembered her gently—her striking good looks, her exquisitely rounded slimness, and the air with which she wore her smart slacks. This very afternoon Chris said that Jade had put on her best slacks for dinner—her best slacks in which to meet death. Never again would she church-steeple her hands to keep them from getting red. He remembered only her beauty and the little pathetic things that had made her human, forgetting the threat he had felt in the air when she passed in the woods, forgetting the cat cruelty that so often lighted the beautiful green eyes now bulging and congested. His stomach squeezed sharply, and he clenched his jaws together.

"Her own head net," Art muttered, pointing.

Around the girl's slim neck was a tight band of black. F. Millard's eyes sought the canvas hat beneath the west window. There was no net on its brim. He noticed again that the window was open. It hadn't been open last night. Had Jade herself flung it up, feeling death coming nearer, for a last despairing cry toward the cabins across the water? And help hadn't reached her in time.

He cursed the long minutes he had stood at the inch wide crack of his door waiting for some move to give the murderer away. Well, the murderer had made the move, but it hadn't been directed at F. Millard. Was that why he'd been warned? To keep him in his cabin so the killer could strike unobserved?

Art squatted to bend the still, out-flung arm. "Twenty- four of two," he read from Jade's wristwatch, "and the crystal's broke. What time you got,

Smyth?"

"Two o'clock. A spring must have snapped when her arm hit the floor, just a minute after she screamed."

"You're sure you couldn't recognize the fellow on the road?" Art asked thickly.

F. Millard shook his head. "It could have been Jade herself. Except—didn't I tell you—?" His hands went to the small of his back like the figure that had passed between the trees.

"Bella," said the deputy instantly.

"But anyone could have been tucking in his shirt or adjusting his belt. Or he might have seen me at the window and made that gesture to point to Bella."

"Who'd want to do that?"

"Jade might. They hated each other."

"Then that'd mean it was Bella—" Art stopped and looked down at the stricken huddle at his feet. "It don't seem like one of the girls..."

"But Bella made that Dipper," F. Millard sighed. "And Bella's a big girl, and strong."

"It wouldn't take a hell of a lot of strength—just to get the net around her neck, and jerk."

Both men looked at the overturned, pulled-askew furniture.

"She wasn't—easy—to get." F. Millard's voice was shaky.

"Once the net was in place, even Chris could've done it."

F. Millard remembered the sturdiness of Chris's little body, her brown, muscular hands.

Art sighed and stood up. "Damn near half an hour since you heard her scream. Plenty of time for whoever did it to get home. But I'll have to take a look around."

F. Millard followed him again through all the rooms. In the bedroom where Jade lay, a sudden thought made the grocer bend, squinting along the floor. But the dust was polka-dotted more thickly than a leopard-skin coat with indistinguishable tracks. He straightened and called to Art. "Whoever did it couldn't have left in a boat. Do you think there might be a footprint in that bare ground this side of the trees?"

They went out the front door and worked back, Art on the east side and F. Millard on the west. But broken stone, grass, and other low growth kept the soles of their shoes and the shoes of anyone else who had passed from leaving impressions. As they came near the trees, F. Millard yelped.

Between two boulders where the thick woods-moss thinned and ceased to grow, lay an arrangement of eight small stones—the Big Dipper, with the North Star.

Art's grunt was enough like a gasp to satisfy F. Millard. The eyes that finally met the grocer's were glassy with stupefaction. "Well, by God, Smyth," he said weakly, "I guess you were right."

Too generous to rub it in, F. Millard only asked—in the manner of a humble detective speaking with a great one, but definitely on the plane of two detectives together—"What do you think we ought to do next?"

"There's not a damn bit of use going through the woods, but I guess if I didn't, this'd be the time the murderer'd drop his handkerchief, or his hat—or his pants, for all I know. Come on, if you want to." He plunged into the brush, still grumbling. "It's going to be like looking for a needle in a haystack and just about as smart, but it'd cost me my job if I didn't."

That walk was very different from the grocer's homeward scramble last night, or his outbound trip made in scurries and crouches. Now he was not only on the side of the law but had the Law right with him. Openly he and Art beat the hillside for signs of the murderer's passage. Torn moss, skid marks in the leaf mold, even broken twigs, gave evidence of traffic, but whether left last night by his own round trip, or Jade's, or that of the person who hid behind the door, or this morning by the murderer, F. Millard couldn't tell. In the deep shade, after two nights of rain, they all looked damp and fresh.

If the murderer had dropped a handkerchief, the two men didn't find it. By the time they got back to the point, the sun had climbed well up in the sky, gilding the weathered boards that had witnessed murder.

"May as well take her home," Art said gruffly as they paused at the edge of the trees. "I'll have to walk out to a road camp and send for a plane. How long's that damn road going to be out?"

"The phone's fixed!" Too many other things had crowded from F. Millard's mind the eerie sound of the telephone reaching out for a human voice in the daylit, lonely night.

"That's something to be thankful for," Art muttered. He gave a black look and a wide berth to the Dipper between the two sentinel rocks and made his way to the house. Once more F. Millard followed.

Funny, no one had come from the other cabins, the little man reflected. Even if they didn't have boats, they'd had twice as much time as they needed to come through the woods. But no feet except his own and Art's had rustled the fallen leaves or snapped dead twigs on the hillside; no boat except the canoe Art had borrowed from Ethan rode the water at the foot of the trail. Perhaps no one else but the murderer had heard that thin scream. Perhaps F. Millard's feet, pounding by the Thornes' cabin, the only inhabited one on the way to Art's, had made less noise than he'd thought. Had there been no one else awake except F. Millard and the murderer and Jade, who would never wake again?

The rasping groan of the kitchen door flung him back into the nightmare. A nightmare in which Jade's body must be straightened and carried down the cliff. A nightmare in which watching the treacherous water that beckoned so far below the narrow path was preferable to looking at the distorted dark face or the wild fair hair trailing so softly over his wrists. He tried frantically to look at neither the thing they carried nor the water, but to fasten his eyes on Art's broad shoulders a yard ahead.

At last, they were down and arranging Jade's body as well as they could in the bottom of the canoe. Then, cautiously, the men climbed in and picked up the paddles.

They were well out in the lake before F. Millard saw the other boat. The two figures at the oars looked like women, but their backs were turned as they rowed.

"Guess it's Chris and Abby," said Art. "They put out from Thornes' landing."

One figure was smaller than the other. Then F. Millard caught the red gleam of her hair. The straight slimness of the second back must be Abby's, since Jade lay here at his feet—he could never confuse them again. He dragged his eyes away from the bottom of the canoe and fixed them once more on the rowboat. The sight of Abby's net-trailing canvas hat made the grocer scratch his neck and forehead. When that thin, far scream had pierced the night, he'd given no thought to head nets, and in their early morning search of the woods, mosquitoes had feasted unchecked. In the bow, the back of Art's neck, too, showed welts above his striped pajamas.

The rowboat was now within hailing distance. The two women drew in their oars and turned around. The canoe shot rapidly closer.

"Art! Art Heggarty!" That rich voice could only be Abby's, calling through the black veiling. "Anything the matter? What were you doing on the point?"

F. Millard heard the deputy grunt and drove his paddle deeper.

They were close enough now, so Abby didn't have to call. "I woke up feeling something was wrong—something terrible."

Inside F. Millard's mind an alert, cold-hearted sentry reported, *Pretty convenient to wake up with a feeling after the murderer'd had plenty of time to get back and rested up.*

"Where's Jade?" Chris demanded. "She isn't home."

"She's here," Art said harshly, jerking his thumb toward the bottom of the canoe.

"We—we saw you carry something down the bluff." Abby's voice was as strained as her rigid body.

"You don't mean—?" whispered Chris. Her eyes were round with the question she couldn't ask.

"I mean—" the deputy's tone was harsher "—she's dead."

Chris gave a shocked little "Oh!" and paled, till across five feet of water, F. Millard could see the freckles on her nose. Abby's veiling hid the color of her face, but she sat like a piece of snow sculpture, white fingers gripping the gunwale.

"The murderer got her," said Art tightly.

His back was still toward the grocer, who wondered if the Irish eyes above the long, stubborn chin were watching the two women as closely as his own.

"See anyone pass your place last night?" demanded Art.

Chris gave a passionate, "No!" and Abby came out of her paralysis long enough to shake her head.

"Hear anything?"

This time, both heads shook.

"No scream?"

"Good God!" Abby gasped. "Did she scream?"

Art nodded. "Smyth, here, was awake."

"How was she—?" Abby moistened her lips and tried again. "Was she shot?"

"Strangled," said the deputy briefly.

The little redhead's expressive face contorted. But strangely, it seemed to F. Millard that Abby Thorne's rigid body relaxed.

"Take a strong man, then," she said abruptly. In her voice, too, he sensed less tension, and now he understood it. But she didn't know that the manner of Jade's strangling would exonerate neither herself nor her treasured daughter.

"Wasn't done with hands," returned Art heavily. "Anyone could do it once they got the net around her neck."

"N-net?" stammered Chris.

"She was strangled with her own head net."

A weighted silence fell over the lake. The cabin on the bluff and all those strung along the shore seemed to watch the two boats—empty cabins with eyes, empty cabins that signaled, empty cabins that turned into tombs or funeral pyres.

In the silence, the two boats drifted closer, and the thing that lay on the bottom of the canoe became visible to the women in the rowboat. Chris gave a choking gasp and turned her head. Abby's only movement was in the knuckles of the hand that gripped the gunwale as they stood out sharper and whiter.

Art raised his paddle. "Got to phone town."

Chris automatically murmured, "You can't; the line's down."

F. Millard said it had been fixed.

"Then that's what I—" Abby stopped, frightened eyes on the grocer.

The little man blinked. If she'd heard the phone when he did and the sound of his running feet, why hadn't she appeared before now? Had she been afraid to leave her cabin, or had she started out, and passing through the main room, found that Chris wasn't in bed? Or—anyone calling near two a.m. must be anxious to get his party— what if the phone had still been ringing, or ringing again when Abby Thorne came back? It could have been Abby who had used Jade's net on the point.

If Chris was the one she was a better actress than her mother. But no matter how hard she might be trying to hide any other emotion than horror, F. Millard could see wild fear looking out of the big-pupiled eyes in the white face below the red hair.

Art dipped his paddle again and glanced back over his shoulder. "If you girls'll come home, we'll leave Jade in her room. And after I phone—" his voice went grim "—I'm going to round up everyone to meet in your cabin. I'm going to get the guy that did this if you folks have to stay here all summer. You better be thinking up some alibis, yourselves."

Chapter Fifteen

More nightmare effort brought Jade's body from the canoe to her bed. Art started to untwist the black mosquito net, and F. Millard stepped outside.

"Just like I thought," the deputy said when he, too, left the bedroom, "the net had simply been jerked tight and twisted till everything was over."

"You—you say you want to get the others?" F. Millard faltered. He opened the door and hurried down the trail toward the Kingdoms'.

"Wouldn't have taken a hell of a lot of strength," Art reiterated behind him. "The furniture must of been tore up just while he was trying to catch her. Once he got the net over her head, she couldn't of put up much struggle."

"Listen, Art—" F. Millard began desperately.

"I'm calling the killer 'he,' but it could've been a woman."

A woman's voice—Bella's—echoed in F. Millard's ears:

If I was going to kill anyone, wouldn't it be the King or Jade? He drew his stomach muscles tighter and raised his voice. "Someone returned that magazine I lost—with a message."

That brought Art to a halt, but Bella came out of her cabin a few yards up the trail with old North padding behind her. F. Millard blinked—North wouldn't have followed Chris that first night or the thin woman who must have been Abby or Jade, but if one of the Kingdoms had made the sound on the road, any of the three—

Art said softly, "We'll take up the magazine later. I want to see these folks as soon as I can."

"For heaven's sake, Art," called Bella, hurrying toward them, "are you walking in your sleep?"

The deputy glanced down at his wrinkled pajamas. "Sure wish I was," he said somberly.

The girl's eyes widened. "What—has anything happened?"

"You bet something's happened," the deputy growled. "Jade's been killed."

F. Millard was put to it to identify the changing emotions in her face—first a glaze that might mean shock, speculation, or hidden knowledge; then a gleam almost like triumph, and at last sheer terror. She began to shake. "I—I didn't have anything to do with it."

"Go on down to Thornes' and wait," directed Art. "Get your own alibi cookin' with theirs. Where's King?"

"He—he and Ethan were going with Benny and the boys to snare rabbits. If you hurry, you may catch them. He—Virgil didn't have anything to do with—"

But the men had already started. Bella's protests died away in the distance.

Rabbit snaring sounded like an innocent diversion, thought the little man, humping himself to keep up. But everyone looked innocent on the surface: a schoolteacher and her mother, a university instructor and his wife, an orderly Boy Scout camp, a convalescent soldier—with their swimming parties and walks, their shared past that went back to childhood. And now three grown men are joining the boys to snare rabbits. It sounded innocent enough—but last night, someone had been woman-snaring—with a black mosquito net.

F. Millard feverishly swatted a new batch of banqueting fiends on his unprotected forehead and hurried to catch up with Art. They burst past the Frazee fence just as the boys were starting into the woods and the men halfway across the Scout Camp clearing. Benny carried a wooden box and Ethan a coil of light rope; King, as usual, walked unburdened.

Art yelled, and the three men turned. Even if none of them was guilty, the sight of Art's pajamas would have shouted that something was up, and they had time to arrange their expressions before the deputy and grocer came close.

Staring at Art, King began to whistle, "I Saw a Dream Walking," and Ethan asked flippantly, "Who's dead now?"

But his eyes weren't flippant. F. Millard could see tension in them and in the hazel eyes above King's mocking whistle. The knuckles of Benny's hand gripping the box were almost as white as Abby's had been on the gunwale.

Art took Ethan's "Who's dead now?" in earnest. He answered tersely, "Jade."

They all seemed to tighten under their clothes. If he could only have told them separately, F. Millard mourned; he couldn't watch all three at once.

Benny spoke first. "You don't—you don't really mean that, do you?" His grip on the box looked strong enough to crush it.

"I mean it, all right," Art growled. "Killed on the point." He jerked his head toward the bluff with its lonely, weathered topknot.

"Look here," began Ethan abruptly, "just because Jade's been throwing out remarks about that will, you needn't think I had anything to do with it."

"Didn't say you had." Art stared so hard at the soldier that F. Millard expected to hear the word "yet" flung down like a gauntlet between them. Then, he included the others.

"The women are waiting at Thornes'. I want you all to get down there, too. I'll be along soon as I get into some clothes and phone in a report to the office."

"Phone?" King's handsome eyebrows shot up. "Has the line been fixed?"

"So Smyth says. He heard it ringing. Better call those kids and get down there."

The instructor's eyes brightened. "Road okay, too?"

"Don't know," said Art. "Wouldn't do you any good if it was. You folks are staying right here till I find out who killed Jade and Trigger Joe. Call those kids back, Benny."

Under cover of the Scoutmaster's hail, F. Millard heard King murmur to Ethan, "If we stay till Art finds the answer, we may as well send for our snowshoes."

"Come on," said Art to the grocer. "Let's get going."

As they started, the boys galloped out of the woods.

"For Pete's sake," Benny yelled after Art, "if the road isn't open when you phone, tell them to send a plane for the kids."

Before rounding the birch stockade, F. Millard looked back. He could see the Scoutmaster talking and the open mouths of the listening Scouts, and it wasn't hard to imagine the rapturous horror that must be lighting their faces.

"I'll stop and get dressed," Art flung over his shoulder. "You go on and get that magazine. I want to have a look at it before I talk to the Abby Association. I'll wait in the phone booth."

He turned in at his cabin and F. Millard trotted on down the trail. As he passed the Thornes' a woman's voice called, but he hurried on.

In his cabin, he picked up the newspaper-wrapped copy of *Flatfoot* and got his hat and head net. He paused for a wistful look at a can of baked beans, then, remembering Jade, looked quickly away and hurried back by the road.

Three bombers droned overhead. This morning, death hadn't needed their drumbeats for cover. This morning, death had been silent.

He could see Art's legs, now properly trousered, beside the stick legs of the booth, before he heard the deputy's telephone-roar. The receiver banged as F. Millard hurried up.

Art unwrapped the magazine and gingerly opened it to the page number F. Millard gave him.

"That's sure as hell the house on the point," he grunted. "And sure as hell telling you where to head in. If there's any fingerprints, I'll get them in town, but whoever drew it would've been a damn fool not to wear gloves, and the picture's just that clumsy."

"What about trying an experiment?" F. Millard ventured. "While they're all together, why not have them each draw something—?"

"The house on the point? And see if it looks like this?"

"Well—" the little man paused. "Why not say any cabin at the lake? Might be interesting to see which they choose."

"Maybe you've got something there." Art's tone was grudging, but F. Millard pinked behind his mosquito net.

"I—" he hesitated. "Wouldn't you like to have them make the Dipper too?"

Art's eyes narrowed. "You must be right about the Dipper having something to do with the murders. But what's it going to get you—just

131

eight dots on paper?"

"That's it—whether they make eight dots or seven, the first Dippers I saw didn't have the North Star—only the one behind the burned cabin, and the one night before last at the end of the morning."

"Hmmm," said Art. "I might tell them to draw the Alaska flag... Say, why don't you do the suggesting? Maybe they won't catch on, if it comes from you." He started toward the Thornes' cabin. "Let's get it over."

"You—you tip me the wink," F. Millard stuttered.

Inside, already eddying with cigarette smoke, the room looked crowded, but there was one chair less than when they'd gathered after Trigger Joe's death. The door to Jade's bedroom was significantly closed.

Art spoke gruffly. "Got those alibis ready?"

Chris stood up. "Can't the boys go back to camp, Art? Surely there's no need for them to—to listen to this sort of thing."

"They'll be all right with—with—" Abby bogged down.

"With the murderer here," finished Art. "Sorry about the kids, but we have to check on Benny too."

All members and near-members of the Abby Association looked slowly around the room. Each glance, as eyes met eyes, slid away.

Then began the second recital of alibis, so like the first, after Trigger Joe's death, except that now Jade's high-pitched laughter and malicious green eyes no longer mocked the others. This time, there was no guesswork about the hour of the murder. F. Millard had been looking at his watch when that cut-off scream vibrated through the night, and only one minute later, at twenty-four minutes of two, Jade's wristwatch had been broken.

No one but F. Millard would admit to being awake at that time. But the middle-sized Scout said he'd wakened at twenty of two, and all outdoors around the Scout Camp had been still.

"Was Benny in bed?" Art demanded.

Two nodded.

"Did you see his face, Two?" asked F. Millard.

"No, just the hump in his sleeping bag. But I heard him snore."

Blanket-stuffed bags didn't snore, reflected the grocer, so that schoolboy trick was out.

"I saw his face," Three volunteered, "when I woke up at quarter past two. He was sitting on his cot rubbing tonic in his hair."

With Jade gone, there was no one to laugh at Benny's wishful thinking. Even Art's "At two-fifteen?" was serious.

F. Millard looked away from the flush that must have been painful, flooding Benny's forehead to the encroaching v's in his hair. "Forgot to use it when I went to bed."

Had Benny, too, seen Bella's husband embracing another girl?

But Art's speculation was less romantic than the grocer's. "If Three, here, hadn't seen you in bed when Jade must've been dying, I'd sure look into your being up last night."

"Gosh!" Benny drew a gusty breath. "I only got up to get the tonic when I woke and remembered I hadn't used it."

"What I'd like to know," said Bella, "is how the Scouts know what time it is whenever they wake up. I never do."

"There's a big alarm clock by Benny's cot," explained One, eager to make up for sleeping through all the excitement. "And with the nights like days, you can't help looking at it."

"You didn't see King last night, Bella—" Art pounced on another victim "—rubbing tonic in his hair? Or a hump in his blankets?"

"Not after I went to bed," said Bella firmly. "I told you I was asleep."

F. Millard still felt that Art was violating *Flatfoot's* code by not examining suspects alone. Still, the first mass interview had brought out things, though this time, Jade wasn't able to show up her former playmates.

Art hammered in vain without shaking any story. As long as each insisted he'd been asleep, King and Bella couldn't alibi each other, neither could Abby and Chris. F. Millard wondered, as he saw the white-haired woman trying not to watch her daughter and Virgil Kingdom's wife trying not to watch her husband, if Abby and Bella wished they could change their stories. The deputy finally gave up and sat down beside F. Millard.

King leaned forward. "Did you find out if the road's fixed?"

The bush of hair on Art's forehead gave a negative swing.

"Still out. Wouldn't do you folks any good anyhow," he said morosely. "You're all going to stay awhile."

Again, the roomful exchanged oblique glances, like thrusting swords.

Art turned to the grocer. "Got something on your mind, Smyth?"

Slowly, F. Millard stood up. "Do you have a tablet, Mrs. Thorne, or some sort of writing paper?"

Abby looked up sharply. "I suppose whoever killed Jade left a note, and you want to see if it came from this house?"

"If he left a note," scowled Ethan, "bet he signed my name."

"Now don't jump to conclusions, folks," F. Millard soothed. "I just thought we'd all appreciate getting our minds off murder for a while, and alibis, and—and—" he began to flounder "—I thought we might play a little game."

"Game!" exploded Chris.

"For God's sake!" cried Abby. "Who wants to play games this morning?" Her eyes turned toward the south bedroom's closed door.

Frantically, F. Millard ransacked a blank mind. Half the suspects were standing up. Art started to rise—and things clicked.

The little man raised his voice. "Listen, folks, that's not the idea. It's not a game. If we could only—please listen!"

Both hands in the air, Art stood up and bellowed, "Sit down!"

They sat. Art gave F. Millard a scowl and sat down, too.

The grocer was left standing alone. He swallowed. "It isn't a game, and it might help solve the murders. I read someplace that drawing helps concentration."

Art's face began to clear.

"I'm sure you're all anxious to get things straightened out." All of them but one, the grocer thought—or two—or maybe— He glanced around the circle of strained faces and hurried on. "I want you all to draw a picture and see if it sharpens your wits. Do you have some paper, Mrs. Thorne?"

With no second protest, Abby took a writing tablet out of the table drawer. A general search produced pencils.

"Suppose we all draw one of the cabins here at the lake," said F. Millard.

"Any special cabin?" asked Bella.

"Just any that comes to your mind."

Some pencils scratched and others were chewed. Grunts, exclamations, and schoolboyish sighs filled the room. He could hardly hope, thought F. Millard, to disarm the murderer enough for him, or her, to draw the house on the point. But if he, or she, was disarmed enough to forget to fake a different style one object would be accomplished.

He and Art drew, too. If this was an exercise in concentration, they would need it as much as the others. Even the Scouts had pencil and paper.

The cabin that came to F. Millard's mind was, of course, the one on the point; his result, he saw, to his horror, too much like the picture in *Flatfoot*.

He waited till the last pencil stopped scratching, then rose to collect the papers.

"Thought this was just an exercise in concentration." King's mocking eyes said he hadn't believed that story in the first place. "What do you want the drawings for?"

"Why, I—I was just curious," F. Millard said lamely.

"I'll bet you were!"

The drawing King surrendered was unmistakable.

Even if the pencil strokes had been less skilled, anyone at the lake would have recognized that cabin. Only one had a fence that ran out in the water. What had brought the Frazee place so strongly to his mind?

The three Scouts held out their papers, all pictures of the Scout Camp. F. Millard had to remind himself to look at them and at Art's, another view of the house on the point.

Abby, who had laid down her pencil first, gave up a picture that F. Millard had to blink over a few times to identify. Then he almost gasped. The telephone booth! Didn't that show a guilty conscience about the ringing this morning?

Benny's drawing was almost as well executed as his brother's, not quite, of course—King would do better. F. Millard's eyes sought Bella, for the Scoutmaster had drawn his brother's cabin.

The little man reached for Bella's paper—and got a shock. Those black, lopsided walls, those door and window openings hopelessly askew, that roofless shell, could only be the burned cabin, where Trigger Joe had met death.

His eyes narrowed when he saw that Ethan had drawn Blaine's cabin. Was this linked up with night before last and that crouching run down the beach? Or those scraps of the will in his teapot?

But F. Millard's biggest shock came from Chris—a picture of the house on the point, though it was neither as crude nor as square as the drawing in *Flatfoot,* and the bluff less like a woman's skirt. That house must have been in everyone's thoughts this morning, with Jade lying on the other side of the closed bedroom door, yet only Chris had drawn it. Did that show innocence or guilt?

As F. Millard stood jouncing his handful of papers on the table, he heard Benny ask, "What are we going to do about these kids, Art? Did you tell the office to send out a plane?"

"And—Jade." That voice was King's. They might be able to suppress thoughts of the place where she'd died, but not of the girl herself. "You'll be sending her back?"

"There's Trigger Joe's icehouse," Abby said practically.

"I've sent for a plane," said Art. "If there's room for the kids after they get the body in, they'll take them."

"After Ja—after the body," Benny corrected himself. "Don't you see the Scouts have to go home—so there won't be any twelve-year-old bodies?"

"Geeeee," breathed Three.

Two gave a nervous giggle.

"We grown-ups have to take our chances, but it's not right for kids." The Scoutmaster's gray eyes were bleak. How much of an effort did it cost him, F. Millard wondered, not to look at Bella?

King and Abby stood up, and the others began to uncross legs and push back chairs.

"Wait!" F. Millard cried. "Wait, I'm not through!"

"For God's sake," frowned Ethan. "You made your test—whatever you got out of it."

"Still want to play games, Smyth?" jeered King.

136

"Just one more picture," begged F. Millard.

"I don't know why we should do everything you ask," cried Bella. "You're not the deputy marshal."

"And we're not guinea pigs!" Chris tossed flaming curls.

"But—but you want to find out who did it, don't you?" F. Millard appealed to the roomful. "Don't you realize that you'll all be under suspicion the rest of your lives if we don't find out who did it?"

In the sudden quiet he wondered if they did want to find out who was guilty, or if their main interest lay in keeping it hidden.

"That's Art's job," said Abby sulkily. "We don't have to stand a lot of damn fool nonsense from you."

She started for her bedroom, and King walked toward the front door. The others were on their feet now, hesitating.

Art stood up and bellowed again, "Sit down!" When even reluctant King and Abby had returned to their seats, the deputy said, "This may look like damn fool nonsense to you, but the marshal's office is behind it. You do what this guy says."

Now, they'd all be on guard, but it couldn't be helped.

Art stayed beside him while the little man passed out more paper, while he tried to steady his voice for the coming request.

"I want you all," he said slowly, "to draw the Alaska flag."

The six adults froze. Bella turned as pale as she had when F. Millard saw her lay out the Dipper on the blanket. Once more, the freckles stood out brown on Chris's nose, and Abby's weathered face blotched. The three men sat rigid and still.

"Just dots will do for the stars," F. Millard said as casually as he could. "You don't have to draw anything fancy."

Slowly, each came to life, picked up a pencil, and began to make lines. Lines, thought F. Millard? It was dots— but of course, these people would all carry out the fiction of drawing a flag.

This time, neither Art nor F. Millard made any pretense of drawing, but the Scouts triumphantly brought their papers to the table and tagged after the grocer when he picked up the others.

Bella's, Ethan's, and King's showed the seven stars of the Dipper, plus the North Star, as it was in the flag. Chris, Abby, and Benny had put in only seven stars.

"Hey, look!" cried the chubby Scout. "They forgot the North Star!"

"Why—why," gasped middle-sized Two, "that's the signal Chris told us about last summer while we were still Cubs! The signal they used when they were kids and wanted to see each other!"

Art Heggarty leaned forward. "When who wanted to see each other, kid?"

Two gulped. His eyes stood out like gobs of blue paint. "C-Chris and Benny's brother."

Chapter Sixteen

A crackling silence followed Two's words. Art and F. Millard stared at Chris and King, whose eyes leaped to each other's and clung, the little redhead alarmingly pale. Abby and Ethan jumped up and strode to separate windows. Benny and Bella sat with eyes fixed on King.

"What's the matter?" asked the middle-sized Scout unhappily. "Was that something I shouldn't have told?"

Art lunged across the room to tower over the chairs in which Chris and King still sat. "Well?" he demanded.

Two tugged at F. Millard's sleeve. "Ought I have kept still?" he whispered.

F. Millard arranged a sickly smile and a reassuring pat on the shoulder. "Don't worry, kid. We had to find out. Art's through with you boys now. Why don't you go down and skip rocks?"

The door closing behind the Scouts was not so loud as Art's second "Well?"

"Well, yourself," King said finally. "What of it?"

"That's what I'm asking you."

"Your province is murder, big boy." King reached for a cigarette. "Catch the killer and keep your micky nose out of other people's business."

"I'm after the killer."

"Oh, Art," Chris said breathlessly, "you know the King, and I'd never—kill anyone!"

"Someone did," said F. Millard.

The deputy put it more plainly. "We got two too many corpses now. What about these Dippers, King? Where'd you and Chris meet last night?"

"We didn't meet last night," King growled.

Art turned to the girl. "I want the truth, Chris. Where'd you two meet last night?"

She stared back, her rounded jaw set more firmly. "The King's doing the talking, Art."

"And we didn't meet last night," Virgil Kingdom said again.

"But I know you did," Art snapped. "At the house on the point."

Chris gasped. Abby flew back from the window to stand beside her and glare at Art.

"Okay, what time was it?" said Art. "Before Jade came—or while she was there?"

"We didn't—it wasn't—oh, Art—" Chris's words tumbled over each other "—we didn't go *there!* We weren't there at all last night!"

"Where did you go, then?"

"Out to the highway. We didn't go anywhere near the point."

"When?"

"Quarter past one. We were back by two o'clock."

"Then why didn't you do something about that scream?"

"We didn't hear it, Art. Honestly, we didn't. We must have been around the hill. We didn't know anything had happened."

"That's what you say now. A while ago, you both said you were sleeping at one-thirty-five."

King's eyes slid to his wife.

"You wait till you see I know you were out," went on Art, "and cook up a story to put you well away from the scene of the murder. Where'd you leave the Dipper last night?"

"We didn't—" Chris moistened her lips "—we didn't make the Dipper. We agreed where we'd meet beforehand."

"You been signaling with the Dipper. Why not last night?" Art's eyes were like steel probes.

This time, it was the girl's glance that slid to Kingdom's wife.

"Bella tell you not to?"

"Of course not. She didn't know—" Pink colored the pale cheeks beneath the bright hair.

"I'll bet she didn't," said Art dryly, "at least not from you or King. Bella might have told King it wasn't safe to make the Dipper anymore, but my guess is you saw her yesterday, Chris—her and Smyth on the beach."

"What are you talking about?" Chris asked faintly.

"When she made the Dipper on the blanket, and you saw its effect on Smyth. They were right down in front of your cabin. But you must of forgot to tell King, or he forgot to tell you—because one of you made the Dipper last night."

Chris gasped again.

F. Millard could see King's muscles tighten under his tan sports shirt as he leaned tensely to ask, "Where'd you find it?"

"Just out of the woods on the neck of the point, with the handle pointing at the cabin."

A listening hush fell over the room, a hush in which F. Millard could hear the hard breathing of Chris and King.

"Where'd you meet the night before last?" Art flung into the silence.

"We didn't," King said shortly.

"Where'd you leave your Dipper signal?"

"I tell you, we didn't meet."

"The Dipper was down at the end of the trail at that clearing below Smyth's cabin."

Chris sucked in her breath, and her eyes flew to King. Then they swerved to the small brown fingers interlocked in her lap, and she brought her lips together.

"Didn't you have time to warn him, Chris?" Art demanded.

Stillness settled again in the room next to the one where Jade's body lay.

"Where'd you meet the night before?" Art persisted.

Chris looked up quickly. "But that was the night Trigger Joe was killed! It was Jade the King met, Art. Don't you remember? He stopped by the house just a second and talked to me through the door."

"Careful, Chris," warned King.

"It was you I saw that night, King!" exclaimed Ethan. "That arm and leg dodging back of the first cabin, next to Thornes'."

The instructor nodded glumly. "I saw you first and ducked."

"Where'd you leave your signal that night?" the deputy demanded.

"We didn't leave a signal!" the little redhead cried. "I told you he just stopped by the cabin."

"Sure it wasn't the burned cabin you met at—with Trigger Joe?"

"Art!" Chris cried indignantly.

"The Dipper was back of that cabin, pointing right at it."

The girl gasped. Abby, behind her, went rigid.

"And the night before that," Art plowed on, "in front of Smyth's cabin—you made that Dipper, Chris!"

Her gaze leaped to F. Millard. "Oh, did you see me? I tried to be so quiet. But I had to let the King know."

"Let him know what?" the grocer asked gently.

"That we couldn't meet in your cabin. I saw you come that afternoon."

So hers were the eyes F. Millard had felt when he walked down the road. Her feet and Virgil Kingdom's had made those tracks on Blaine's floor. She or King had sat on that dustless chair.

Art took up the questioning again. "Did you make the Dipper on the road that night, too, back of Smyth's cabin?"

The red curls bounced as she nodded. "I remade it. The King made it first, but after Mr. Smyth came, I had to change the pointer. Besides, he dropped his magazines and messed it up."

F. Millard leaned toward her. "How many stars do you and Kingdom put in your Dippers?"

"Why, seven, just like the real Dipper."

"Not the North Star?"

She shook her head. Just the stars of the Dipper itself."

The grocer scrabbled through the papers on the table. "Is that why you didn't put in the North Star when I asked you to draw the Alaska flag?"

"Why, I guess so. I didn't think. I just made the Dipper the way we used to make it so often—so long ago."

He glanced at Abby and Benny. They, too, had drawn Dippers with only seven stars. Neither spoke, and his gaze returned to Art.

"It's swell for you to say you don't know anything about the other Dippers—just the ones made the night no one was killed. But somebody made those other Dippers—" the deputy paused "—and who else would it be but you?"

"Somebody's up to something." The words came tightly between the instructor's stiff lips. "Chris and I had nothing to do with those signals."

"What you two been meeting about?" demanded the deputy marshal.

"That's our business!" growled King.

"The hell it is! Any place there's been two murders, it's my business. Come on, King—give."

But Virgil Kingdom's chiseled lips were as motionless as a rock sculpture.

Benny shifted uneasily, troubled eyes fixed first on his handsome, defiant brother, then on Bella a couch length away.

"Okay, Chris." Art turned to the red-haired girl. "You tell."

Mouth tight, Chris shook her head till her short curls whipped.

The deputy tried another tack. "Look here, Chris, if you don't show a reason for meeting King, it looks like you've got something to cover up."

"Something to cover up?" Abby's hoarse voice above her seated daughter stirred flame glints in the bright hair.

"Maybe murder," said the deputy harshly.

Chris swallowed. Eyes on King, her lips parted.

"Don't say anything, Chris," he warned. "We can refuse to talk till we see a lawyer."

From outside came the beat of a plane. F. Millard catalogued it briefly as a solitary fighter.

"You'd better send for a lawyer, hadn't you, King?" broke in Benny. "Don't wait till the road's fixed. Get him by plane."

"I've a damn good notion to arrest you both," barked the deputy. "That'd look swell in the paper—Fairbanks teacher and University instructor jailed on murder charge."

"The lake's short of jails," drawled Ethan. His lips were as tight as King's and his bronze tan the same lemon yellow it had been yesterday on the beach.

Art snapped, "My cabin's got a lock."

"Oh!" For the first time, Bella spoke. "You wouldn't lock them up together!"

"Don't worry, Bella," the deputy snorted. "I'd ship them to town—to a real jail. I'll bet that'd make them talk."

Virgil Kingdom abruptly recovered his own lazy drawl. "Better think it over, Art. You don't want to get mixed up in a suit for unlawful arrest. Didn't that happen to you once?" He leaned back and stretched out his long legs.

Art's heavy lashes batted. "The old saw about give a criminal enough rope, and he'll hang himself's not so bad either. I guess you two'll come in handier right here on the spot."

The door burst open, and the Scouts tumbled in.

"The plane's landing!" one of them shouted.

"By God, it's the one I sent for!" Art leaped for the door, and the others streamed behind, down the boathouse steps to the beach.

The plane was already on the water, taxiing toward them. When the pontoons hit the shingle and the motor died, the dapper doctor and rangy pilot who had come for Trigger Joe jumped out and held out their arms to a woman in the doorway.

"Mom!" the chubby Scout yelled.

She was chubbier and pinker than he was and very little taller. Watching her embrace an unwilling son was like something out of Walt Disney.

Then she counted the other two boys and drew a fervent breath. "Your mothers and I—when we heard there'd been another murder—you kids are coming back by plane." She turned, bright-eyed, to Art. "Was it really that actressy Lothrop girl that was killed? I thought she killed Trigger Joe."

"We don't know yet—" Art began.

"Bet she's mixed up in it." Her eyes fell on F. Millard. "This the gentleman that was with the Senator's party last winter? Heard he was here."

"Mrs. Quinn—Mr. Smyth," Bella murmured.

"We'll have to get together sometime," she beamed. "You boys get your clothes and sleeping bags."

"Guess you might as well," Art said helplessly, "while we—"

He broke off and steered the doctor toward the boathouse steps. The tall pilot started to follow.

"I'll go with the kids," said Benny.

Agitation bubbled in F. Millard, and as they started to leave, burst out in a shout. "Wait! Art, Benny, wait!"

They stopped and turned. "Look, Art, I—I—there've been two murders here! Do you think the suspects ought to wander around as they please—with a plane right on the beach?"

"Hell!" Art snorted. "Jim here's the only pilot, and he's no suspect!"

Red spurted into F. Millard's cheeks. "I—I—maybe I'm nuts, but young folks seem to know as much about planes as cars these days."

"I'll stay with the crate," drawled the pilot.

"That suit you, Smyth?" The deputy's tone was heavily ironic. "Can the rest of us go about our business now?"

"Well, I—" the little man's flush deepened "—what if there was something the murderer wanted out of the way? Not destroyed, but—"

Art snorted again. "Well, he sure wouldn't send it to town with all the woods to ditch it in!"

"Well, I—I just had a feeling…" The sense that someone here had a special interest in the plane came more strongly to F. Millard.

"The Scouts can get their own stuff together," said Benny suddenly, "if my going looks suspicious."

"I'm with you," said Ethan, "right here on the beach where Jim can see I don't stow away on the plane, and Smyth can see I don't sneak any evidence aboard."

Chris tried to laugh and muffed it. "I—I guess we'd better all stay."

"If this isn't a lot of malarkey—" King began.

Art interrupted. "Smyth may be right at that. After last night, I got some respect for those 'feelings' of his. Guess King and Benny and Ethan better stay right here —and Abby and Chris and Bella too. Doc'll come with me. Can you kids pack up by yourselves?"

"I'm going with them," announced Mrs. Quinn. "I came out to see that nothing happened to my boy."

"Aw, no one's going to hurt us, Mom!" objected Three.

Art and the doctor clumped up the boathouse stairs. "They'll be safe, Mrs.

Quinn," F. Millard assured her, "with all of us here on the beach."

For the first time, the plump, blond face, so much like Three's, looked disconcerted. "Why, I—I guess—"

"Someone here killed Jade and Trigger Joe," F. Millard finished.

Eyes darting from man to woman and on about the circle, she took a backward step. "C-come on, boys." Then suddenly, maternal indignation flooded out all other emotion. "The idea of keeping three children with a bunch of murderers! They should have sent you back the first day instead of the body."

Her voice floated down from the bank after she and the boys were hidden by the trees.

One foot on a pontoon, long back hooped to prop an elbow on his knee, the pilot grinned at F. Millard. This Jim, the grocer noted, was as silent as his lady passenger wasn't.

The others were equally silent, only scratching matches to light cigarettes as they watched the Thornes' cabin door. Once Benny said to his brother, "God, it'll be a relief to get the kids away from here!"

King didn't bother to answer.

Benny looked dragged, F. Millard observed, perhaps more than anyone but Abby, whose weathered skin seemed to be all that held her together. But the responsibility for the children had been Benny's. Chris looked white and apprehensive, Bella dark-faced and smoldering. Except for the muscle that twitched at the back of his jaw, Ethan's bronzed face was impassive, though F. Millard sensed tightness in the broad shoulders under the G.I. suntan. Virgil Kingdom's lordly laziness had disappeared. He was now as alert as his brother, but with the tension so evident in the others either absent or under control.

Even when brief remarks broke the silence, the eyes of the Abby Association kept going back to the Thornes' closed door.

The Scouts and their chattering guard returned before it opened. Mrs. Quinn's voice preceded them down the trail ahead of her briskly switching skirt. The boys dumped sleeping bags, sweaters, birds' nests, and unidentifiable pieces of machinery on the beach. Two clutched a cage that held a cowering rabbit.

"Hey, you kids haven't been in my garage, have you?" King demanded.

Waiting for one door to open, all turned with relief to the hodgepodge. While the men rummaged through it Chris brought a sympathetic handful of grass to the rabbit, and Bella and Abby, flopping down on two bed rolls gave absent-minded answers to Three's mother.

Then, at last, the Thornes' door opened. Though it gave no warning groan like those in the house on the point every eye was fixed on it. The doctor came first, silver-fox hair still sleek in spite of the blanketed burden he shared with Art, who swung up the hair on his forehead with an angry jerk. His hat lost its precarious balance and rolled down the boathouse steps. Scowling more blackly, he kicked it. What could have happened, F. Millard asked himself, to set off the deputy's temper?

The two men marched past the staring group on the beach and hoisted their burden into the plane. The Scouts began to gather up their litter.

"Don't load that stuff yet, kids," Art ordered. "Give it here."

As the heap of belongings rose beside him, the others crowded forward.

Unrolling a sleeping bag Art scowled. "You folks keep back. Jim, you and Doc and Mrs. Quinn get in the plane. The rest of you stay over there by that boulder."

"I'm not going back without my boy—" began Three's mother.

"Okay, you're not," agreed Art, "but right now, you're getting in that plane."

Mrs. Quinn looked at the open door above the pontoons. All the fight went out of her. "There—there's only a body—"

"You can keep it company," glowered Art. He rolled up the bag and tossed it through the door. "Any of these folks give you anything when you came back from the Scout Camp?"

Her eyes went as round as Three's. "Why, no, we've just been talking."

"Get in, then. Jim and Doc'll be with you... These folks give you anything, Jim?"

The pilot shook his head and leaped inside. The dapper doctor followed. Art re-rolled the second sleeping bag and swung it after them.

"What—what you looking for?" asked the biggest Scout.

Art only grunted. He examined the rabbit cage before setting it inside the door, glanced at each bird nest and piece of machinery, felt in sweater sleeves and pockets.

The watching group came closer.

"Get back," he repeated, eyes like glacier splinters. "I'm not kidding."

King reached for Ethan's cane and marked a groove in the pebbles. "Cross that line at your peril, men. The penalty—" he paused dramatically "—is papa spank."

Chris giggled and couldn't stop.

With a sharp smack, Abby slapped her.

Chris caught her breath, and the only sound on the beach was the jingle of pebbles as Art turned to fling the last sweater into the plane.

He swung around. "All right, kids, you're next. Come over here, One, and I'll search you."

"S-search?" gasped Two.

Chris, with one cheek still red, took a quick step forward.

The deputy motioned her back. "Don't go near those kids."

The dark Scout crossed the line in the pebbles, and Art turned out the contents of his pockets, prodding lightly over his clothes. He waved him toward the plane. "Okay, Two, you're next."

Huddled beyond King's mocking line the others waited. Like going through fumigation, F. Millard thought—the uncontaminated safely apart; and the contagious, the pestilential—himself and his neighbors— quarantined beyond the line in the pebbles. He swallowed, the sound loud in the waiting quiet.

Finally, Art waved the last boy aboard. "Okay, Jim. Happy landing."

Scrambling inside, the smallest Scout protested, "Aw, Mom, if you hadn't made us go home, we might've found out who done it."

The deputy slammed the door and stood back as the motors roared.

For the second time, a plane taxied away with a blanket-wrapped body and left the dwindling survivors. As it rose from the lake, F. Millard wondered if the others, too, felt the pull of loneliness and insidious nag of fear growing larger as the plane diminished. It cleared the farthest hill, became a speck in the arch of blue, and vanished.

No one spoke while the plane was in sight. Then Art turned his back on the water. "Now you folks get yours," he said grimly.

"Get ours?" Bella's tone showed the inference she drew.

"What the hell are you looking for?" King demanded.

"Someone here knows." The deputy's voice was still grim. "And I wouldn't be surprised if it was you."

"But you haven't found anything, Art," Chris said wearily. "The idea of searching those children!"

"Don't worry, I'll find it. No one's had a chance to get rid of it and won't— now the kids are gone."

"But, Art," F. Millard murmured, "wouldn't their mothers have found whatever it was when they unpacked?"

"And burned it up for junk," snapped Art. "That's what whoever took it counted on."

"But if you knew about it, you could have phoned."

Art sniffed. "You can bet your bottom dollar if that stuff had gone out on the plane, someone'd be starting something right now that'd keep me away from Thornes' and the phone long enough for the Scouts' things to be unpacked and the stuff destroyed."

"Keep you away from Thornes'?" F. Millard echoed.

"We slipped up, Smyth—both of us, though you had the right hunch. Somebody hung back when we all rushed out to the plane and pinched the drawings, we made this morning."

Before pebbles rolled under shifting feet, F. Millard heard a gasp.

"That's why I searched the Scouts' things," said Art, "because whoever pinched the drawings had to follow the rest of us out. There wasn't any fire in Abby's stove and if he'd taken time to hide them or burn each one with a match, I would of smelled a rat, though I went through the cabin to make sure. His only chance was to stick them in the kids' truck and hope whichever mother found them'd take them for kids' scribbles and burn them up."

"And when you didn't find them—" F. Millard began.

"Whoever took them's still got them... So I'm searching all of you."

The group, as one man, stiffened.

"You first, King," said Art.

Insolently silent, Virgil Kingdom permitted the deputy's hand to feel in his pockets, to prod, slap, and massage.

Art looked disappointed as he waved the instructor over the line in the pebbles. He hesitated, eyeing Chris. His glance traveled on to Ethan, until this morning, his favorite candidate.

It was Ethan who received the next probings and slappings, also to be waved across the line. Art's eyes went back to Chris, then on to Benny.

F. Millard blinked. The Scoutmaster was the only one who had tried to leave the beach, and his attempt had not succeeded. Had he been frustrated also in hiding the papers among the boys' things? But Benny had no drawings.

Once more, the Irish eyes turned to Chris. With a single step, the three who had been searched moved forward.

"You won't paw my wife and Chris," flung out King.

"Keep your dirty hands off the girls," warned Benny.

And Ethan said firmly, "One of the women will have to search the others."

"Fat chance," scowled Art. "The women are suspects, too."

"Look here—" King began again.

"Shut up!" snapped Art. "This is murder, and I'm a deputy marshal. I've got no time to be a gentleman. You first, Abby." He glared at the three tall men. "Don't forget I've got a gun."

But he didn't have to use it or search the girls. Because, beneath his prodding fingers, Abby's flat bosom crackled.

Chapter Seventeen

"All right, Abby," the deputy growled. "You take them out or I will."

With eyes like a cornered animal's, Abby Thorne reached into her dress.

Art ran through the creased papers and rammed them into his breast pocket. "Okay, they're all here. Whatever you had to make all this trouble for..."

Pebbles jingled again as the group on the beach shifted uneasy feet.

"I'd like to give that layout on the point a gander," King murmured. "Got any objections, Art? Even if you and Smyth went over it this morning, sometimes another pair of eyes are a help."

The two exchanged glances, Art's measuring, King's bland.

Chris added, "Why don't we all go over?"

The deputy frowned. "What do you think this is, a picnic?"

A bright flush ran up in her cheeks and slowly faded. "That wasn't fair, Art. After—what happened, even if we didn't like Jade, we—we've got to stop this killing."

He looked from the red-haired girl to the handsome instructor, then consideringly around the circle, and strode over to pick up his hat, still lying where it had dropped when he and the doctor carried Jade to the plane. He tapped it on as he flipped up his hair.

"Okay, folks, we'll all go. I'll pay out some of that rope for the murderer to hang himself with."

"We'll have to get head nets," said Abby, and the group began to scatter. F. Millard looked quickly at Art, but the deputy, too, was making for the trail. The little grocer shook his head. At such a critical time, would Flatfoot Flannagan have permitted his suspects to go off alone? Oh, well, he tried to shrug it off; it was Art's business, not his. He had his own net, but there might be time for a sandwich.

Perhaps they'd all had snacks—or drinks—he thought when they met again in front of the Thornes'. They all seemed to look better.

To the grocer's surprise, King offered to row the girls over. Physical exertion didn't seem quite his line.

"You think the murderer made the trip on foot?" Benny asked the deputy marshal.

"Must of," Art grunted.

"I'll walk over with you then and see if we can find any traces."

As F. Millard and Art exchanged glances, Ethan said, "I'll walk too."

"But your leg!" Chris exclaimed. "There's no trail."

"I can make it," said Ethan grimly. And the deputy and grocer exchanged a second look.

At the clearing below the Blaine cabin, Benny told North to lie down. The old dog raised worshipful, begging eyes. "It's too far, old boy," the man urged gently. "Wait here." Reluctantly half-crouched, North implored his master to change his mind. Then Benny dropped his handkerchief, and the dog settled down beside it. They left him breathing asthmatically over his Benny-scented treasure, and F. Millard felt his brooding eyes follow them into the woods.

Perhaps King's anticipation of this scramble, the grocer thought as he wriggled through a scratchy thicket of wild roses and struggled over a windfall, was the reason he'd offered to row. Again, it hadn't seemed right to F. Millard's *Flatfoot*-trained mind to split up the group, especially to let the others reach the point first. But at least in this second splitting, no one had gone off alone. The foot party was only halfway over when he saw the row boat tied up at the foot of the cliff and the three women and Virgil Kingdom climbing the narrow path till it disappeared around the north face.

Ethan, he noted, wasn't holding back the men on the hill. With his cane, which he remembered to use, he made as good time as Benny. Though, when they reached the point, they had no more to show for their efforts than Art and F. Millard had earlier.

The others greeted them gloomily. "We've been all through the house, and there's nothing in it that doesn't belong there but Jade's hat," Bella told them.

"If we had an expert and all the apparatus, we could go over the room where we found her for fingerprints," Art said glumly. "But you're in Alaska, folks, not New York. The office'll get the ones on the gun, if there are any, but a whole room—" He shook his head.

"Our own prints are all over the house now anyway," said Bella.

F. Millard's eyes turned toward King, who had offered to row the girls over, whose idea this trip had been.

Benny and Ethan insisted on making an examination of their own. The others followed them through the dusty rooms.

"I haven't been over here for years," said Bella, "not since the Potters left Fairbanks. Did they ever sell this cabin?"

Benny shook his head. "Always said they were coming back. Remember the time Dink Potter had that Midnight Sun picnic, Bella and the boats got caught in a squall?"

"If it hadn't been for you," said his brother's wife softly, "our canoe would have capsized."

"Benny, the hero," gibed King. "It's a wonder the whole damn cabin hasn't blown off; it's built so near the edge."

"Especially on the east," added Chris. "I'll bet you could dive from the window where you're standing, King, right into the lake."

"Except I remember a flock of rocks below it. Benny and Dink Potter and I considered it once. By the way, Art—" the instructor moved toward the open front door and cupped his hands to light a cigarette "—did you look outside the house? The murderer might have sneaked around on the other side from the cabins."

"Hey, hold that match!" The deputy, too, bent over the flame. "I walked around there and didn't see anything."

"Well," said Benny doggedly, "we came over here to look." He started out the front door, King followed, and the others crowded behind them.

Outside, F. Millard murmured, "My gracious," as he peered around the northeastern corner. This morning, when he came panting up the trail with Art, he'd been so intent on the house and what might be in it that he hadn't even looked at its surroundings, and when they'd been hunting for footprints, Art had taken the east side of the house and F. Millard the west. Not more than a yard of margin lay between the east wall and the bluff. It made the stretch of ground on the west across from the cabins look like a vacant lot.

"Oh, be c-careful," squealed Bella, flattening herself against the house. "It'd be so easy to fall over. Don't—don't go near the edge, Virgil." Her voice rose sharply.

King instantly stepped closer.

Chris, Ethan, Benny, and even Art stepped closer, too.

"Don't be silly, Bella," said Abby. "You ought to go sheep hunting sometime."

"Oh, I couldn't," wailed Bella. "This makes my head reel."

"Ground's too rocky for footprints," said Art.

"Oh, Virgil, please come back," his wife begged, huddling flatter against the wall.

The others couldn't go farther without stepping off the cliff, but as one man, they all leaned forward, and the grocer's gasp mingled with Bella's.

"Remember how fussy the Potters used to be about throwing things in the lake?" said Chris. "You could tell they aren't here anymore by the litter in the water."

Ethan laughed. "You wouldn't call one shiny thing a litter, would you, Chris? Those cans are so rusty you can hardly see them."

"Funny that thing's still bright," King said.

"It's not a can," said Art. "Looks like—" he broke off. Abby and F. Millard deserted Bella, the little man resisting an impulse to get down on his hands and knees. Below, on the tumbled rocks sloping into the water from the bluff, something gleamed white and small and oblong—reminiscent, F. Millard thought ghoulishly, of a finger bone without the flare at the knuckles. But a bone that white would have to be bleached and this was under water.

"Looks to me," repeated Art, "like that thing's just been dropped."

"Wouldn't we have heard it splash?" asked Chris.

"Not across the lake," said the deputy dryly, "at half past one this morning."

"You—you mean—" Chris swallowed.

"The murderer might have dropped it, and after Jade screamed, he wouldn't have had time to get it back."

Chris swallowed again.

King stepped back from the edge of the cliff. "What do you say I pick it up, Art? I was going swimming this morning and I've got my trunks on under my pants. I'll row the boat around."

He stepped into the house and came out in bathing trunks, the muscular body beneath his tanned face far whiter than his brother's—like Ethan's the other night. King in swimming trunks, F. Millard mused, watching him take the sharp-angled turn at the start of the trail and sink out of sight as he rounded the bluff—King, who hated cold water.

He heard the creak of oarlocks before the boat shot around the point in long, rapid jumps as King stretched powerful muscles.

Even Bella crept cautiously forward to join the others and lay flat to peer over the edge.

The man in the boat looked up. "Can't see it from here."

"Couple more strokes," called Art. Then, "Okay."

King shipped the oars and lowered himself over the side till his feet found the slope of the cliff. He climbed among the slippery boulders while the others called directions.

"Around that rock," Art shouted, throwing his cigarette stub. "Look out for cans."

King bent, his body dripping in the sun, only up to his shins in water, and the small oblong that had gleamed whiter than his torso disappeared in his brown hand.

The watchers on the bluff stared at the bent black head while the man in the water stared at the thing he'd picked up.

"What is it?" Art yelled.

King's voice sounded muffled and strange. "It's a knife."

"A pocket knife?"

The head below bobbed.

"Whose is it?"

The line of watchers waited and stopped breathing.

King's hand slid into the pocket of his swimming trunks. He buttoned the flap and looked up. "Guess I better bring it around."

In silence—a silence that strained at the leash like a dog too dangerous to bark—the others watched him go down the rocks, swim out to the drifting boat, and climb in. The oars dipped slowly now, shallowly, no longer in the deep bites of the outbound trip.

The watchers followed along the bluff. Even Bella got up off her stomach and came near enough to the edge to keep the boat in sight. But as if all dreaded the news the boat brought and tried to put off hearing it, no one went down the trail.

King landed and climbed slowly. F. Millard tried to watch the rowboat rocking gently on the water instead of the mounting man, but his eyes kept returning to the white muscular body and the proud black head and the faint bulge in the swimming trunks pocket.

They all shuttled back to the top of the trail on the other side. There, Art held out his hand. Slowly King unbuttoned his pocket flap and laid in the big palm a closed jackknife with a walrus ivory handle carved like a seal.

F. Millard heard gasps, quickly stifled.

The deputy marshal's slitted eyes measured each close crowding face. "Okay, folks. Whose is it?"

No one spoke.

Again, Art's dueling glance crossed the others'. "Give," he said briefly.

At last, King said hoarsely, "It's Ethan's."

Chapter Eighteen

F. Millard saw knowledge in every face. He didn't need the gunner's stiff, "It's a damn funny thing that I haven't had that knife for two days. I loaned it to Bella Kingdom."

The eyes, all fixed on Ethan, turned to Bella.

"I didn't—I didn't—" Her skin looked greener than it had on the edge of the bluff.

"I don't say you did." The soldier's words came out clipped and separate, like staccato gunshots. "But it's a damn funny thing that your husband suggested searching outdoors."

Now, the eyes turned to King.

"No," Chris whispered. "He wouldn't—"

"The hell he wouldn't. The great Virgil Kingdom would do anything to save his own skin."

"But, Ethan, you can't think—"

"The hell I can't! Why would he point at someone else—if his own neck wasn't in danger?"

"Perhaps he knew—" Chris stopped again, her eyes on Bella.

The soldier's laugh was a bark. "Listen, beautiful, the King doesn't know the Age of Chivalry ever existed—or a thing like sportsmanship. I took a licking once when we were kids for something he did. I only took it once, but Benny was the goat a lot of times, and once, Chris— you." He gave another barking laugh. "I was ready to kill Abby when she licked you for going into that old shaft after King dared you to."

"For Pete's sake," muttered Benny, "we're grown up now. Just because a

157

kid gets other kids in trouble doesn't mean—doesn't mean—" He licked dry lips.

"Doesn't mean he's a murderer?" F. Millard suggested.

King groaned. "Now we're all getting juvenile. Let's hope Art's still got sense enough to consider the source."

"The source, Virgil?" murmured Bella.

"A fellow whose knife was found on the scene of murder, a fellow already accused of one murder—by the girl who became the second victim; the fellow—"

"Wait a minute, King," broke in Abby; "what are you trying to do?"

"Get me arrested for murder," said Ethan.

"The fellow," continued Virgil Kingdom as if there had been no interruptions, "who was the first victim's only heir."

"K-King," stammered Chris, her vivid face puckered, "you mustn't talk like that. Don't you know what you're doing to Ethan?"

"He knows all right," the soldier grunted.

"You don't want a murderer to go uncaught, do you, Chris?" King's tone was reasonable, even gentle. "Two of the people you've known all your life have been killed. Do you think it'll stop with two?"

"But—but, King—"

"I know it's hard to think the killer is someone else you've known all your life, Chris. But don't you see—"

"Very touching little scene," jeered Ethan. "Now suppose we turn the matter over to Art without any so-called help from us."

"Don't let me interrupt," Art grinned. "Sure you're through calling each other names?"

"Let's—let's go where we're not so near the edge," entreated Bella. She sidled along the front of the house toward the wider space on the west.

Art herded the others behind her. He stood a minute staring down at the rowboat tied at the foot of the trail. "So the knife belongs to Ethan," he remarked. "And Bella borrowed it."

"Look here—" began Benny gruffly.

"But—but I returned it—or thought I did." No blue showed now in Bella's

158

eyes.

"How could you *think* you returned it?" Art demanded.

"Yesterday afternoon, Chris and Ethan stopped in for a drink, and I remembered the knife and laid it on that shelf Virgil calls his bar, under the cupboard where we keep the liquor, and went to wash some glasses—" she stopped for breath "—and when I came back, the knife was gone. So I naturally thought Ethan had picked it up; he's always so fussy about that knife."

"Was he in the room where you left it?"

"Oh, yes. They all were, you know our cabin's like Abby's—a main room and a bedroom on each side. I just went to the sink to wash some glasses, and Chris and Ethan, and Virgil were all roaming around talking. It would have been so easy for Ethan to have noticed the knife and picked it up, and that's just what he would have done too, because he never could bear to let it out of his sight. He only lent it to me to clean fish when I didn't have anything else."

"But I didn't get it," said Ethan.

King spoke quickly. "Bella doped it out. He saw the knife and picked it up on the q.t.—so he could pull this very stunt."

"Pull this stunt?" cried Abby. "Hell's fire, you mean to stand there and say Ethan Frazee wants to get himself arrested for murder?"

King laughed. "His scheme backfired. Instead of proving someone else had the knife and dropped it here, he's only got himself in deeper."

"There's another angle to that situation," said Abby slowly. "If Ethan could of picked up that knife without being seen—so could someone else. You could of yourself, Virgil Kingdom—and planted it over here!"

Bella gasped.

But Abby's voice went on, as inescapable as doom. "Coming up here a while ago, when we got to the top of the bluff—right there at the switchback, just a few yards north of that knife—you stumbled, and Chris heard a splash. You could have thrown it in then when you said you kicked over some rocks."

"Oh, no! Oh, no!" whispered Bella.

"That's not the only other angle, Abby," Art said suddenly. "Chris and Bella

159

were in the room where the knife was, too, and you all climbed the bluff together."

Once more, a hush settled over the bluff top.

With an impatient jerk of his wide white shoulders, King flung up his head. "This is all a lot of malarkey. What's the matter with Art, letting Ethan get around him like this? I can see how he'd get around the rest of you—the blue-eyed boy in uniform, the childhood pal—but a hard-boiled deputy marshal! Art, I'll bet you didn't even know Ethan's been after Trigger Joe for two years to get the money for that dairy!"

"To borrow it!" Ethan corrected sharply.

Chris cried out, "King, you've got to stop! If you can't talk without accusing someone of murder, keep still!"

"Atta girl," said Benny. "King's just shooting off his mouth."

"Shooting off—God, even my own brother sticks up for him! Chris, Chris Thorne—" the man's gleaming broad shoulders and proudly held head towered over the red-haired girl "—don't be a sucker for blue eyes and a uniform. Just because a fellow still treasures a knife you gave him when you were ten, don't let it get you! Use your head. Ethan's the logical suspect. Ethan could have done all—"

"Virgil Amos Kingdom!" she cried, shaking with fury, "if you say one more word about Ethan, I'll tell why you and Jade were meeting! I'll tell why you came to me! Talk about people in glass houses!"

"Chris!" he rasped. "Shut up!"

"Shut up—when you've been—*sky-writing* about Ethan! I'd have kept still till I died, I'd have been arrested myself before I told your sickening secret, if you'd had the decency to keep still. But you had to accuse someone else—for all you know, an innocent man! And how do I know the thing I've been hiding for you doesn't have something to do with the murder?"

"Oh, God, Chris!" King caught her shoulders. "I was only guessing about Ethan. Maybe he is innocent—as innocent as I am. For God's sake, don't—"

"For God's sake, indeed!" She jerked free and grasped the deputy's arm, leaning back for a last shot at King: "If Ethan's no more innocent than you are, I'm sorry for him! All right, Art, I'll tell you what you want to know.

The night Trigger Joe was killed, the King met Jade to—"

A strong brown hand clamped over her mouth. "You'll keep still till I get Bella out of here!" blazed King.

Chris gave a muffled squeal, and F. Millard found himself leaping forward with Ethan.

Other voices rose. Art's drowned out the rest. "Keep your shirts on, folks," he yelled. "Chris'll tell what she's got to say, all right. But if King don't want his wife to hear, he's got a right to say so."

King released Chris, and the hubbub died. F. Millard was suddenly conscious of husband and wife staring at each other.

"You—you don't want me to hear it, Virgil?" No quiver in Bella's quiet voice, yet the grocer found difficulty swallowing.

King's tone should have been humble, to go with his, "Oh, God, I've been a fool," but it was embarrassment rather than humility that F. Millard heard.

"Is it something Chris knows about you?" asked Bella. "Both Chris and Jade and not me?"

"But you're my wife, Bella. It's because you're my wife that I don't—won't you please go on home?"

Wordlessly, the tall girl turned, her hat with its dangling net in her hand. F. Millard watched the neat roll of hair at the back of her neck and the swing of her strong young shoulders as she started for the woods.

"The—the boat, Bella. Take the boat," said Abby faintly.

The up-tilted dark head didn't turn. Defiance in those swinging shoulders, thought F. Millard, watching and desperate loneliness.

A squawking groan made him whirl. Art had opened the front door. "Come on in, folks, and we'll find out what Chris has to say."

Chapter Nineteen

Silently, the group on the cliff top filed inside. F. Millard stepped over the untidy heap of clothes King had left on the floor.

Art sat down on a dusty couch. "Okay, Chris," he said grimly. "Shoot."

But Chris Thorne was no longer a redheaded fury. She trembled now only in spasmodic shivers. The flush of anger had ebbed, leaving the freckle-dust clear and distinct on her nose.

"Got something on King, Chris?" asked the deputy.

Her voice, when it came, shook too. "J-Jade did." Jade—who now was dead.

"How do you know?" the deputy barked.

"He—he told me. The King did."

"Tell you what it was?"

"Ask him," she said faintly. Then her voice strengthened. "I told him to tell Trigger Joe. If the old fellow knew how serious it was, I thought he might give in about selling the Abby Association, and then the King could pay off."

"Pay who off?"

"Jade."

Benny bent forward abruptly. "The King and Jade had some sort of deal on?"

The girl said scornfully, "I wouldn't call it a deal."

"What would you call it?" Art asked. "Blackmail?"

Chris nodded.

"Blackmail!" Benny's voice and Abby's were like simultaneous shots.

F. Millard blinked.

Art broke the lengthening silence. "Then Trigger Joe was killed so the sale would go through just the same."

No one spoke.

"And Jade was killed so the hush money wouldn't have to be paid."

"Hey, Art," objected Benny, "that's saying the King—"

"Oh, hell," his brother muttered, "what's the use? Art's made up his mind that I did it."

"That you did it?" began Ethan. "Why, I thought—" His mouth clamped suddenly shut.

Abby gave him a sympathetic grin. "You and me both, soldier. You're afraid Art thinks it's you, and I'm afraid he thinks it's me." But F. Millard saw her eyes go to Chris and knew the fear she admitted wasn't only for herself.

Benny made a sheepish grimace. "Guess that's what we all thought. About ourselves, I mean." He stopped, his eyes far-seeing. F. Millard remembered the high-tilted dark head and defiant shoulders swinging up the point toward the woods.

"Say, King!" In a rush of returned alertness Benny ran a hand over his forehead that was getting higher each year. "Did you see Trigger Joe? And tell him about Jade?"

"Sure I did," his brother returned. "And that's all the good it did. Old coot lost his temper and tried to kick me out."

"Was he on the prod—all burnt up—sizzling?"

"On the prod?" King repeated. "That baby was loaded for bear."

"When was it that you saw him, King?" asked Benny tensely.

Every muscle in Virgil Kingdom's nearly naked body was tight. Then he shrugged and relaxed. "Oh, well, as long as you know so much. I saw him the night he was shot. Chris had been hounding me to, and I finally figured I couldn't be any worse off unless Jade—" He interrupted himself. "There was a chance that Trigger Joe'd help me out. If he'd only agreed to a sale of the Abby Association... Well, you know how that came out. I went to his cabin sometime before eight and left in five or ten minutes. He was all steamed up at me, but the way he talked about Jade was something to hear. I almost stayed to listen."

"So that was why he tore up that will," said Ethan. "By God, Kingdom, you did me a favor."

"I didn't see him tear up any will," King said sharply.

"But it was somewhere between eight and nine when I went in," said Benny, "and he was sore as a boil at someone—I didn't get who—and threw that torn paper at me."

"You don't know what time you were there, Benny," pointed out his brother. "Ethan may have been in ahead of you and worked on him to tear up the will. For that matter, we don't know what paper he threw at you. He might have torn up something else, and Ethan saw his chance to substitute the will."

"King!" choked Chris.

"We know it was the will, all right," said Art. His eyes, for a moment, met F. Millard's. "Though Ethan might've high-pressured the old man to destroy it. But you're not through yet, King. What was it you told Chris and Trigger Joe? What was it Jade had on you?"

Virgil Kingdom shot a lightning glance at the red-haired girl.

She began to shake again. "If you don't tell him, King, I will."

"Hell, women make such a fuss. Oh, all right, here it is. You men'll understand. Jade and I once had a little—" he eyed Chris and Abby sideways "—shall we call it an 'interlude?' "

"Don't be so ladylike!" Art snorted. "The girls can take it. You mean you and Jade lived together?"

"Well, yes, for a while."

The room was so still F. Millard could hear someone's hard breathing.

"When?" Art demanded. "How long?"

"Oh, about a year ago. It lasted a couple of months."

"A year ago!" Benny's voice went up shrilly. "When you went out after Dad died?"

His handsome brother nodded. "Jade was back in Seattle then. The movie stuff had gone phtt."

"After—after—" Benny choked. "You and Jade— after you and Bella were married!"

"Hell, Benny, don't be a sissy!" But instead of achieving nonchalance, King's tone sounded defensive.

"You and Jade after—" Benny's face was livid. He was shaking harder than Chris. "Why, you filthy—"

Abruptly, he brushed by them all. They heard running steps and the back door's agonized wail. Then stillness again settled over the house on the point.

King was the first to break it. "Two down," he said bitterly. "Now, little brother's mad."

"So it wasn't just to get on the good side of Trigger Joe that Jade came back to Alaska," Art said thoughtfully. "She thought she had two sources of revenue instead of one. She hated the place so, it sure made me wonder."

"She didn't collect—or maybe she did," said F. Millard before he could stop. The picture came back too vividly of the distorted, purple face and the fair hair that trailed on his wrists.

"How much did she want?" Art asked abruptly.

"Five thousand."

"No wonder you were so crazy to sell the Abby Association. Was she going to tell the University authorities or Bella?"

"The University. A job meant more to her than a marriage. Guess she figured the same way for me."

And was nearer right than King would admit, thought F. Millard.

"Pretty handy for you when the old man was killed, wasn't it, King?" Art remarked.

"What the hell do you mean?"

"So the Abby Association could be sold."

A foot away, F. Millard heard the instructor's teeth grate together.

"And handier yet when Jade went where she didn't have to be paid."

"You said that before," growled King.

"Keeps getting more noticeable," Art returned.

Abby bent over the heap of clothes on the floor. She held out a pair of trousers. "Better put on your clothes, King. May not be any pretty nurses in the pen if you get pneumonia."

165

He thrust a furious foot down one leg hole.

"Don't mind Chris and me," she murmured.

"Don't be silly," her daughter exclaimed. "He's not—it's not as if—"

"Not like he was starting from scratch," admitted Abby. "But still and all—"

Virgil Kingdom jerked on the other leg, shoved feet into shoes, snatched up his shirt, and stalked out the way his brother had gone. The groaning slam of the back door left open by Benny underscored the third departure.

"Guess that's three down," Art commented.

"No need for the rest of us to stay either," declared Abby. "Now we've got down to just five we can all go back in the boat."

"Just a minute," said F. Millard. "Remember that storm a few nights ago? Not the one that put out the fire —the one the next night. Did you meet Kingdom that night, Chris?"

"Why, I was going to, and then it rained so hard it seemed silly to go all the way to the point."

"The point?" F. Millard tried to keep his voice down. "You were going to meet here?"

Chris nodded. "But I didn't go. And I guess the King didn't either."

"Did you make the Dipper signal that night?"

"No! No! No!" Again, her curls made bright little whips in a frantic head shake. "I told Art this morning we didn't. I wouldn't let the King railroad Ethan, but neither will I railroad the King."

"I wouldn't want you to," F. Millard soothed. "I'm only trying to get at the truth. Surely all of us—who are innocent, want to." He stopped to let that thought sink in. "Did you get hold of Kingdom, Miss Thorne, to let him know you weren't going?"

"I didn't think he'd go in that storm, but in case he'd already left, I went in one of the empty cabins and signaled."

"How—how did you signal?"

"With a flashlight. It was plenty dark in that storm to show up on the point."

Involuntarily, F. Millard's head turned toward the bedroom behind him. Sunshine now poured in the dusty cabin, but he heard again the drum of

166

rain and saw the quick flashes and longer, steady beams of light across the cove. His eyes hadn't been the only pair watching. On the other side of the wall, in the room where the chair had been moved...

He blinked and controlled a shiver. This morning, that room had witnessed far more than the moving of a chair, and the girl he had seen the night those lights blinked, the girl who had slipped so noiselessly through the woods before the storm, was now dead.

He cleared his throat. "Were you meeting Jade that night too—you and Kingdom, to talk things over?"

"Lord, no. It was all I could do to be polite to Jade at home. I didn't want her to know that I knew—about her and the King."

But it didn't have to be King who had watched those lights and moved the chair in the room next to F. Millard. Even Chris doubted his presence on the point.

Abby rattled the doorknob. "Let's get going while we've still got enough men to row the boat."

F. Millard closed the front door as the others started down the switchback below it on the east. This, he told himself, would be the last time he'd hear the wail of either door leading into this house of horror.

Ahead, rounding the north face of the cliff, Chris and Abby, the deputy and the soldier, swung along as carelessly as if they were on a paved highway. F. Millard leaned toward the inside as inconspicuously as he could and wondered how Bella would have made the descent. At least her fear of heights should clear her of the charge of dropping Ethan's knife. She'd never have gone near enough to the edge to drop it accidentally. But if it had been planted—she could have thrown it from a window or crept to the edge of the bluff as she had a while ago. Her giddiness could even be a pose.

By the time F. Millard reached the boat around on the western side, Art and Ethan were holding the oars, and the little grocer had to wedge himself in with the women.

As they pushed off and rowed in silence, F. Millard slid back into thought. Bella and Virgil Kingdom... Up to now it had seemed to be the wife who had the stronger motive, while the husband had the cartridge shell. But now—blackmail fitted only too well with the presence of that twenty-two shell in Virgil Kingdom's pocket. King could have picked up Ethan's knife when Bella laid it out yesterday. Or Chris. Or Ethan himself—not, as King had suggested, to plant the knife on himself, which seemed to the grocer too devious—but he could have picked it up and accidentally lost it, stalking Jade.

F. Millard thought back to the morning Virgil Kingdom had poured him a drink after Trigger Joe had been killed. The bar shelf was not near a window.

He leaned quickly toward Chris. "Did anyone else come in yesterday when you and Ethan were at the Kingdoms'?"

"Not while we were there," she said positively, "from about four to five-thirty."

From four till after five-thirty he and Abby had been hunting. And during that time the knife had disappeared, if—mentally he stumbled—if Bella had told the truth.

Scalp-prickling in that silent boat on that silent lake, before those hushed, empty cabins and the memory of death twice-told, came Art Heggarty's chuckle. "What'd I say about giving you folks enough rope to hang yourselves with? Boy, King sure put his neck in the noose!"

"Oh, oh, Art, don't!" Like a child, Chris threw her arm up over her face and burst into sobs.

All F. Millard's outstretched detective feelers curled up. Abby's arms reached for her daughter, and the rowers dug their oars deeper. The lake glinted green in the sun, and hills pressed green to the water's edge. While the empty cabins watched, the sobbing beat in F. Millard's ears was like a clamoring pulse—the pulse of doom.

The opposite shore came nearer. Abby, facing forward with Chris and the grocer, said suddenly, "What the hell's the matter with Bella? She's all in a lather down there on the beach in front of Smyth's."

Art and Ethan raised their oars and turned around. Chris choked back her sobs.

Bella stood under the bank in front of F. Millard's cabin; one hand cupped around her mouth, the other arm making sweeping beckons. Now that the sobbing and the creak and splash of oars were stilled, her hail came over the water—a drawn-out "Halloooooo," unhappily recalling Jade's last thin scream in the night.

Art swerved the boat toward her.

Chris's weeping lessened to hiccups as a new dread dried her eyes.

They were still well offshore when Bella cried sharply, "Virgil! Where's Virgil? What have you done to him?"

"What have we—?" echoed Art. "My God, what do you think?"

Bella gave a strangled gasp and stepped toward them, ankle-deep in the lake. "Where—? What—? Oh, what's happened?"

"He's all right, Bella," Chris said quickly. "He's walking back."

The other girl retreated up the beach, shaking impatient wet feet. "Then he— Oh, thank God, he's all right! I've got to—Benny—I couldn't—" She began to run up the bank.

"Bella!" roared Art.

"I've got to see Virg—" came back to the boat, and Bella was off. F. Millard could see the navy blue of her slack suit darting by the trees on top of the bank, and she jammed on her hat and head net as she ran. Then she was out of sight, before the boat had landed.

"What the hell?" the deputy muttered. "What's biting her?"

The keel grated on gravel, and Ethan jumped out. Chris and the grocer stood up, but Abby and Art sat still.

"I can understand it," said Chris. "When she left the point, the King was on the spot. And then we show up without him—"

Ethan grinned. "She could hardly think it was a necktie party with the deputy marshal right there."

"She mentioned Benny," F. Millard said slowly. "He left the point after she did. Do you suppose she saw something happen?"

"Happen to Benny?" Abby unrolled the mosquito net from her hat brim. "Guess if it had been a broken leg she'd of told us."

"It was King she was worried about," Art said positively.

"But don't you think it had something to do with Benny?" F. Millard persisted. "Or why would she drag in his name?"

"Damned if there's any accounting for women," Art said crossly.

Ethan sighed.

F. Millard climbed out of the boat. "I wonder where Benny is. Mrs. Kingdom must have seen him, or why would she speak of him? But if she saw him, why isn't he here? It was all because of her—"

"Maybe she didn't want him to stay after he told her—about the King," suggested Chris.

"Or maybe," said Abby slowly, "he was too upset to tell her."

"Poor Bella." The other girl's voice was soft. "No wonder she's nearly nuts, if she doesn't even know."

"Looks like your sympathy for Bella's a little late," observed Art.

Chris, climbing out of the boat, spun around as her feet struck the shingle. "Late? I don't like your tone, Art."

"How do you think Bella liked you hanging around her husband? All those meetings in the middle of the night? All those walks to the highway and—"

"Art Heggarty!" Small, brown fists beat on the gunwale as she glared at the big man still sitting in the boat. "I told you I was meeting him to help him out with Jade! You talk like—like I was trying to get him away from Bella!"

"Well?" Art's tone must enrage the little redhead, thought F. Millard. "Weren't you?"

"No! No! No! I told you no!" She stamped with a clatter of pebbles. "He came to me about Jade because—because of our old friendship. He couldn't tell Bella, and he had to have help—so he came to me. He knew he could count on me. I was proud to help him. It wasn't—I certainly didn't—"

Bright pink, she began to flounder, and her gaze met the little grocer's. He could almost see, mirrored in those copper-brown eyes, the picture before his own—the picture of Chris beneath the trees, held close in Kingdom's arms.

"Oh!" she cried. "You make me so mad—every damn one of you!" She tore up the bank and flew down the trail toward her cabin.

"If that don't prove what I just said about women!" scowled Art.

"You hadn't any right to talk like that!" It was Ethan now whose bright eyes blazed at the deputy. "You stick to murder and leave morals alone! It could have been just like she said—not the way you hinted at all!"

"You'd like to believe that, wouldn't you? By the way, Sergeant—" from Art's pocket came the ivory-handled jackknife "—don't count too much on my figuring someone else dropped this. You had as good a chance to pick it up as anyone."

No pebbles rattled now. The sound of Chris's running feet had died away. Motionless on the beach, Ethan and the little grocer stared at Abby and Art in the boat.

"Wish I knew what Bella meant about Benny," F. Millard murmured. "I wonder where he is."

Abby stood up. "Hell, now you're getting me in a sweat, too. Let's go down to the Scout Camp."

"Wait for Bella," said Art. "They ought to be along any minute. King left the point quite a while before we did."

Four fighter planes darted over the hill F. Millard's eyes were searching. As the beat of motors faded, voices came down from the bank and sunlight found King's tan shirt in the clearing at the end of the trail.

Abby jumped over one side of the boat and Art over the other. The deputy might say he wasn't uneasy, but he beat all but F. Millard up the bank. They were waiting in front of his cabin by the time the Kingdoms arrived.

Eyes on the path, the man strode moodily ahead.

"Oh, forget it, Bella," the waiting group heard him mutter. "He was just upset, I tell you. He's all right."

"He didn't look it," his wife insisted. "North jumped up as soon as he got to the clearing, and Benny didn't even see him—and you know how crazy he is about that dog. He just shot by—"

As she was speaking, King looked up at the watchers in front of the cabin. He said something to the girl behind him, too low for the others to hear.

"I can't help it, Virgil," she answered. "I'm worried about him. Now I know you're all right and he wasn't accused of the murders, I don't see what harm it can do to let them know how upset he was. They must have seen it when he left. After all, if it was something he heard about you—" Then at last Bella stopped talking.

King scowled at Abby and the three waiting men and started to detour around them.

Art let him go and caught the girl's arm. "What are you in a stew about Benny for, Bella? Anything happen to him?"

"It's according to what you mean by 'happen,'" she burst out. "I don't know what you did over there on the point. Virgil says when Chris told—whatever she did, Benny went off mad, but mad's hardly the word for the way he shot past me."

Involuntarily, F. Millard cried, *"Past* you?" When it was because of Bella that Benny had flung off so furiously?

"He didn't even see me. I was sitting in a patch of larkspur near the clearing at the end of the trail, and I heard something crash through the brush like a charging moose. Before I'd even picked out a tree to climb, Benny tore by without so much as looking at North, who jumped up and started for him. He didn't even turn his head in my direction. And he looked—oh, he looked terrible!"

"Why didn't you go after him?" asked Ethan.

"I—I was afraid to. He looked so—" She stopped again.

Afraid of Benny, F. Millard wondered? Of what he might do to himself if she pushed him too far? Or to her? Did Bella think it was Benny they had to fear?

She hurried on, "I was afraid something might have happened to Virgil—" her eyes followed her husband's receding back, now almost opposite the burned cabin "—and Benny couldn't bear to tell me. I was just going to start back through the woods when I saw your boat. And then—Virgil wasn't with you, and I was certain something had happened."

"Now you know we haven't got a third victim on our hands," said Art, "what are you still stewing over Benny for?"

"Oh, I don't know." Bella started down the trail after her husband. "But I've got to see he's all right."

"Me too," said Abby abruptly, bumping into F. Millard, who had already swung in behind Bella.

Art and Ethan followed. The girl's pace was so fast that they began to gain

172

on King. In silence, they filed by the empty cabins, a silence unbroken even when they passed the still pungent charred logs of the house where they'd found Trigger Joe.

At the Thornes' Chris opened the door. "What's going on? First the King, and now all of you come pounding along like you're late for work. Has something really happened to Benny?"

Bella gave her only a glance. She reached the next cabin while Chris was still talking, Abby and F. Millard close behind.

"God knows what it's all about," the grocer heard Ethan tell Chris. "You'd think, the way Bella's carrying on, that Benny was one of the Scouts. But I don't want to miss anything. Come along."

As they crossed the parking space that divided the two rows of cabins, Bella waited for Abby and F. Millard. "North started to run after him—poor old North who can hardly walk. He must have felt the way I did—that Benny was in pain."

F. Millard looked back. Chris, too, had joined the parade.

They passed more empty cabins, the red wallboard of Art's, and started by the Kingdoms'. A voice from a birch clump at the side of the trail made the whole procession jump. "What do you make out that is, Ethan? Looks like a man's head to me." From behind the trees King leaned over the bank toward the water, pointing far out in the lake.

The soldier narrowed his eyes against the glint. "Someone swimming. Must be Benny, but it's farther out than—hey, there's someone else!"

For a heart-flipping second, the thought of Jade's husband popped into F. Millard's mind. But even if Art hadn't been so convincing, it was Chris, not Jade, who had signaled, and she'd meant it for King.

As the thought blazed up and was quenched, he heard Bella murmur, "The Scouts are gone," and Abby's sudden shout: "That's not a man! That's North! He followed Benny out!"

"By God!" cried Ethan. "The poor old boy. Hey! Hey, King, look! He's not swimming. He's—"

King was already ripping off his shoes and slacks. He plunged in and struck out toward the dog.

Bella gave a soft, drawn out, "Ooooh," and Chris said gently, "Poor old boy."

"If he stopped swimming—" F. Millard began. "If he stopped swimming after Benny—" Ethan spoke with respect, as he would of a man he admired "—that means the old dog's dead."

"He never should have gone out so far," murmured Chris, watching King's dark head and flashing arms draw nearer the dog.

"He's too old to swim like that," Art said.

"That's what I've been telling you," cried Bella. "He saw Benny was upset. North hasn't run for ages either, but when Benny burst into the clearing coming back from the point, North ran after him—actually ran! I could hear the poor old fellow wheeze. And now—you can see how he tried to follow Benny out there."

As she spoke her husband reached the dog. The six on the bank saw him turn and start towing in the lighter colored dot that was North. Far out beyond them bobbed the third dot that was Benny.

"If North's dead, we ought to call Benny in," said Bella. "You know how crazy they've always been about each other."

"Maybe North's all right," F. Millard said hopefully.

"If he is," returned Sergeant Ethan Frazee, "I'm a brigadier general."

King was near enough now to answer questions. He shook his head at the one that, audibly or not, all asked.

When his feet touched the bottom, he lifted the dripping gray-tan body in his arms. The others came down the bank and gathered close as he laid the old dog on the pebbles.

Chris and Bella were near tears. Abby, Ethan, and King looked deeply sad. Concern showed even in Art's face. F. Millard swallowed past a lump in his throat and then swallowed quickly again at the thought that reared up like a full-grown weed among the funeral flowers. This was the first death at the lake that had brought out genuine grief. The visible reaction to Trigger Joe's had been one of shock more than grief. And Jade's... Hastily, he uprooted the weed.

Across the body of the dog Bella looked at her husband. "We'll have to call

Benny."

King frowned, but before he could speak, Ethan cupped both hands around his mouth and shouted over the water. Art's bellow roared out, too.

At last, the distant dot moved shoreward. But it was a long time before Benny was close enough to stand up in shallow water. The others were still grouped around the dead dog.

"What's the matter?" he panted. "Has anything happened? Has someone else been—hurt?"

F. Millard peered at the wet brown face as the Scoutmaster splashed up the shingle. The fury that had twisted it was gone, leaving it weary and sad. The little man looked down at the soggy fur at his feet. Was it possible that even this dog's death played a part in the tragedy at the lake?

Then, someone pushed Bella forward. "Oh, Benny, I hate to tell you." She held out a commiserating hand. "It was too late when we saw him. Virgil went out—"

"What?"

The close group parted, exposing the gray-tan fur.

Benny leaped forward, stumbled in the dry pebbles, and flung himself down by North's body. "Forgive me, North! Forgive me! No woman's worth this." His head fell against the wet fur.

Chapter Twenty

"Poor Benny," said Bella softly.

The last spadeful of earth had been rounded over North's body. The Abby Association that had gathered to bury the old dog was beginning to scatter. From the grave on the hill above the Scout Camp, F. Millard saw Abby, Benny, Art, and King all striding off alone while Ethan walked down beside Chris.

Bella still stood with the grocer, looking down at the freshly turned earth. He wondered if she was thinking, as he was, about the almost ritualistic burial they had witnessed. Benny himself had carried the furry body to this spot on the hill that he chose. Both Ethan and Art had lent a hand digging; even King had brought a spade. There had been a moment after the hole was ready when F. Millard wondered if the Kingdom brothers would come to blows over who should lay the dog in it. Then Bella had caught her husband by the arm to let Benny lower North into the hole. Afterward, King elbowed Art and Ethan aside and, with Benny, filled up the grave while the others watched in silence. With the thud of each dark spadeful, F. Millard had found himself fighting emotion—he didn't know whether laughter or tears—half expecting someone to strike up a hymn.

To him, there had been something spine-tingly about it all, something not quite healthy and, at the same time, faintly ridiculous. Here were all these grown men and women so dolefully paying their last respects to a dog when two of their own kind—a man and woman like themselves—had been murdered. F. Millard was reminded of the funerals children give dead robins with flowers and a candy box for a coffin. Yet in the five days he had been at the lake, death had struck twice—murder without the decent dignity of normal death. Perhaps this creepy hint of ceremony was to satisfy some race instinct in themselves that death had made active and murder had not assuaged.

"Poor Benny," Bella said again.

F. Millard jumped. He'd forgotten the girl standing so quietly beside him.

"He was so fond of North," she said softly. "Virgil was fond of him too, but I'm afraid part of Virgil's attentions were to wean him away from Benny."

Again, F. Millard started. So Bella's devotion to her husband didn't blind her after all!

"I'm very fond of Benny." She began to walk down the hill, with the grocer hurrying to keep up and miss nothing. "He taught me how to make the most of my good points. If it hadn't been for him, Virgil never would have seen me for dust."

"Benny's a discerning young man, but what a back-handed favor he did for himself that time, Mrs. Kingdom."

Bella sighed. "You can't marry a man for gratitude. Not when you're—in love with his brother."

"Do you think you could have loved Benny? Suppose King hadn't fallen for you when Benny—uh—made you over?"

"I think I could," she said slowly. "At least I could have if Virgil hadn't given me a rush. Sometimes I think now if—" She broke off abruptly.

When she spoke again, they were past the Scout Camp. "Won't you stop at the house for a drink?"

"Sorry, I promised the Thornes to go there." His first drink at the Kingdoms' in the early rain-darkened morning and the red-hot knot it had made of his stomach were too closely tied up with fire and storm and a singed, mummy-like corpse for pleasant recollection.

"You won't get anything stronger than coffee at Abby's," Bella told him. "She always blamed her husband's getting mixed up in a rockslide on liquor. You know it's wonderful that now she won't have to be dependent on Chris."

F. Millard looked up quickly.

"Abby wasn't trained for anything and when the mine closed down, she got a job cooking for another operator, but she told him how to run his mine and got fired. Chris nearly had a fit about her mother's working, and Abby's so crazy about her, she finally promised she'd never work for wages while Chris could support them both. Everything she had was tied up in the Association, and when Trigger Joe wouldn't sell—well, you can guess what it's been for Abby."

F. Millard stumbled over a bare root. He could guess what dependence had been for Abby—fiercely independent Abby Thorne.

"That's why I thought it would be nice—" Bella's glance was suddenly too innocent "—if she married again and had a husband as well as her share of the money from the mine."

F. Millard drew his breath in sharply. Those words hit home and roused his sluggard wits. Beneath all this smooth palaver, was Bella knifing Abby in the back? She hadn't been as blatant as King and Jade with open accusation, but she kept on slyly suggesting. This gossip about Abby, now he'd stopped to think it over, could be a hit below the belt. She'd been tattling on them all, all but her precious husband, and it was time Bella Kingdom learned to keep her shapely nose out of other people's business. He braced himself to teach her.

"I shouldn't think," he said harshly, "you'd be such a strong advocate for marriage."

She gasped, and her dark face paled. "What do you mean, Mr. Smyth?"

His conscience gave a twinge. He had to remind himself of her dagger-thrust in another woman's back. "There's no use pretending I don't know about your husband's—meetings with Jade and Chris—what's been going on. That's not my idea of a happy marriage."

Her smoke-blue eyes went black. "What do I care what you think about us? It's not your marriage! It's none of your business. And the Abby Association's none of your business either—or—or the murders. I warn you—I'm warning you now—keep out!"

The Kingdom house was only a few yards away. Bella tore down the trail and slammed the door behind her.

F. Millard stood blinking. When at last he moved on he was tempted to crouch and run when he passed the Kingdom cabin. But neither bullet nor blunt instrument whistled by his head.

Abby—but it had been Chris who asked him in for coffee. Once before he'd wondered if Chris was with Bella in a conspiracy to get him and Abby married. With a stepfather to share her mother's estate, Chris would lose money, but she might gain—life, or freedom from the penitentiary, or safety for someone she and Bella both sought to protect.

Another thought made him stub his toe. He hadn't turned on Bella until she attacked Abby. Was it possible that he was beginning to take a special interest in Abby Thorne?

By the time he reached her cabin, he could hardly speak to his hostess. But all the conversation he heard at the Thornes' concerned another man.

Coffee turned out to be lunch, with Ethan also invited. Funny to think so much had happened, and it was only lunchtime. As the four sat down at the table and he saw how the soldier looked at Chris, the little grocer was struck stammering again with the intimacy of the four some.

But the note of the luncheon table was the note on which Bella had begun: poor Benny.

"Poor Benny," said Chris gently. "He ought to have a wife, and then he wouldn't take on so over a dog."

"If you can't have the wife you want—" began Ethan.

"Oh, Ethan," Chris interrupted, "I'm so sorry! I didn't mean to pour so fast." She picked up his sloshing coffee cup and saucer and hurried to the crude sink.

Abby renewed the first topic. "But Benny's always been like that. Things mean more to him than they do to the King."

As Chris set a fresh cup before the gunner, it rattled in its saucer. She slid into her chair. "Remember when Mary died?" said Abby.

"How Benny took on then?"

"Mary?" F. Millard asked.

"Mary Kingdom, the boys' mother." Abby popped half a biscuit into her mouth. "She was killed in 'Thirty-five in an accident on the Circle Road. I thought Benny'd never get over it."

"But Mrs. Kingdom and Benny were especially close,' said Chris. "You remember how they were, Ethan."

The man who had had Jade's mother for a stepmother nodded.

Chris held out a plate of fuchsia-red jelly to the grocer. "Wild raspberry, Mr. Smyth. Do have some. Abby made it."

He passed it on quickly, unspooned.

"When Mr. Kingdom was killed—" Chris turned back to Abby "—the King took it harder than Benny."

"But Benny wasn't as close to his father as he was to Mary. Besides—" the weather-beaten face beneath the white hair changed in a way the grocer couldn't define "—the King was there when his father was killed. Had you forgotten he was on that hunting trip?"

F. Millard hadn't forgotten, nor had he forgotten that Ethan and Abby herself had been on that hunting trip, too.

Anyway, whatever fleeting strangeness had been in her face was now gone. "Benny may not have taken his father's death like his mother's, but remember the day Bella was married?"

Chris winced, then made her face blank. Benny wasn't the only one who had suffered that day, the grocer reflected.

But Abby was looking at Ethan. "Remember how he waited right up to the very day, and then, an hour before the wedding, he took a plane Outside?"

"I saw him off," said Ethan. "He tramped up and down like a wild man till the plane was ready to start."

"Poor Benny," Chris sighed again, "it should have been *his* wedding day."

"He stayed in Seattle till spring the next year," Abby told F. Millard. "And when he came back, he was still haggard and thin."

Chris had something else to add, and the voices went on while F. Millard sat musing. Funny how it took tragedy to bring some men into the spotlight. Benny's name must have come up more frequently today than in an ordinary month. And the things that were said—Bella first, and now these three were talking as if Benny were the dear departed instead of North—or Jade—or Trigger Joe.

The grocer's musings hit a rock. This wasn't a case of dear departeds. The

180

old dog was the only one at the lake who had died from natural causes. This was murder, two murders—so far. Did speaking of Benny the way people speak of those who are dead have any significance? Did it mean—F. Millard swallowed—that Benny would be next?

He came out of his abstraction with an echo of sound in his ears. Sitting straighter he blinked around the table and knew that the sound had been his own swallow. The three who had been chattering as volubly as the chubby Scout's mother were utterly silent now. Chris sat staring at her plate, crumbling a biscuit; Abby's glazed eyes were on a window, gazing off into space; Ethan's, half hidden by sunburned lashes, were fixed on the small, brown hand demolishing the biscuit.

Outdoors a twig snapped, and both women jumped.

However they might fill the hours with what appeared to be casual talk, no one at the lake shore, F. Millard saw, was casual. Each was well aware of danger, of the presence of death. It was strange that, in the shadow of lurking menace, the Abby Association still clung together—the innocent with the guilty, not the innocent with the law.

Abby rose to clear the table, but the grocer's meditations had left him unable to enjoy her blueberry pie made of last summer's berries that, Chris pointed out, her mother had picked and preserved herself.

While Ethan stayed to dry dishes for Chris, F. Millard made an excuse to leave. With no definite goal in mind, he followed the road up the hill behind Art's cabin and the Kingdoms'. Where it dipped toward the Scout Camp, he paused, thinking wistfully of the high, white mountains to be seen from the top of this very slope where he'd hunted ptarmigan with Abby. Then, from the Kingdom garage, fifty yards farther on, came the clink of metal. F. Millard walked on, stubbed his toe, and scattered gravel. The clink of metal stopped.

F. Millard stopped, too. Was it coincidence that the sounds of work ceased with the rattle of rocks? Why should Virgil Kingdom not want to advertise that he was working on his car? Or was he watching for someone, with eyes even now at a crack between the boards? Or maybe it wasn't King inside the garage.

The little man hesitated, controlling an impulse to run. But if anyone was peering through a crack, F. Millard had already been seen. Squaring his shoulders, he put one foot ahead of the other, then the second ahead of the first—left, right; left, right; left, right. He was past the garage, going on down the hill. Whoever was there was evidently not looking for him. He was getting to be an old granny, he scolded himself, imagining the simplest things cloaked menace.

Two bombers thundered overhead. If only their motors made less noise than rifle shots! If it weren't for past associations—and future possibilities—their frequent flights could go almost unnoticed.

He was abreast now of Trigger Joe's fence where the skirting trail nearly touched the road. He heard no sound within the stockade and saw no sign of life in the Scout Camp beyond it. Poor Benny, he thought in the words he'd been hearing so often, he was probably off moping over North. And where more likely than at the dog's grave?

F. Millard started up the hillside behind the camp but when he reached the low, freshly turned mound he saw no mourner beside it. A shovel lay nearby in the trampled grass, and past it, half hidden by a bush, he saw something black and squarish. Walking around the grave he picked up a man's billfold and flipped it open to look for a name.

Words sprang at him from the center of the card in the window pocket: "In case of accident, notify Mrs. Mary Kingdom. "A woman, he told himself with a prickle at the back of his neck, who had been dead for seven years.

The isinglass was too cracked and cloudy for him to read through the name of the identification card holder, though he could see a Seattle address. Below "Mrs. Mary Kingdom" was the same Seattle address.

The leather, too, showed wear. Hooping the window pocket, he worked his fingers inside and had just drawn the card out far enough to read the name Benjamin Kingdom when he heard a voice.

Without stopping to deliberate he thrust the wallet in his pocket and whipped behind a big alder. Not that he wanted to keep the thing, he assured himself, trying to stand thinner than the tree; he'd never yet stolen a wallet. But he wanted a chance to examine it before it must be returned.

The voice came nearer and was joined by another. Now, F. Millard was an eavesdropper, too, as well as a temporary thief. He stretched himself still thinner.

"But I tell you," came King's voice, "he's always been jealous of me. Even when we were kids, he was all burnt up when I beat him wrestling or running. And with me leader of the gang—"

"Well, of course—" F. Millard recognized Art's voice, roughly sarcastic, "—you were only a head taller and thirty pounds heavier and a year or two older. He's damn near as big as you now."

"What the hell?" Behind his tree, F. Millard could at most see King's impatient head-jerk. "He thinks he's safe with a uniform and a wound."

So it was Ethan they were talking about. The grocer's first thought had been Benny.

"I don't suppose you *would* try to beat up a wounded soldier," the deputy remarked.

"Don't kid yourself, Art. Ethan's leg's a damn sight better than he lets on. You said yourself he didn't hold you back any on that rough ground to the point. Listen, Art. Ethan was a kid with Chris and me. He knew about our Dipper signal. He's hated me for years. What's to prevent him making the Dipper each time he kills—to make it look like me?"

F. Millard blinked.

"Chris," returned Art promptly. "That's what'd prevent it. He's too crazy about Chris to run the risk of involving her."

Behind the tree, F. Millard nodded, then suddenly caught his breath. Ethan had been hopelessly in love for so many years—what if that frustrated love had gone sour? He might have seen his chance to get even and one up on the girl who had always turned him down and the man who was behind it.

With this thought racing through his mind, he heard the sharp crackle of twigs and pressed closer to the tree trunk.

A new voice exploded in the woods. "I heard you, Virgil Kingdom—trying to throw Ethan to the wolves! I saw you come out of your garage and nab Art as he went by. I was just coming over the top of the hill."

"Don't be dramatic, Chris," drawled King, "I only remembered I left my shovel where we buried North and caught up with Art for company."

"Phooey!" said Chris. "I've known you too long; you don't hunt company without a reason. And you needn't think Ethan's going to take this lying down. You needn't think any of us—"

"Excuse me," said Art loudly. "Got to see a man about a dog."

Nothing on earth would have induced the grocer to leave if he'd been Art. He doubted that either of the others even heard the deputy go.

"I'll tell you right now I'm not going to let you get away with it," the girl rushed on, "not if I have to track down the murderer myself!"

King laughed, and the sound wasn't pleasant. "What's that you've got in your arms, beautiful? Wild roses and larkspur? No wonder you came around by the road so you wouldn't have the whole lake laughing at you for bringing flowers to a dog's grave."

F. Millard heard a choked little sound and knew King had scored.

"You with your flowers for a dead dog," the jeering voice went on. "And not caring who suffers just so the guy that's been faithful to you ever since you were ten gets off! You with—God," he interrupted himself, "you're as sentimental as Benny!"

As Benny, who still kept his mother's name on his identification card.

"It's just too bad a little of that sentiment wasn't spread around the Kingdom family!" Chris flared. "When I remember—oh, when I remember how wonderful I've always thought you were! When I think of all the really good men, I've turned down because I couldn't get you out of my system! When I think—oh, damn, damn, damn!"

"Tut-tut, my girl, is that the way to show proper respect for the dead? Throwing down your flowers like that. What if it is just a dead dog? All God's children get wings, you know."

"Oh, you—you blasphemer!" Those snapping twigs, F. Millard guessed, would be Chris stamping frenzied feet. "I might have known when you told me about Jade. You'd already cheated on Bella. Why would I think you wouldn't cheat now—about murder! Listen to me, Virgil Amos Kingdom." Her voice had suddenly lowered, but every word was distinct to the man behind the alder. "There's one thing I haven't told Art. I haven't figured it out yet myself. But there was something awfully phony about you being so late for our appointment last night. How could my watch be half an hour faster than yours?"

The woods were as still as F. Millard himself.

Into the stillness King's voice crept—low and incredibly chilling. "You'd better look out, beautiful, that something doesn't happen to you."

Chapter Twenty-One

F. Millard stood rigid behind his tree long after Chris's faint cry, hardly more than a gasp, and the crackle and thud of her running feet had died away.

He waited, remembering the smell of smoke and leap of flames, an old man's singed body—remembering a high, thin, chopped-off scream, and a purple-faced girl's body. Horror fouled the summer air—fear and hate and menace crowding out normality—clamoring, enlarging… Someone would have to stop it.

At last, King's footsteps retreated down the hill.

Waiting a few minutes longer, until from his vantage point he saw the tall instructor striding up the road, F. Millard scuttled across the Scout Camp, past Trigger Joe's fence, and on along the trail on the lake bank. No one from the Kingdoms', Art's, or the Thornes' accosted him, and he reached his cabin with Benny's billfold still heavy in his pocket.

He flipped it open as soon as the door was shut, but the gesture was purely automatic. Wallets, dead dogs, jackknives, and Dippers all shrank to rice-grain size compared to his decision. For all Art's bluster, he'd made no arrest; Jade had been killed right under his nose. The Abby Association seemed strangely fearless, almost as if they thought they were safe, as if they thought the killings over. Art was too slow; the others blind. It was up to F. Millard now.

At the table, he emptied the wallet, his mind turning over the phases of his problem as his fingers turned over papers. But even a casual glance showed that the identification card in the window pocket was more yellow than the others: two lodge membership cards, a draft card, a driver's license, several insurance-rate folders. Only the identification card gave a Seattle address; the others all read Fairbanks.

Seattle, Fairbanks, everyday normal existence—and here at Harding Lake, two murders—two, so far—his own life at stake, along with Art's and the lives of five of the six remaining members of the group from Abby Creek. His life—what if he risked it first, before the murderer claimed it?

The moisture that should have been in his mouth— and wasn't—came out in the palms of his hands.

He tried to swallow, but his mouth was too dry—if he wanted, would he, F. Millard Smyth, stand a chance of winning the jackpot? But the jackpot would be catching the killer. Slowly, F. Millard shook his head. That might be the jackpot for a six-foot-two deputy marshal with a gun in his shoulder holster, but a five-foot-six, fifty-six-year-old, weaponless grocer didn't sit in on that kind of game. A jackpot for F. Millard would be learning the killer's identity, so Art could make the arrest.

On the table only a little stack of paper currency remained to be examined. One, two, three five-dollar bills, a ten, a check... The grocer gasped—dated yesterday, for $109.16, on Virgil Kingdom's account!

Was this an innocent insurance payment—fifty miles from a bank, with the road washed out? If Benny had found out something... The nine dollars and sixteen cents tacked on to the hundred could be an added flourish for the benefit of bank clerks. King would already be conditioned to blackmail. Perhaps Jade's only mistake had been in demanding too much.

Finally, F. Millard sighed and put the papers back in the wallet. Deduction, the fitting of pieces, had a place, but now was the time for action.

Most of all, the murderer would want immunity. And if he thought only one little grocer stood in his way—F. Millard's anticipatory shiver became a full-sized chill. He mustn't run too great a risk. A lot of satisfaction he'd get out of extinguishing murder if the murderer extinguished him! It would have been nice if he and Art could lay their plans together, if the deputy could be the hunter in the blind while F. Millard became the decoy. But it wouldn't be hard for the murderer to check, and if the hunter was out stalking, the quarry would stay at home.

Propping his head in both hands he began to worry his hair. If one little grocer stood in the murderer's way... If F. Millard made them all think he knew something... Then the one that responded...

When at last he stood up, his watch said half the afternoon had gone by. Pulling the accustomed roll of *Flatfoot* out of his hip pocket, he laid it on the table, caught up his hat and head net, and hurried out.

But what if Art and the Abby Association wouldn't follow his lead? What if they saw the halter rope? His feet faltered in the path, and his eyes sought the green, silent lake. Across the cove, sunlight beat on the house on the point. He jerked his gaze back and it fell on charred logs. Murder on both sides—murder lurking in a cabin—murder behind a tree—

He began to run.

At the Thornes' Ethan answered his knock. Abby turned sharply from a window, and Chris, at the table, dropped the dipper back in the water bucket.

The grocer tried not to pant. "Have you been swimming yet?"

Abby shook her head, and Ethan remarked, "Today spoiled the girls' taste for swimming."

"But when an aviator crashes, they make him go right up again." F. Millard took a deep breath. "Don't you think the longer Benny puts off going in, the harder it'll be, with the memory of poor old North always nagging?"

"You've got something there, Smyth," said the soldier.

"But what if Benny won't do it?" Chris demurred. "If we go swimming, what if he won't even come down to the beach?"

"Why not swim from the Scout Camp beach?" F. Millard asked. "That'd do Benny the most good, because that's where North was drowned. I'll get Mrs. Kingdom to ask him."

"Oh," Chris said abruptly, then stiffly, "Do they have to come too—the King and Bella?"

They certainly did, if the grocer's plan was to work. He said quickly, "We all ought to be there. We were when it happened. And King brought in the dog."

Chris still hesitated.

"Besides," F. Millard added, "we'll need Mrs. Kingdom to get Benny to come."

Sighing, Chris gave in.

They agreed to meet at the Scouts' beach in half an hour, and F. Millard scurried on.

He passed Art's cabin, soft-footed, his face turned away. But no voice roared after him, and he broke into a trot for the Kingdoms'.

Bella opened the door, King just behind her. Remarkable, F. Millard thought, to find them both home at once. Neither asked him in.

But when he explained his errand, one pair of hostile eyes softened. "I'll go right now and ask him," applauded Bella.

F. Millard looked at the man. "You'll come down too?"

"I don't see—" he began.

"Of course he will," his wife interrupted. "He's Benny's brother." Her needling look at her husband made the little grocer blink.

He started back, but he passed three empty cabins before he heard the Kingdom door close and, over his shoulder, saw Bella set out for the Scout Camp.

The job before him now was harder. If Art didn't swallow the bait, all this groundwork would be useless.

Again, he passed the deputy's cabin. At the cut in the bank where the road came in from the highway, he paused with his eyes on the telephone booth. Then abruptly, like a man in a hurry to answer the phone, the little grocer bustled into the clearing.

Just as he stepped inside the booth, he heard a door close, and Abby's hearty voice call out, "Be with you in a shake." Shouting from a window after Ethan—F. Millard gulped. One house to pass, and Ethan would be coming down the bank to the clearing! And when he didn't hear a ring—

F. Millard grabbed the old-fashioned handle and cranked out the Harding Lake ring. "Hello," he said loudly. "Hello. What? Want me to see if I can find him? All right, I'll take the message." He paused. "What? How do you know? Who is this? Hey, who is this? Hey!"

He banged up the receiver and rubbed both wet palms down his trousers. Already, two tan-clad legs and a cane showed under the three-quarter wall. Luckily, this wasn't the kind of phone that had operators waiting to pounce on lifted receivers, or a lot of farm wives to rubber at every ring, only a few road camps, all busy with repair work.

He stepped out of the booth just as Ethan came around it. "N-nice, the phone's fixed, S-Sergeant," the little man stammered. "I just got a message for Art."

They climbed the north bank together and walked on down the trail. At the red wallboard cabin, while Ethan went on, F. Millard stopped and knocked. Or were those hollow thumps made by his heart instead of knuckles on wood? If he failed in what he was trying to put over, what would Art do about it? For that matter, the way F. Millard had to go about it, what would Art do even if the grocer succeeded?

The door swung open, and the big deputy peered out, hair matted like black excelsior.

Must have been asleep, F. Millard thought enviously. Ethan's unexpected appearance had thrown him out of his stride, and he couldn't remember his opening speech.

"I was just p-p-passing the ph-phone and heard it ring, and—and—"

"Well? What's the matter?" Art demanded.

"It was for you, but he—I took the message."

"Who was it?"

"He w-w-wouldn't say."

"Wouldn't say!"

"No. He just said he thought he heard his ring, and when he took down the receiver, he heard someone say, 'I'll meet you where the road turns in to the lake at five o'clock.' " F. Millard pulled out his watch. "This fellow that called didn't know what it was all about or if they meant Harding or Birch Lake, but he thought with a couple of murders at Harding, he'd better let you know. So he phoned, and I was just passing, and—"

"Hold everything," Art commanded. "If this guy wouldn't give a name, whose voice did he claim to hear?"

190

CHAPTER TWENTY-ONE

"He didn't say. Just gave the message and hung up."

"Not even if the voice was a man's or woman's?"

F. Millard shook his head.

Art looked at his own watch; "Four-forty-five. I'll just have time to get there."

"How'll it be if I keep tabs on the Abby Association? Find out who isn't around..." The grocer's voice eased off significantly while he wrestled with mental discomfort.

"Swell." Art picked up his hat.

"Whoever it is may be late if he thinks I'm snooping around." F. Millard tried to look guileless, hating himself for it, hating everything he was doing and planning to do. But when it came to stopping murder, you couldn't be squeamish, even if it seemed to put you outside the law.

"I'll hang around an hour or so." Art flapped him out the door. Then, to the little man's horror, turned the key.

Dashed, he watched the big deputy stride down the trail.

But there were other ways to get into houses besides doors. F. Millard circled the red wallboard cabin. At the back, a small window was open, with a mosquito bar tacked on the inside. He couldn't get in that way and tack it up again. The other windows were unbarred but shut. He struggled vainly with each. It would have to be the back window. Pushing in the net, he loosened the tacks, fortunately, thumbtacks, and squeezed himself through the gap.

Inside, he shook down his clothes and drew a long breath. Flatfoot Flannagan would never have locked a door and left a window open. Then his own face stung.

What would Flannagan think of a man who tampered with evidence—or stole it?

Above hot cheeks, his spectacles made a circuit of the room, and he saw he had done Art one injustice. The bed had not been mussed. Some papers spread out on the table explained the deputy's tangled hair. Each sheet was headed with a name: Bella, Benny, Chris, King, Abby, Ethan. He straightened one crushed into a ball, and his conscience gave a toothache twinge as he crumpled it again. How long would it be before Art wrote Smyth at the top of another?

Outside, a twig snapped. Then he heard voices and breathed again—the Thornes on their way to the Scout Camp. But he'd better hurry. Art might smell a rat or remember the open window.

At last—here it was, in the newspaper he'd wrapped it in himself. He leafed through the rain-blistered pages till he came to the sketch of the house on the point, with the bluff like a woman's skirt. No other copy of *Flatfoot* would have the same meaning for one of the group now gathering on the beach. Fingerprints, if any, must be sacrificed for the greater good.

He picked up Art's pencil and drew a heavy cross through the keep off the grass sign beside the picture. He stood thoughtfully, licking the lead. Nine o'clock? Too early. So was ten. Would he have to wait till midnight? Another midnight of eerie daylight and the isolation of the point? Eleven ought to do, he decided with a shiver. He made a circle on the other side of the cabin and put an eleven inside it. The picture looked now even more like a child's, with the circled eleven like a sun. The midnight sun—of course, it would be a disguise! Quickly, he drew a curved line like a hill through the circle with straight ones raying out of the upper arc. And to avoid suggesting the morning sun he gave the page the points of the compass. The two straight marks of the figure eleven might be part of the decoration. To the wrong person it would look only like a child's drawing. To the right one, it would carry a message.

F. Millard refolded the newspaper and laid it back in Art's bureau drawer, rolled the blistered copy of *Flatfoot* with the picture outside, and shoved it into his pocket. Then he wriggled through the window and tacked the net outside. It might be days before Art noticed, and tonight should be long enough.

For a minute, his eyes squeezed shut. *Tonight must be long enough. Dear God, let it be long enough.* If it wasn't, Art's discovery of the disturbed mosquito netting or even the theft of the magazine would come too late to hurt F. Millard.

He shook himself and hurried down the trail. Rounding Trigger Joe's fence, he saw the Abby Association gathered on the Scouts' beach.

"Well!" Abby sounded aggrieved. "Thought you'd be here first."

"I—uh—was delayed." He noted the wet bathing suits on the girls and both Kingdom brothers. "I see you've already been in."

"Yes, and it *was* a good idea," approved Bella.

F. Millard glanced at Benny, stretched out on the blanket beside her. He still looked sad and tired, but a little of the tension seemed eased in his strong, tanned body.

The grocer pulled out his watch. Five-fifteen. Art should have reached the highway and been waiting fifteen minutes. Could F. Millard count on another half hour? He didn't want to begin too abruptly.

He sat down on the blanket by Abby. That ought to please Bella, but he only wanted to ask a question. Chris said something to one of the others, and he murmured, "Do you know where the Kingdoms lived in Seattle, Mrs. Thorne?"

"The Kingdoms? Benny and the King weren't Outside together." Her voice was so low the grocer wondered if she, too, felt some compulsion. Anyone who listened could have heard them, but the louder conversation went on.

"The time Benny was out with his mother," F. Millard specified.

"Benny was only out once, four or five years after his mother died. Mary was never Outside."

"Never Outside?"

"She was born in Douglas in the early mining days before the Klondike."

F. Millard glanced again at the outstretched brown man beside Bella. So his mother had never been in Seattle except in Benny's heart.

Taking out his watch, the grocer leaned toward Chris. "Did you bring your watch, Miss Thorne? I'd like to check on mine."

She held out her hand to Abby, who took a gold wristwatch from her pocket.

"Ten minutes of five," said Chris.

"No wonder you've been late all day. According to this—" her mother nodded at F. Millard's watch "—you're half an hour slow."

The burnished head turned slowly. "What time—do you have, King?" Her voice was strangely jerky.

For a minute her gaze held his, then he reached for his wife's handbag on the blanket beside his brother and took out his own wrist watch. "You *are* half an hour slow, Chris. I've been telling you your watch was haywire."

"Yes, you've been telling me." Some peculiar quality in her voice gave each word significance. "When—" She broke off.

F. Millard drew a deep breath and mentally finished the sentence—when King told Chris last night that her watch was half an hour fast.

Abruptly, Bella stood up. "Anyway, it's time to start dinner."

The little grocer reached out his hand and drew it back. That scanty bathing suit... "While Art isn't here—" he paused. Maybe there was something significant in his own voice, for Bella sat down and waited with the others. "While Art isn't here," he began again, "there's something I'd like to ask you—all of you."

No one spoke. Each pair of eyes impaled him.

He made himself laugh. It came out like a croak. But he wouldn't be expected to seem at ease. "I'm afraid an officer of the law'd be prejudiced. But you folks will understand—I think." He paused again. "If you—I mean, I was reading a detective story the other day and came across an interesting problem. If you—I mean in this story the—uh—hero wasn't a detective, but he stumbled on something and didn't know what to do. All the suspects were closely connected by blood or marriage or long friendship, and if the—uh—hero told what he knew, one of them would be convicted of murder."

He paused again, longer this time, while the six pairs of eyes bored deeper. In his mind, he'd been over it a hundred times. Anyone could lose a button, or snag his clothes, or throw down a cigarette stub. Think how it would have been for Benny if he'd lost his wallet near the house on the point instead of North's grave! "The—uh—hero happened to be by himself for a while at the scene of the crime right after the murder, and he—uh—found something. Something he couldn't possibly miss knowing the owner of."

Still, no one spoke. A bird gave a noisy chirp, and F. Millard jumped.

"The fellow didn't know what to do," he went on.

"It seems—according to the story there was some justification for the murder—if it can be justified—and if any one of them was convicted, it was going to wreck all their lives. He liked them; they were basically fine folks, even the murderer—who believed he was justified. And—well, the fellow didn't know what to do. Should he turn this thing he found over to the police, or give it back to its owner and let all these fine people go on living their full, rich lives, unaffected by the stain of murder?"

He hoped he wouldn't gag; it was a wonder no one else had. They must all see through this performance, yet each watched and listened gravely, intently. Perhaps they were just pretending to be taken in to find out what he was up to.

At last, the long silence was broken. "Are you asking us?" Abby demanded. "Or telling us what the hero decided to do?"

"I'm asking you," said F. Millard, "what most of us would do in his place."

Abby stood up briskly. "I'd give it to whoever lost it so fast it'd make your head swim." She held out her hand to Chris.

But her daughter went on staring at F. Millard.

Behind his spectacles, the little man blinked. And then blinked faster and faster, his pulses hammering in his ears like riveting machines. "I m-m-might add," he stammered quickly, "in c-case the killer got other ideas, that when—when the fellow in the story went to meet him, of course, he took a gun."

A hush fell again. Abby shifted her feet, and the rattle of pebbles was loud.

The grocer thought, *My gracious, she's going to leave.* He pulled out a handkerchief, reaching with his right hand to his left hip pocket, knocking out *Flatfoot* on the way. It fell at Abby's feet. Chris, still seated, leaned to pick it up.

F. Millard seemed not to notice. The way it had been rolled would make it fall either sketch or jacket side up. And the jacket would mean enough to one person, so he'd turn the magazine over.

Out of the corner of his eyes, he saw Chris turn it over. She looked for a while at the penciled sketch and held it out to the grocer. "You dropped your magazine," she told him.

"Oh, thank you, Miss Thorne." Fumbling to take it, he knocked it clumsily toward King.

The long, well-shaped fingers twitched and stilled. F. Millard saw the brilliant eyes fixed on the drawing, bright in the sun, before King turned away and Ethan picked up *Flatfoot.* He glanced with apparent carelessness at the drawing, ruffled the pages, and held the magazine out to F. Millard. "Guess this is. yours."

F. Millard re-rolled it, drawing side out and thrust it insecurely into his pocket. As he scrambled to his feet, it fell between Bella and Benny. Both reached for it. For a minute both heads bent above it. Then Benny returned it to the grocer.

Funny no one made any comment. He looked anxiously at his watch. Art might be back any minute, and if he found this copy of *Flatfoot* making the rounds…

The grocer slid in the pebbles, and the magazine, loosely held in his hands, fell for the second time before Abby.

"For God's sake," she said crossly, "can't you keep hold of that thing?"

So she hadn't missed its gyrations. Perhaps she had already seen all she needed to, but F. Millard picked it up and pointed to the drawing. "Kids nowadays don't have any respect for other people's—"

"Break it up!" roared Art's voice from the bank.

F. Millard clapped the magazine shut and jammed it guiltily and very securely into his pocket.

"Smyth!" yelled the deputy. "What do you mean by sending me off on a wild goose chase? So you could all put your heads together?"

"I—I—" the little man stammered.

Abby came to his rescue. "What do you mean yourself, Art, by 'putting our heads together'? We've just been swimming and sunbathing like we do every day. What's wrong with that?"

"Don't think you're fooling me any—you, Smyth—and your telephone calls!" The big man spat down the bank in a high disgruntled arc. "After I waited at the road for damn near half an hour, I came back and got on the phone myself and called all the camps till I found the fella that heard you."

"The f-fellow that heard me?" F. Millard's voice was feeble.

196

"You didn't think you could use the Harding Lake ring after there'd been two murders out here—and get away with it, did you?"

That ring he'd been stampeded into making! Why hadn't he at least had the sense to leave the receiver on the hook? He could have got his talking over before Ethan arrived. "But I thought—" he began.

"Yeah, I know what you thought—that central wouldn't answer and there's no farmers' wives on the line. But some of the road camp phones are in the cook tents. And if you think even a man cook's not going to burn the biscuits and listen in on the ring for a place where there's been two murders, you're nuts!"

The Abby Association was listening wide-eyed, as innocent as a nest of baby vultures.

Again, the deputy spat his high, angry arc to the beach. "That ring sure cooked your goose. When you took off the receiver, the cook heard every word you said and told me there was no one else on the line!"

"You—you mean, Art," stammered Chris, "that Mr. Smyth faked a telephone call to take you away?"

"Damn right."

"And damn nice of him, too," declared Abby. "We sure needed a rest from your Sherlocking all over the place. The way you sit around chortling every time someone takes a step nearer the gallows—"

"You know what it means to be an accessory, Smyth," Art interrupted ominously.

F. Millard swallowed.

"Look here, Art—" began Ethan. But Benny, who had sat up at the deputy's arrival, was on his feet. "I'm afraid it's my fault, Art. Smyth did it for me— Smyth and all the others. They thought I needed a rest. And I did. I'm grateful to them."

"Yes, Art, you mustn't blame him," urged Bella.

"Well—" the deputy looked like he was going to spit "—he could of said so. Why hand out all that hog-wash?"

The others began to fold up blankets and pick up spray guns and sweaters. "Come have dinner with us, Millard," urged Abby cordially.

But F. Millard shook his head. The time had come when the little grocer must be alone—and stay alone to stop death.

Chapter Twenty-Two

I n the hours that followed that incredible scene on the beach, F. Millard caught himself thinking wistfully again and again of Abby's invitation. If only he could have accepted and been sheltered now by the presence of others, wrapped and diapered and tucked away in a cradle of safety. Catching criminals wasn't his business. But by the time Art snapped the handcuffs, someone else would be dead. The little grocer was as conscious of approaching doom as he was of his own pulse, ragged and racing, leaping on toward the hour that was set.

A flight of pursuit ships roared overhead. He glanced at his watch and stepped out on the porch. Nine o'clock sunlight was bright across the lake, though his own cabin was in shade and the hill where he'd hunted with Abby made a long, growing blot on the water, creeping nearer the house on the point.

He'd said eleven, but he must arrive first. He had to be first! Clenching his hands, he counted ten. If he left an hour early... Would it be King, with his arrogant step, who would come to the house on the point, or sensitive Benny, still mourning for his dog, Ethan, leaning on the cane he didn't need, or one of the women? For a minute, he hoped it would be a woman; if anything should happen, if his plan should miscarry—the little grocer would be no match for one of those three big men.

Why hadn't he left well enough alone and kept himself out of this mess? But he still wouldn't be safe. No one at the lake would be safe but the killer— and the danger constantly mounting... All that blather about justification and leaving his bit of evidence—what murderer would let him return?

Thank heaven for that desperately flung-out remark about taking a gun, the only on-key bar in the whole off-key opera on the beach this afternoon. Ironically, the only remark in which there had been no grain of truth. But F. Millard was running enough risk, without the murderer believing him unarmed.

Nine-fifteen now—time yet to back out. If he ran down the trail and told Art—but then the murderer wouldn't come, and the whole mounting horror would increase, with F. Millard knowing for certain that he was marked to go next.

Nine-twenty. But the murderer, too, might go early. F. Millard snatched up his hat, and the net unrolled from the brim. Whoever went through those woods to the point would almost certainly wear a head net. Veil, slacks, and a long-sleeved shirt—a complete disguise for the killer.

The little man slumped into a chair. All those plans— Art successfully sidetracked, the murderer lured to the house on the point, and F. Millard already waiting. If he couldn't tell who—

With a stifled yelp, he leaped to his feet and grabbed the water bucket, swished its contents through a window screen, and began to jerk off stove lids. The murderer would expect to find F. Millard inside the house. He'd go in to look... And to heck with disguises!

* * *

Pail in hand, F. Millard opened the door and silently shut it behind him. The shadow of the northwest hills now covered the house on the point. Beyond, the yet gold southeastern hills seemed far away and unreal. He came to the end of the trail, hurried across the clearing, and, with bucket carefully balanced, plunged into the woods.

It was too bad to hurry; he ought to be fresh for the wild dash back while the killer was searching the point. But if F. Millard didn't reach it first, in time to get his work done and himself safely out of the house, he wouldn't be coming back.

He panted on till he needed more breath. When he stopped, the woods settled back into quiet. No bird twittered in the branches. No leaf brushed another. No rustle, no crackle, no movement to show there was any other living thing on the hillside. Except for the light, it was like that other night he had come to the point, the night Jade had passed while he cowered behind a leaf screen, the night he had heard the thunder of rain on the roof that had also sheltered someone else. That time, too, he had gone just to look and report and, seeing Jade, had thought the house was empty. But this time, he wouldn't be misled. He'd get out of that house of doom just as soon as his work was accomplished. He leaped again into a run.

Once more, he dodged, crouching among the boulders at the neck of the point. Once more, as the back door yielded to his hand, he heard the groaning wail that he'd told himself only this morning he need never hear again. He pulled the door behind him and was wrapped in shadowy gloom.

For a moment, he stood waiting for his breath to slow. The house, too, seemed to wait, stealthily still. He remembered the patter of slackening rain two nights ago, like bird claws on the roof and the creak of the door that had told him he wasn't alone. This house had fooled him before. His hand tightened on the bail of the bucket, and he hurried across to the bedroom where he and Art had found Jade. It was just as they had left it, with the furniture pulled askew. No one hiding behind the pile of boxes; nobody there now, either. No one flattened in back of the door.

He peered into the living room—untenanted but for the dusty furniture and the ghosts of this morning's quarrels.

No one in the bedroom with the door that opened outward.

Thank goodness he'd come early. Thank goodness he was first. Now to finish this job and get out.

To keep his head net from flopping off the brim and getting in his way, he laid his hat on the table beside the front door, then hurried back to the kitchen, dipped his hand in the bucket, and sprinkled a light fan of ash from the door halfway into the room. Light, so no ashes would show above the dust, but thick enough to record the killer's signature—his footprints.

As he worked, pictures crowded his mind: Bella making the Dipper on the blanket—Abby's trapped look when Art found the stolen drawings—King on the rocks at the foot of the cliff staring at Ethan's white knife—Benny's despairing head against North's soggy fur, and his mother's name in his wallet—Chris shaking her brilliant curls into whips to protect first King and then Ethan—the soldier without uniform or cane hurrying through the beach pebbles. But now was no time to fit and correlate. Now, he must finish his infertile sowing and get away.

He shifted the bucket to his dirty right hand and pulled out his watch with the other. Not yet ten o'clock. The murderer wouldn't dare leave too early if someone went to his cabin—or someone else shared his cabin...or her cabin...

He began to scatter ashes in the living room. He'd back out the front door to leave the gray dust free of his own tracks, then whip around the narrow east side and find a hiding place in the woods.

All at once, the bucket nearly dropped from his hand. The pieces of the puzzle that had been whirling in his mind began to jump and spring together, to take form in flashes quicker than words. He took a fresh grip on the bail and, frantically sowing ashes, tried to sweep his mind clear, fearful of the fascinating, growing picture taking shape. He squeezed his mental eyes shut to blot it out so he wouldn't be afraid. It sank back, down, and back behind a curtain of his mind, but he knew it was there waiting for the curtain to be stirred.

And he knew he was afraid, more afraid than he'd ever been in his life.

His eyes searched the room. Where could he hide this unwieldy thing in his hand? He'd spread all the ashes he was going to inside these stealthy four walls! He had to get out of here—fast.

Tilting the back of the Morris chair that stood against the bedroom wall in the corner away from the kitchen, he slid the bucket behind it, turned toward the front door—and heard a sound that he couldn't mistake. The back door was beginning to open! The murderer, too, had come early.

Ribs were all that kept his heart inside his chest. He couldn't go out the front door that wailed as sharply as the back. He sprang for the meager shelter of the bedroom door that opened out and had barely shrunk behind it when the back door stopped groaning.

From the kitchen came the sound of footsteps—light, quick, sure of their maker's power to look after himself. They paused at the first bedroom door, stepped swiftly inside. The murderer would have to make certain that no one lurked behind the twisted box bureau, where this morning he had left his second victim.

Then the steps were coming out, coming nearer. F. Millard shrank smaller and stopped breathing.

Inches away, they paused for a palpitant eternity... Only a thin door, now, between him and the figure that must be bending forward to peer into the bedroom. For a moment, F. Millard's whole structure—bones and flesh and viscera—felt as if it were melting and trickling under the door. Then the steps went on, and the front door groaned.

Hard as F. Millard tried to stay rigid, his head turned irresistibly sideways. But the figure going through the front door had no more reality for the grocer than this twenty-four-hour daylight—there to be coped with but not to be recognized. This was someone larger than he was, but all the Abby Association except Chris were larger than F. Millard—someone who wore the ubiquitous canvas hat with hanging black net, the slacks and long sleeves, and—of course—gloves, that all of them but Chris wore during mosquito season in the woods. The face was turned away, but under the shade of the hat brim, in the further shade of the room, with the point itself in the shadow of the hill behind Art's cabin, features would be hard to distinguish—unless he had a close look, and F. Millard prayed that he wouldn't.

He heard the steps start around the house to the east, their maker screened from the cabins across the cove. Then they died away, and the stealthy quiet fell again.

Suddenly, F. Millard's heart gave another rib-shaking thump. His hat—there on the table! The murderer would know his prey was here, hiding. Another trip through the house—a thorough search—and the mouse would run squeaking from cover—or be stepped on before he could run.

Tense, the little man waited. No sound came from the cabin, no sound from out of doors. What had become of that swift, cautious figure? Was he, too, hiding and watching?

Again and again, F. Millard drew breath quickly and exhaled in lingering silence... Still no sound in the daylit night.

How long would this go on, with the murderer waiting where he was and F. Millard behind the door? He couldn't stand here, taut, forever. But if he moved and the murderer saw him—though by now his stalker must know where he was. If he only hadn't laid down his hat! Now, it was only a matter of time.

Again, he gave thanks for his tossed-off threat of a gun. Even if the murderer didn't quite believe it, he couldn't be sure. The killer himself would be armed—unless he was planning to do what he'd done to Jade. F. Millard's hand crept up to a collar suddenly too tight. But what the killer wouldn't want would be noise. He wouldn't want the report of a gun to carry across the lake, his own, any more than F. Millard's. That gave the little man a chance. The killer would have to get close, and by gracious... F. Millard straightened.

Then why not yell? Someone across the cove might hear; it wasn't very late. Then the grocer sagged. If he yelled—and broke the silence, the murderer wouldn't need to fear the report of a gun. If F. Millard yelled, the murderer's shot would come that much sooner.

Silence still hung over the point—a pall of quiet, a shroud of quiet, a death blanket.

Waiting, straining to hear a step, F. Millard winced. The figure that moved with such light, sure feet had left both outer doors open. There would be no other warning groan. The killer could take off his shoes and creep in without a sound. Only the chance of a creaking board for warning.

Then white-hot hope seared F. Millard. The trail to the landing! Less than a third with the switchback at the top was on the east side of the bluff. If he could pass that perilous sharp angle and reach the north face, he'd be in sight of the farther cabins, in a moment in sight of them all. In this daylight, the murderer wouldn't dare follow. Thank God for the midnight sun! He wouldn't dare follow or stand on the edge and shoot from above. If F. Millard yelled—

His heart dropped again. If he yelled, the murderer could retreat to the wooded hillside and pick F. Millard off like a sniper. But if he made the boat landing and didn't yell, he'd have a chance for his life.

He might have to wait the rest of the night on that sloping ledge above the water before someone across the cove saw him—but at least he'd be waiting alive. The killer must know F. Millard couldn't have seen his face through the net. He'd only have to go back, join the rescue party—and wait for his next chance. But F. Millard would come through this encounter.

The door swung as he slid from behind it. Flexing legs stiff with tension he took a step toward the door. A board creaked, and he jerked back his foot. No boards had creaked beneath the light, sure steps of the killer.

But F. Millard couldn't imitate the murderer's confidence. He scuttled like a calf-sized rat across the room toward the east corner and the open front door. Only a few yards between him and freedom. If he could cover those few yards—if the murderer wasn't waiting now for that very move at the switchback—

On the threshold, F. Millard faltered. A deep breath—a lunge through the door—down that sharp angle to the right…

He took the breath and started to lunge. Something—some shadow or sound must have warned him. As his body swayed forward, one foot over the sill, he jerked back—just as a gloved hand and sleeved arm shot by him.

The glove had hardly passed before F. Millard was in the middle of the room with the feel of death and the breeze of its passage still quivering in the air.

The back door—the back door, too, was near the east corner, but the killer was watching the front!

Again, F. Millard dashed, this time through the kitchen.

And at the back door also the gloved hand brushed his sleeve as he flung himself back just in time.

This could go on for hours. The stalker outside had only a straight line to run between the two outer doors placed, for him, so conveniently near the east corners. The distance F. Millard had to cover was a third again as great, with the door between the living room and kitchen near the bedrooms on the west.

Then hope flared again in the grocer. The windows—what if he climbed out a west window in sight of the cabins? He still couldn't get to the trail with the murderer guarding the top, and he couldn't dive off the cliff to swim to the foot of the trail—only the narrow landing place was free from treacherous rocks. But if he climbed out a window and stayed on the west side of the house, wouldn't that be as good as the trail? If he waited long enough in full sight of the cabins where the murderer wouldn't dare follow, eventually, by tomorrow sometime, he'd be seen.

He hurried into the bedroom where Jade had had her brush with death—and lost. He raised the window higher—the window Jade must have raised to call for help. He thought again of calling, himself, and again discarded the notion. Calling would start shooting—and the end.

But what about planes? Their motors had covered the sound of a shot once before. If one of those frequent flights went over while he was exposed out there—still, if that happened, he could run to the front of the house in view of half the cabins.

The little man slid over the sill and dropped. It was good to touch ground again, to be out of that stealthy house. He took a deep breath of fresh air. But he shouldn't waste time doing breathing exercises. If anyone was still up in those cabins across the cove—even if he couldn't yell, motion might attract attention.

He began to wave frantically at the shadowed cabins peering out from the trees on the lake bank.

He wondered how long the murderer would slip back and forth between front and rear doors before he learned that his prey had escaped. In the upswing of new hope and fresh air, F. Millard almost laughed at his frantic waving unaccompanied by shouts—like the old days of the silent movies.

Then all thought of laughter fled. Something whistled by his ear and splashed in the water over the bluff. No bang of a gun, just a terrifying whizz of something solid that splashed. Then—he gasped—something crashed on his shoulder.

At his feet lay a rock as big as a baseball. He stood dumbly staring at it, and, with terrific force, another hit his thigh. Flattening himself against the house, he saw the next rock coming in time to jerk his head sideways and miss a skull-smashing hit. From one of the boulders dotting the neck of the point between the house and trees, an arm shot out at crouching height, long-sleeved and gloved, the angle of a bent knee, a head draped with a net—and another rock hurtled toward him. F. Millard ducked and began to run toward the front of the cabin. A wall between him and that deadly aim—

An agonizing blow at the base of his ribs brought a groan as he neared the northwest corner. Gasping and panting, he leaped around it for the trail. Now was his chance while the killer had farther to run. One foot in the path—and a wrenching blow on the shoulder—the shoulder that hadn't been hit—told him the other was ready. And F. Millard had to run toward him down that south-reaching arm of the switchback! Stones in a thickening hail—a storm he couldn't face, that he couldn't run deliberately farther into—racking blows on both ankles sent him hopping and crawling back.

Arms up to shield his head, he stumbled back around the corner.

In less than a shuddering breath, missiles came again from the boulders. Again, he tore to the front of the house—to be met again by the killer...How carefully those rocks were thrown to miss the house, to let no echoing thud crash a warning into the quiet!

Battered and gasping, F. Millard dodged back and forth—always followed, some rocks always finding their target. As long as he stayed in the open, the murderer couldn't close in, but eventually—before morning—when one of those rocks thrown with such force got under the guard to his head...

At last, he had to give up. He had to get back in the house and find shelter from this beating. He couldn't go in either door, with the murderer waiting to pounce. Now, the open window he'd come out of seemed impossibly high to climb through. But finally, at the cost of more back and leg hits, he jumped and heaved himself over the sill.

Longing to lie where he fell and do nothing but groan, he forced himself to stumble upright and lurch to the kitchen—he mustn't be caught in this bedroom like Jade.

He got there just in time. The figure with the dangling head net was just coming in the back door. But F. Millard was nearer the living room door. He dived. The other dodged back—and was tearing along the cliff top before F. Millard could make the trail. No use to try—with the first leg of the switchback sweeping them nearer together.

The grocer whirled back into the house—to the door between the living room and kitchen, where he could watch both ways. Panting, bruises throbbing, he waited.

Silence once more shrouded the house on the point—stifling, pulsing silence. Out of doors the nighttime daylight touched lake and trees and the fringe of sleeping cabins. Touched the murderer, too, hidden from the cabins across the cove, waiting on the narrow east ledge of the cliff top to kill F. Millard Smyth.

The little man took a tentative step toward the front door—and a shoulder and half a net-draped head appeared for an instant in the doorway.

Before his new thought was complete, F. Millard began to run through the kitchen as softly as the killer himself. For once, he hadn't had to test out the other's presence at the front of the house. For once, F. Millard knew he was nearer the back door. Lightly, without stopping, he dashed through it and plunged for the nearest boulder— the next—and the next. No gloved hand had brushed him at the door. Was the murderer still waiting at the front? Again, a flash of hope shot through him. He dodged around another big rock, now just a few yards from the woods—and knew his hope had failed.

A large figure in hat and net sprang from behind a boulder. Long-sleeved arms and gloves reached out—F. Millard fled back for the cabin. He might have known the murderer wouldn't be fooled—not anyone so smart, so strong, so determined. The little grocer had been both out-guessed and out-stripped.

The other's feet pounded close. In a frantic spurt, F. Millard hurdled a low boulder and made a desperate fling for the door.

The killer got there first—with his arm across the doorway. F. Millard dodged around the corner and heard a grunt behind him—a grunt of satisfaction! Then he knew the other's plan—why the killer had sprung for the door instead of his victim. This narrow ledge down which he was tearing—the jagged rocks below—his was to seem a natural death.

Desperation spurred him faster. Would it be a sudden shove, with the strength behind those hard-flung rocks? Or here, out of sight of the cabins, would the murderer catch his victim to enjoy every ounce of power—and throw him, like a basketball, over the cliff?

If he could only make the trail—jump for the turn of the switchback… But he wasn't near enough yet—and already felt his pursuer's breath on his neck. There was just one chance—a desperate chance! It might not work—or might kill them both.

He risked a glance over his shoulder—and saw the killer's arm lift.

F. Millard dropped to his hands and knees. The ground mashed his nose as the killer tripped—and went over.

He heard a splash, just a shallow splash, and a hard thud on the rocks.

On the cliff top, F. Millard sagged flat. For long, shaken moments, he lay panting and hearing his heart thump. When at last he tried to get up, throbbing bruises and muscles balked. He turned his head—and looked into blank space. The little grocer shuddered and rolled closer to the cabin.

That picture—the one he'd drawn a mental curtain over —now he could lift the curtain. There was time now to look at the picture. Time now to breathe—and to live.

Then the thumps he had thought were still labored heartbeats became footsteps, and Art's voice roared in the quiet: "My God, my God, girl! They've got him!"

F. Millard raised his head. Chris Thorne's bright curls and terrified eyes showed over the bluff at the switchback. Behind her loomed the big deputy's head and shoulders.

"No! No!" she gasped. "Look, Art, he's alive!"

Slowly, the grocer sat up.

"Thank God you're not dead!" Art cried. "Chris just came tearing to my cabin, yipping that you had a date with the killer."

"It just—it just got through my thick head," stammered Chris, "what that magazine meant this afternoon—that picture you drew."

"T-too bad you didn't think of it sooner," F. Millard sighed. "But I'm glad I didn't hear you now till you spoke, or I'd have thought the killer was coming back to finish me off."

"The killer?" Art repeated. "Then you did—you don't mean you—say, what happened to him?"

Painfully, F. Millard wavered to his feet. He pointed over the bluff before he looked down at himself. The murderer had landed face up. With his hat and veil knocked off, he lay half out of the shallow water while the three on the cliff top stared down. That upturned, still, face was the one F. Millard had known he would see ever since the pieces of the puzzle began clicking together while he was sprinkling ashes—the face of the man who had killed Trigger Joe and Jade and tried to kill the grocer—the face of Benny Kingdom.

Chapter Twenty-Three

F. Millard limped up the road to the highway a little behind the other three. He was glad they made no effort to slow down, to respect his years and wounds. After all—he squared his shoulders and limped faster—he hadn't been too small and middle-aged to catch the murderer.

Ahead, Ethan turned around. He made a very soldierly figure, F. Millard observed, standing with his service cap on the light thatch of hair above his brown face and the cane at last discarded. Chris and Abby, beside him, stopped too.

He grinned with a white flash of teeth. "Want to take a last look at the lake, folks? The bus won't be along for half an hour."

Slowly, the eyes of all four were drawn east.

From the road trees hid the cabins, even, F. Millard saw with relief, the house on the point. The lake was an emerald set in malachite—innocent, green and twinkling in the sun. It didn't seem possible that a shining place like that had been the scene of murder.

"None of it seems possible." Chris echoed his thought aloud. "I'm glad they got the road fixed so the bus can take us away. Even with—oh, I can't think of Benny as a murderer—even with him caught, I wouldn't want to go on staying there."

"Guess that's what the King thought too," said Abby dryly, "the way he and Bella lit out in their car as soon as the dump truck got through, even before the marshal's car picked up Art and Benny's body. I thought the King's motor was out."

"It was," said Ethan. "I saw parts of it all over his garage. Must have assembled it on the q.t. But he couldn't have cleared out in a car even if things got too hot for him here."

"I should say not!" exclaimed Chris. "With Valdez and the ocean at one end of the Trail and Fairbanks at the other—and the road washed out, at that."

"Well, you know how the King is," reminded her mother, "always trying to avoid anything unpleasant, no matter what temporary or childish method he uses."

The copper-brown eyes that repeated the tints of the girl's shining hair looked troubled. "You think he knew his brother'd done the killing and wanted to get out before Benny was caught?"

"I mean, he was getting too damned involved himself," retorted Abby. "It's the King that the King's interested in, not his brother or anyone else. He planted Ethan's knife over the bluff and kept pointing him out to Art to take attention away from himself, didn't he, Millard?"

The little grocer nodded. "We went all over it last night —Art and King and I. He threw down the knife when he kicked the stones over the bluff, like you said, Mrs. Thorne. Got it when Bella laid it out for Ethan that day. He didn't know then about the murder-Dippers, but Art had the shell Kingdom had picked up from the bullet that killed Trigger Joe, and he was afraid things might get uncomfortable for him."

"Boy, they sure did!" snorted Ethan. "Benny must have had it in for him a long, long time to make him plant those Dippers. Not that I blame Benny for hating the King. What makes me so mad is the Dippers' involving Chris, too."

"But it wasn't the Dipper we used to make," insisted Chris. "Ours had only seven stars."

"I think Benny forgot," said F. Millard. "He never used the signal himself in the old days. So when he tried to recall it he naturally thought of the whole group of stars as it is in the flag."

"But Benny made the flag without the North Star," objected Ethan. "I remember when you asked us to draw it, he and Chris and Abby all did."

The grocer smiled at both women. "That was just a holdover for you two, wasn't it? From your years on Abby Creek—when Chris and King had the Dipper for their signal. And lately, Chris had been making it again, and Mrs. Thorne seeing it here at the lake."

"My God," Abby cried, "I sure was seeing it again—all over the place—with murder going on—I thought I'd go wild."

"That's why you destroyed the one behind the burned cabin, wasn't it, Mrs. Thorne?"

"How'd you know, Millard? Wish you'd call me Abby. Sure, that's why I destroyed it—and all the others I found. I knew Chris had been out the night Trigger Joe was killed, and I didn't know when she got back. So when Benny came in from the road camp and said the marshal was coming by plane, I went down to the burned cabin to scout around."

"I saw you," said F. Millard. "You were gone so long I went to see why. You were out the night the old man was killed, yourself. You admitted it to Art."

"I was looking for Chris. That very day, I'd come across the signal she and the King used to make, and—well—I wanted to keep her from getting mixed up with a married man, especially a no-good like that."

A little silence fell on the group in the road. Chris laid down her bundles and pointedly dusted off a rock to sit on; Abby hunched herself on another. Ethan lowered his knapsack and stood straight and still, his eyes on the lake.

"I wouldn't be surprised," he drawled, "if the King had the fear of God put into him these last few days."

"Hmmm," said Abby skeptically.

"What I hope," said Chris gently, "is that Bella's going to have it easier, that the King will reform enough for that."

F. Millard glanced at her sharply. She was looking at Ethan with eyes that held a special glow. Both smiled, and Chris said softly, "It's good to see you without your cane, Ethan."

"I hated to put anything over on you and Abby, Chris," said the soldier, "but by the time my leg began to get better, I could see something was brewing, and my leave wasn't up till the end of the month. The Kingdoms were working too hard on Trigger Joe, and with Jade here—" He turned to F. Millard. "I figured a man that looked out of the running might get hold of something an able-bodied man couldn't."

Juggling his magazines and sack of clothes, F. Millard gingerly sat down on a boulder, too. He tried not to wince. After last night, sitting was as painful as walking. "What were you doing the second night it stormed?" he asked the soldier. "I saw you running along the beach under the bank and thought you'd been at the point till I talked to King last night."

Ethan sighed. "Chris had been talking to Kingdom outside my uncle's fence, and I heard them arrange to meet at the point. I wanted to make sure they didn't leave that damn Dipper where Art'd find it, but after Jade had been yapping about me and my uncle's will, I didn't want to be caught snooping, so I swam around the fence and sneaked under the bank after everyone should have gone to bed. I found the Dipper all right, eight stones at the end of the trail by the clearing, so I messed it up and scrammed."

"It was King I heard that night on the point," said F. Millard. "He told me last night. He started before Chris signaled, but he swore he didn't make that Dipper. Jade! I'll bet it was Jade who made the Dipper to involve King and Chris!"

"Sounds like her," growled Ethan.

"You didn't say why Benny didn't make the North Star the day we drew the Alaska flag," Chris reminded F. Millard.

"There could have been several reasons," said the grocer. "He might have been trying too hard not to repeat the murder-Dippers, or he might even have forgotten the North Star was on the flag, or he might have connected the North Star some funny way in his mind with the dog North and been afraid someone else would too, and tell Art."

Chris gave a strangled gasp. "Oh, of course, of course! I remember when North was a puppy, Benny wanted to name him North Star. Of course, he wouldn't put it in his picture."

"And he drew that stuff in the magazine so poorly," F. Millard went on, "so Art wouldn't suspect Benny Kingdom, who drew almost as well as his brother. And he must have worn gloves, besides. I think Art'll find that out when he has *Flatfoot* fingerprinted. Thank goodness he forgave me for swiping it."

214

"Since you caught the killer," remarked Abby.

"Did Benny draw that picture you showed us on the beach?" asked Chris. "The one I figured out almost too late?"

F. Millard nodded. "He must have found that magazine at the point the morning after I lost it and drawn the picture to warn me away. Apparently, he'd been meeting Jade there. I saw her coming back the night Chris signaled with the flashlight. She must have gone to meet Benny and found King already there. Benny couldn't get away at all that night because the Scouts took turns keeping watch. No wonder he was so anxious to send them home!"

"But why would Benny be meeting Jade?" asked Chris. "It was the King she was trying to blackmail. Do you think she saw something about Trigger Joe's murder and was blackmailing Benny too?"

"I think that was why he finally killed her," F. Millard agreed, "but they must have been meeting secretly ever since she came to the lake."

"Benny and Jade?" Chris gasped. "Why on earth—?"

"Let's clear up some other things first," F. Millard countered.

"Benny might have killed Jade because she found out something, but why did he kill my uncle?" The soldier's eyes were hard and bright. "He may not have made a lot of money, but after Bella married the King, why would Benny care much whether the Abby Association sold or not?"

"Wait a minute," said the grocer. "Did you follow Chris when she made the Dipper in front of my cabin the night I came to the lake, Mrs. Thor—uh—Abby?"

She shook her head.

"Then it was Jade. She always managed not to miss anything. And the footsteps I heard on the road were King's. And the hunting accident when Mr. Kingdom was killed—since Benny was the murderer and he wasn't on that hunting trip—I guess that was a real accident."

Both Abby and Ethan started. "My God, what did you think?" cried the woman.

F. Millard grinned. "Just like King's check in Benny's billfold was a legitimate check for insurance, but it gave me quite a start. And your—

what Jade would have called your screaming meemies, Abby—your wailing about being the next victim—was that real or put on?"

The woman's weathered cheeks reddened. "Afraid those first yips when we found Trigger Joe were real enough, but after that—"

F. Millard nodded. "After that, when you began to see how I might suspect Chris, you were trying to throw me off the track. Like you heard me run by the night Jade was killed, when I went to get Art and the phone was ringing, but you couldn't admit it because Chris was still out. Like swiping the drawings all of you made because you didn't know what Art and I were up to and thought Chris's might count against her. Like trying so hard to sell me a good opinion of her the afternoon we went hunting."

Defiantly, Abby nodded.

"You were as bad about Chris as Bella was about King. Everything she did was for him." *Including,* the grocer silently added, *trying to marry me into the Abby Association.* "I thought Bella was going to faint the day we were down on the beach, and she accidentally made the Dipper on the blanket. She remembered that childhood signal, all right, and she, too, had been finding it again. Did you see her, Chris, on the beach? Art said that was why you told King not to make it anymore."

Chris nodded. "But I don't understand now why the King had me set my watch back half an hour—since it was Benny who killed Jade."

"Because King heard her scream. He didn't know who was after whom but he wanted an alibi for that time. He'd been working on his car after he thought everyone was in bed, and that's why he was late to meet you and heard the scream. So he set his watch back and got you to change yours."

"Okay, Smyth," said Ethan abruptly. "We've let you satisfy your curiosity about all our acts and motives—now what about Benny's? Why did he kill Trigger Joe?"

F. Millard drew a long breath. "What you said a while ago about his hating his brother for a long, long time applies to the rest of it, too. I don't mean just hating King, but Benny's whole character. You know what King's like—handsome and smart and strong and utterly selfish, and Benny, being his brother and not so handsome and not so smart and not so strong, has had

216

it rubbed in all his life. Benny may not have been as brainy as his brother, but he was one jump ahead of him in psychology. Look at the way King's always been with North. The dog preferred Benny—one of the few cases on record—and King, up to the last hour of the old fellow's life, tried to wean him away. Benny knew all about that trait. My gracious, he knew only too well. So when it came to the most important thing in his life—getting the girl he loved, he knew how to handle King."

"Then he certainly bungled the job," exclaimed Chris. "Because Bella married the King."

"That's just what Benny wanted," F. Millard returned.

"What he wanted!" the other three gasped.

"Benny wasn't in love with Bella." The little man kept his voice down and his face poker calm, but he couldn't resist a quick flick of the rolled pages of his hip pocket *Flatfoot*. "It was all a brilliant idea, part of a masterly plan. He could see the possibilities in her and taught her how to bring them out. Then, apparently, under his love and attention, she blossomed into a beauty all ready to fall for the man who had brought it to her. That was too much for King—Bella, who'd always been beneath his notice, turning out a beauty and falling for his brother! So King went to work. And Bella, who'd never been popular with any group and only tolerated by the younger generation of the Abby Association, had the Cinderella-like experience of having the Crown Prince himself at her feet."

"Poor Bella," said Chris softly.

"'Poor Bella' nothing," retorted Ethan. "She got the guy she wanted. And she's still got him."

"But what about Benny?" Abby demanded. "You said he was in love, even if it wasn't with Bella."

"He certainly was, and you can imagine how he worried for fear something might slip up to stop that whirlwind courtship of King's and the hurry-up marriage. That's why he waited till the very day of the wedding, so his competition wouldn't be withdrawn, and King loses interest. No wonder he was pacing up and down like a wild man when Ethan took him to the plane."

"You mean Benny just left town to save his face?" demanded Chris. "But he stayed Outside all winter! And looked worse when he came back."

"No wonder," said the grocer. "He didn't go Outside to save his face. He went for his girl."

"Outside!" Chris exclaimed over Abby. "A girl in Seattle?"

"The girl Benny's always been crazy about, now, with her needing money and King safely sidetracked, he thought he stood a chance to marry—was Jade Lothrop."

Again, his audience gasped.

"She must have fascinated him even when they were children, and then when her family came back the summer she was seventeen, he must have fallen for her so hard he never got over it and always managed to keep in touch with her. I suppose Jade's business sense made her answer his letters just for the sake of an anchor to windward. Benny knew if King ever discovered his interest in Jade, he'd go for her himself, so he had to get his brother tied up first. And then Benny took the first plane out."

"Poor Benny," said Chris, "he missed again. That was the year Jade married someone else."

"I kept feeling Jade's husband had something to do with this mess," F. Millard said slowly. "That he might be the murderer."

"Too bad he wasn't," sighed Ethan. "I'd rather it had been the Big Ape any day than Benny."

"But it was the Big Ape," said F. Millard. "Benny was Jade's husband."

The others goggled.

"B-B-Benny was the B-B-Big Ape?" stammered Chris. "Goo-Goo?" asked Abby faintly.

F. Millard nodded. "You can imagine how he must have felt all the time Jade was getting in those digs about her husband, and she never missed a chance. I happened to be looking at him one of those times and I thought I'd never seen a more unhappy looking man, but he remembered to play up and keep his eyes on Bella. Her marriage to his brother gave him the perfect excuse for looking unhappy when Jade was running down matrimony."

"But why on earth didn't he tell us?" cried the girl.

"Jade wouldn't let him. You remember when Benny went Outside, he hadn't been going to college like the rest of you? He'd been making money on insurance. Jade was in Hollywood trying to crash the studio gates. Bella told me once that none of you had ever been anyplace in the States except Seattle, but Benny didn't write anyone about going to Hollywood till he found out if Jade would accept him. Art, King, and I went all over it last night. Well, when Benny hit Hollywood, Jade's cash was hitting rock bottom, and when he offered marriage with money in his pocket, she snapped him up. But she made him promise to keep still for fear it would hurt her chances with the movies. By the time she finally gave up all hope of making the grade, Benny'd run out of money. I'll bet the first time he had to refuse her a check she told him she was through."

"To think," murmured Chris, "that Benny Kingdom had been married and divorced—to Jade, of all people, and we never even knew it."

"Married, yes," agreed the grocer, "but not divorced."

"Not divorced?" cried Ethan. "Don't you remember Jade's song and dance about the Big Ape and how she had to divorce him? She was always talking about her divorce."

"That was just to put the screws on Benny, poor devil," F. Millard sighed. The deep breath made his lower ribs pain sharply, and at the memory of those hard-flung rocks, his tone hardened. "That's where his special character comes in again. He hadn't told about the marriage while Jade was living with him, and after she left, he couldn't tell without admitting defeat. Benny's ego couldn't take it, he was already known for too many defeats. He must have kept on sending her money after he came back to Alaska, so she wouldn't try to divorce him and make the whole business public, and I'll bet he was plenty careful not to give her any grounds. All that stuff about the Big Ape she just invented to torture him. Benny'd be Goo-Goo, all right, but never the Big Ape with Jade—till the very last."

"It sounds like the McCoy the way you dope it out, Smyth," said Ethan, "but Jade and Benny are both dead, so it's only speculation. The King wouldn't know any more about it than you and Art."

"It's easy enough to check with the police in Las Vegas and Hollywood and Seattle, but we had more than that to go on. I thought it was funny that a healthy, single man like Benny hadn't been drafted. Flat feet or bridgework isn't enough reason these days. My own registration certificate doesn't have a classification, and without any sons or close friends in the draft age, I wasn't familiar with the figures on Benny's draft card—as long as they weren't 1-A or 4-F—till Art explained last night and compared Benny's card with King's. They're both the same classification—married men without children. And besides, Benny had an identification card in his billfold to notify Mrs. Mary Kingdom in case of accident—"

"That's his mother," Abby broke in. "Or was his mother before she died. Don't you remember I told you?"

"That's what steered me wrong. I thought, of course, it was his mother when I saw the card, and I believe his devotion to her was part of the reason for using the name Mary, and the other part was to keep from pointing at Jade. Her full name—I heard Chris call her that once, but I'd forgotten it—was Jade Mary Augusta Lothrop. And the address on the card, King told us last night, was Jade's address in Seattle."

"For God's sake," said Abby simply.

"I can see now," commented Ethan, "why Benny was so wild when he heard about King's affair with Jade—why he took that long swim that killed North. No wonder he said no woman was worth the life of such a friend. I'll bet he was trying to kill himself then and was too good a swimmer to drown. He was smart enough to lay his being upset on his interest in Bella, but it wasn't her marriage being violated that got him; it was his own. Poor devil."

"Would that be enough to make him kill her?" Chris began, then cried abruptly, "But he killed her before he knew about it!"

"Remember she was still dressed the night of the fire?" F. Millard pointed out. "She must have been snooping and found out something about Trigger Joe's death. I think she was completely confident of Benny's being so crazy about her that he'd never hurt her no matter what she threatened, and she must have used her knowledge about Trigger Joe's death to try to get the money from Benny without going back to him as his wife. Of course, we'll never know—he might have killed her to save his own skin. But I think when the realization hit him that he'd committed murder for the money to lure his wife back and found she not only still scorned him but threatened to tell Art, he must have just gone berserk and instinctively put an end to all her cruelty. It must have been Jade who passed on the road the night she was killed."

"But if she knew Benny killed Trigger Joe," exclaimed Chris, "why did she accuse Ethan? You remember—about the torn-up will?"

"Just my stepsister's sweet disposition," the soldier murmured.

"I think so," F. Millard agreed. "Of course, Benny killed Trigger Joe for the same reason any of you might have—so the mine could be sold. But he wanted his share of the money to coax Jade to come back to him."

"Poor Benny," Chris said again.

"How'd he get Trigger Joe down to that cabin?" Ethan asked abruptly.

"That scrap of the will in the cuff of his slacks really gave him away if Art and I'd only known it," F. Millard began indirectly. "Benny claimed he didn't know what Trigger Joe was raving about when he threw those scraps of paper, but he must have known all the time. He may even have influenced the old man to tear up the will. But the important thing is that he knew the will was torn up and wanted to make sure Jade knew it too, so she'd have to come to him for money. You remember the morning after Trigger Joe was killed, and we were having coffee at your house?" He looked at Chris and Abby. "Remember how King and Benny wrangled about who was going to the road camp? They both had something else to accomplish. King wanted to get that cartridge shell out of the jacket he wouldn't lend me after he remembered it—that's why he left so soon after Benny and only rang the phone once in his hurry to go home for that shell—and Benny wanted to hide his pocketful of will scraps. After he killed Trigger Joe, he must have gone back to Frazee's cabin to return the gun while Ethan was walking to the highway (he'd have taken it before Ethan came back from duck hunting), and he saw the scraps had been swept up and dumped in the fireplace. He wanted Jade to know right away she'd been disinherited, so he picked up a handful of scraps—they had ashes on them too, just like the others—and when he started for the road camp, he went around by my cabin and hid them in my teapot."

The women caught their breath, but Ethan laughed.

"Benny didn't know I don't drink tea," F. Millard went on, "but Art found the scraps, and anyway, the others weren't destroyed. When Benny made his visit to Trigger Joe after King's, he must have found out the old man was mad at Jade because of something King had told, but not what it was; so I figure Benny must have told Trigger Joe that Jade was meeting King in that empty cabin and offered to hide him there to see for himself.

So while the old man was waiting, Benny, too, was waiting where he could see him through a window for one of those frequent flights of bombers— waiting with the old fellow's gun. And after it was all over, he set the cabin on fire."

"Hell's bells," cried Abby, "there's something screwy somewhere! Don't you remember the Scouts testified that Benny was in bed at the time of both murders? Once they just saw his hump in the sleeping bag, which could've been stuffed blankets, but the other time they heard him snore!"

"That snore stuck me too," soothed F. Millard, "till last night, while I was in the house on the point, everything began to come clear, far too clear for comfort. Benny really gave himself away the night Trigger Joe was killed when one of the Scouts saw him rubbing tonic in his hair hours after he was supposed to have gone to bed. He always did that when he went to bed, and the habit was too strong."

"But," Chris broke in, "the hump—"

"You remember how North and Benny were," said F. Millard. "The old dog would do anything for him. Remember how he breathed—a cross between a wheeze and a snore? Benny left him in his bag for a substitute, with the inner blanket pulled up around his head. North was the hump in the sleeping bag, and it was North who snored."

"For God's sake," said Abby again. And a hush fell on the hill.

"For God's sake's right," said Ethan briskly. "If we don't snap into it we'll miss the bus." He adjusted his knapsack and picked up half Chris's bundles. She jumped up with the sun-like flame on her hair, and the two started on down the road.

Abby picked up her bundles while F. Millard balanced his tottering copies of *Flatfoot* and struggled painfully to his feet. She smiled after the two ahead. "Thank God the King finally showed himself up to Chris. Now she and Ethan are going to get married."

"How s-swell." F. Millard's voice suddenly broke. Here they were again—that intimate foursome—with Abby and him behind.

A familiar drone began in the sky, and a flight of bombers swept overhead. Involuntarily, the little grocer waved, and his shoulder hurt. No longer did the Abby Association or anyone at the lake need to fear that the beat of motors might cover the sound of a shot.

"You planning to stay in Fairbanks, Millard?" Abby asked. "Going to buy Blaine's grocery?"

For a minute, F. Millard looked back at the lake. Six days ago he had come here to decide about buying a grocery. With six days and four deaths, if he counted the dog's, all thought of groceries had been knocked from his mind. Groceries—Alaska—Abby—his mind leaped to successive peaks. How could he give up a country he loved as much as this, a country where he didn't have to read *Flatfoot* for excitement? Two murders and the capture of a criminal within fifty miles of town! But Abby—if Abby Thorne lived in Fairbanks...

"Myself," said Abby calmly, starting after the others, "I'm going to sink my Association money in another mine. I can't live in town after the creeks. A fellow can't hardly breathe."

F. Millard could, and did—a long, deep breath. His problem encountered a week ago had been settled in less than a minute. "Guess I can meet the payments," he said as they rounded the hill and left the lake behind. "I'm going to buy Blaine's grocery."

A Note from the Author

From 1944:

   Harding Lake is real, but the individual cabins and the characters in this book are not.There is a real point with a house on it jutting into the real lake, but the point told of here, with the trail up the bluff, is fictitious. For the many pleasant hours my friends have given me at Harding Lake I thank them and apologize for liberties taken with it here.

It's great to be back in print (80 years later)!

If you enjoyed the book, please post a review on the sites where you read or buy books such as Amazon, Goodreads, Barnes and Noble, etc. Thank you.

Elizabeth Reed Aden

About the Author

Eunice Mays Boyd (1902-1971) spent twelve years living in Alaska from the late 1920s until the onset of American engagement in World War II. She was born in Oregon, the granddaughter of George C. Ainsworth and great-granddaughter of John C. Ainsworth, the scion a prominent pioneer family. She was raised in Berkeley and graduated from UC in 1924. She married George Lloyd Boyd, an attorney whose career took them to Alaska. They divorced in the 1940s and she worked for UC President Sproul and later at UCSF in the Department of Preventive Medicine.

Her goddaughter, Elizabeth Reed Aden, secured the literary rights to her novels and has published three manuscripts written between 1948 and 1971 (*Dune House, Slay Bells* and *A Vacation to Kill For*). She also secured the rights to Eunice's out-of-print books which are being republished. She was a co-author with Anthony Boucher, among others, of *The Marble Forest* which was made into the movie *Macabre*.

SOCIAL MEDIA HANDLES:
  FB: https://www.facebook.com/ElizabethReedAden/

AUTHOR WEBSITE:

www.EuniceMaysBoyd.com
https://www.elizabethreedaden.com/eunice-mays-boyd

Also by Eunice Mays Boyd with Elizabeth Reed Aden

Featuring F. Millard Smyth
   Murder Breaks Trail (1943), Honorable Mention, 3rd Mary Roberts Rinehart Mystery Contest
   Doom in the Midnight Sun
   Murder Wears Mukluks (1945)

Co-author of: *The Marble Forest* by Theo Durant

Books by Eunice Mays Boyd with Elizabeth Reed Aden
   Slay Bells
   A Vacation to Kill For
   Dune House
   One Paw Was Red (an F. Millard Smyth Novel) - to be published

Other books by Elizabeth Reed Aden
   The Goldilocks Genome
   HEPATITIS Beach (in process)

9 781685 126193